Roddy Doyle

Love

ALFRED A. KNOPF CANADA

PUBLISHED BY ALFRED A. KNOPF CANADA

Copyright © 2020 Roddy Doyle

Published in 2020 by Alfred A. Knopf Canada, a division of Penguin Random House Canada Limited, Toronto. First published in 2020 in the United Kingdom by Jonathan Cape, an imprint of Vintage, part of the Penguin Random House Group, London. Distributed in Canada by Penguin Random House Canada Limited, Toronto.

www.penguinrandomhouse.ca

Knopf Canada and colophon are registered trademarks.

Library and Archives Canada Cataloguing in Publication

Title: Love / Roddy Doyle.
Names: Doyle, Roddy, 1958- author.
Identifiers: Canadiana (print) 20190239506 |
Canadiana (ebook) 20190239514 | ISBN 9780735279889 (softcover) |
ISBN 9780735279896 (HTML)
Classification: LCC PR6054.O95 L69 2020 | DDC 823/.914—dc23

Typeset in 12.4/15.1 pt Plantin Std
by Integra Software Services Pvt. Ltd, Pondicherry
Cover design by Leah Springate
Image credits: (cello) © Mark Berndroth / 500px,
(hand on cello) © ASphotowed / iStock,
(wood) © Wachirawit Jenlohakit / Moment, all Getty Images

Printed and bound in Canada

2 4 6 8 9 7 5 3 1

Penguin
Random House
KNOPF CANADA

For Belinda

There stands the glass –

Fill it up to the brim –

'Til my troubles grow dim –

It's my first one today –

'There Stands the Glass' by
Russ Hull, Mary Jean Shurtz,
Audrey Greisham

He knew it was her, he told me. He told me this a year after he saw her. Exactly a year, he said.

—Exactly a year?

—That's what I said, Davy. A year ago – yesterday.

—You remember the date?

—I do, yeah.

—Jesus, Joe.

He saw her at the end of a corridor and he knew. Immediately. She was exactly the same. Even from that far off. Even though she was only a shape, a dark, slim shape – a silhouette – in the centre of the late-afternoon light that filled the glass door behind her.

—She was never slim, I said.

He shrugged.

—I don't even know what slim means, really, he said.

He smiled.

—Same here, I said.

—I just said it, he said. —The word. She was a tall shape – instead.

—Okay.

—Not a roundy shape.

—She's aged well, I said. —That's what you're telling me.

—I am, he said. —And she has.

—Where was the corridor? I asked him.

—The school, he said.

—What school?

—The school, he said again.

—We didn't know her in school, I said.

I knew he didn't mean the school we'd both gone to. We'd known each other that long. I'd said it – that we hadn't known her in school – to try to get him to be himself. To give back an answer that would get us laughing. He was the funny one.

—My kids' school, he said.

—Hang on, I said. —It was a parent–teacher meeting?

—Yeah.

—The woman of your dreams stepped out of the sun and into a parent–teacher meeting?

—Yep.

—Thirty years after the last time you saw her, I said. —More, actually. Way more. Thirty-six or seven years.

—Yeah, he said. —That's it, more or less. What did you say there? That she stepped out of the sun.

—I think so, yeah.

—Well, that's it, he said. —That's what happened. She did.

I didn't live in Ireland. I went over to Dublin three or four times a year, to see my father. I used to bring my family but in more recent years I'd travelled alone. The kids were grown up and gone and my wife, Faye, didn't like flying, and she wasn't keen on the drive to Holyhead and the ferry.

—Your dad never liked me, so he didn't.

—He did.

—He did not, she said. —He thought I was a slut. He said it, sure.

—He didn't say that.

—More or less, he did. You told me that, yourself, remember. I'm not making it up. He never liked me, so I won't be going around pretending I like him. I hate that house. It's miserable.

—She kissed me, Joe said now.

—In the school?

The man I knew – I thought I knew; I used to know – would have answered, 'No, in the arse,' or something like that.

—Yes, he said. —She remembered me.

I didn't know Joe well.

I used to.

We left school for good on the same day. He got work; I went to college, to UCD. He had money, wages – a salary. I had none until after I'd graduated. But we kept in touch. We both lived at home, a ten-minute walk from each other. We listened to records in my house about once a week, in the front room. He bought most of the records; mine was the house where we could blast them out. We played them so loud we could put our hands on the window glass and feel the song we were hearing. My mother was dead and my father didn't seem to mind. He told me years later he just wanted to see me happy. He endured the noise – the Pistols, Ian Dury, the Clash, Elvis Costello – because he thought it made me happy. I'd have been happy if he'd hammered at the wall with a shoe or his fist and told me to turn it fuckin' down. I'd have been happy if I'd felt I had to fight him.

We went drinking, myself and Joe, when I had the money. At Christmas and in October, when I came back from working in West Germany and London, before I had to spend the money I'd earned on books and bus fares. We'd get quickly drunk and roar. I rushed straight into anger. I thumped things, and myself. I let myself go, glimpsed the man I could become. I pulled back, and copied Joe. He drank, I drank. He laughed, I laughed. I roared when he roared.

—She remembered you?

—Yeah, he said. —She did. Immediately. Like I said.

I looked at him again. I could see why she'd have recognised him. The boy – the young man – was still there. His head was the same shape. He'd worn glasses back then and he still did – or, he did again – the same kind of black-framed glasses. He still had his hair. It was grey now, most of it, but it had never been very dark. He'd put on weight but not much, and none of it around his face and neck.

—Where were you? I asked him.

—In the school, he said. —I told you.

—Where, though?

—Outside the maths room, he said. —Waiting.

—For your turn with the teacher.

—Yeah, he said. —There were four or five people – mostly mothers – ahead of me. And I'd no one else to see – I'd seen all the others. We divided the list.

—Hang on, I said. —Trish was there as well?

Trish was his wife.

—Yeah, he said. —She was somewhere else. Queuing up for another teacher.

—You kissed the love of your life while Trish was in the building?

—Big building, he said. —It's a fuckin' school – in fairness.

That was more like the man I thought I knew. The man I'd wanted to be.

—You kissed her, I said.

—She kissed me.

—Where was Trish, exactly?

4

—Exactly, Davy? *Exactly?* Is this a murder investigation?

—Okay.

—For fuck sake, Davy.

—Okay – sorry. Go on.

—The home economics room, he said. —Or woodwork. Somewhere else. We took four teachers each, to get it over with as quickly as possible. Even at that, it took all afternoon. It's the only chance the teachers get to talk to adults. So, they fuckin' grab it. I was lucky.

—How come?

—I got to meet the maths teacher, he said. —A gobshite, by the way. But I was outside his door. I just happened to be there.

—And she walked in while you were waiting.

—Right place, right time. Yeah. Like I said – I was lucky.

—One of your kids does home economics and woodwork?

—What?

—You said home economics or woodwork. Trish was in one of those rooms.

—You're being Columbo again, Davy.

—Lay off.

—I just meant – like, for example. The rooms. Trish was somewhere else, in one of the other rooms, you know. Way off somewhere in the building.

—Which kid was it?

I'd never met his children and I didn't know their names. We told each other about the kids, brought each other up to date whenever we met, and then forgot about them. I hadn't seen Trish in twenty years.

—Holly, he said.

—You sure?

—Yeah, he said. —Of course, I am. Fuck off.

—Okay.

—You're being a bit of a prick, Davy.

—I'm not.

—You are.

—It's a bit of a shock.

—Why does it even matter?

—Okay.

—To you.

—I know.

I'd never seen him with his children but I knew he was a good father. And I knew what that meant. He was reliable. He'd given them their routines. He'd come home at much the same time every evening. He'd picked them up from football or gymnastics and he'd always been there on time. They'd seen him filling the dishwasher and the washing machine. They'd seen him cooking at the weekends; they'd probably preferred his cooking to Trish's. He'd served them Fanta in wine glasses on Saturday nights. He'd told them he loved them, twice a day, start and end. He'd read to them – the same book, again and again – gone swimming with them, slept on a chair beside them when they'd been kept overnight in Temple Street Children's Hospital. He'd read about asthma, eczema, OCD, intersexuality. He wasn't a man who didn't know what subjects his kids had done in school. He would never have pretended that he was that man.

He was right. It shouldn't have mattered. I shouldn't have cared. But it did. And I did.

We saw her there the first day, at a table under one of the windows.

We'd found a pub that liked us. We'd wandered the city centre for months, every weekend, starting after work on Friday and ending ten minutes before the last bus home on Sunday night. This was after I graduated and had new money in my pocket. We'd escaped from my front room and the record player. I could buy my round. We were peers now and we could become the lifelong friends we hadn't really been before. Getting drunk together, sneering at the world together, aching for the same women, denying it. We became the same man for a couple of important years. Before I left. Before he met Trish. Before I met Faye.

That day, the day we saw the girl who became the woman he saw years later, we got lost in the basement of Mercer's Hospital. We'd left Sheehan's on Chatham Street at the start of the holy hour – the pubs used to shut for an hour in the afternoon – and we'd wandered up to the Dandelion Market. But we were already too drunk – not drunk, exactly; more oiled – to flick through second-hand books and records. So we left, went back out on to South King Street. We got a bowl of chilli in a tiny place long gone and without a name; I'll never remember what it was called. It was so small, it didn't have a toilet. That was fine back then, normal, a res-taurant or café without a loo. We were on South King Street again. We were the same man and we admitted we were bursting for a piss, really bursting, half an hour before the pub doors would open. Mercer's Hospital rose before us and we went in, trying to look like young men visiting a sick relative, and – I don't know why; I don't think I ever knew – we went down the stairs to the basement, instead of up to the wards. I remember the ceiling being low, just above our heads. There was

7

no one else down there, no charging men or women in scrubs. There were no stretchers or abandoned wheel-chairs – I can't remember any. One corridor became two corridors, and another two – and no toilet. We ended up pissing into an enamel bucket in a broom cupboard, first him, then me; there was only room for one of us at a time.

We passed a toilet on our way back out. We didn't laugh. We were quickly ashamed – *I* was. The pubs were open when we got out into daylight, through a different door.

It was right in front of us. We'd never noticed it before. It had its own corner. We must have walked past it once or twice but we hadn't seen it.

—Looks okay, said Joe.

And it did.

We were sober again. It was early winter, afternoon. The sky was clear and the sun was making blocks of yellow and grey – the last few hours before night, the perfect time for drinking. Mercer's Hospital was behind us. Literally behind us. A pint would cure us, drown the shame. We'd start laughing again after the second.

We were twenty-one.

We looked in the window. It was plain inside, but a bit more than the standard Dublin pub. There was less wood, more light. There was one man sitting at the bar, his back to us. He was wearing a suit and there was a grey ponytail resting on the back of the jacket. It was the first time I'd seen a ponytail on a man who wasn't on *The Old Grey Whistle Test*. There were tables along the other wall, under a line of win-dows. Only one of them was occupied, by four people – a man and three women. There was a cello leaning against the wall between two windows, and three violin

8

cases sat on the table beside them. The women were drinking pints.

She was one of those women.

—Do we go in?

—Definitely, said Joe.

The double door was on the corner, under a porch. He went for the right side, I took the left. Both doors opened when we pushed, then walked in side by side – and sideways. The doors swung back into place behind us. We heard them creak, and rest.

There was no television, no horse racing. No radio, no music.

No one looked our way.

The man with the ponytail was reading a magazine. It sat on the counter between his gin and tonic and an ashtray. The musicians were talking quietly. I didn't know it then but the College of Music was around the corner, on Chatham Row. I heard strings and a trumpet coming from an open window the next time I passed it, the following Monday, when I was off on a wander during the lunch break. I'd been walking past the building for months.

There was no barman.

We stepped closer to the counter. We passed the musicians, went further – deeper – into the room, and took two stools at the end of the bar. We sat, and saw him. He was down on his hunkers, filling the lowest shelf with bottles of Britvic Orange. He heard us and turned, stood up, groaned, and smiled. It was the first time a barman had smiled at us.

—Gentlemen, he said.

He was happy to see us.

We stayed there for months.

★   ★   ★

She walked right through the thirty-seven years as she got nearer to him. The age crept across her face. Her back took a very slight stoop.

—But she was beautiful, he said.

Beautiful wasn't a word we'd ever used. The women we'd liked were always gorgeous. But we saw her the first time and she was beautiful.

—And she knew me, he said. —She came right up to me.

—Was it the first time you'd seen her?

—What do you mean?

—It wasn't the first parent–teacher meeting you've been to, I said. —Was it? And the school concerts, the football, hockey – all that stuff. All your kids went to that school, didn't they?

—I know what you mean.

—You've been going up there for years then. Was this the first time you saw her?

—Yeah, he said. —Yes.

He said Yes; he'd changed Yeah to Yes. He was in the witness box.

—How come? I asked.

—How come what?

—All those meetings and matches and you never saw her.

—You don't know the school, he said. —It's huge. There's over a thousand brats go to that place.

—Yes –, I said.

I was at it now, playing the prosecutor.

—Yes, but parent–teacher meetings aren't convened for the parents and guardians of every child in the school, are they? This one, when you saw her, it would have been just a form – a year group. Am I right? What class is Holly in?

—It was a year ago, he said. —She was in Transition Year.

—What's that again? I asked.

He looked at me.

—I don't live in this country, I reminded him.

—She was sixteen, he said.

—Four years' worth of meetings and sports and cake sales and sponsored walks.

—And I never saw her.

—How come?

—Maybe I wasn't looking, he said.

Now I stared at him. Was he making this up?

He shrugged.

—There's no answer, he said. —I don't know. It's a big school. It's possible.

—But improbable.

—Okay.

—Was it the first time she saw you? I asked.

—It's not really –.

He stopped. And started again.

—It's not really the point, he said. —The fact is, she saw me and it was like she'd seen me the day before. The way she behaved, the way she spoke to me. Like it was 1981, or whenever.

—Okay, I said. —But had she ever kissed you before? In 1981?

—Back off a bit, Davy, he said. —Just listen. She came up to me and kissed me.

—How?

—The cheek.

—One cheek?

—You didn't hear me, he said.

—I did, I said. —What do you mean?

—She kissed *me*, he said. —She didn't – whatever – offer her cheek for me to kiss. She kissed mine.

He was right; I hadn't been listening.

—Lips, he said. —Her lips kissed me – made actual contact with my skin. Not the air near my skin. Do you remember her well?

—Yes, I said. —I do.

—Do you remember her smile?

—Yeah, I said. —I think I do.

—Well, she smiled – while she was kissing me.

—Did she not smile when she saw you?

—She was smiling when she got there, like we'd arranged to meet – like she'd expected me to be there when she arrived, leaning there against the wall.

—Did that not worry you – a tad?

—No, he said. —Why would it have?

—Well, it was so – like – out of nowhere.

—I felt the exact same way, he said. —It made complete sense.

—Well, I said. —No offence. But it makes no fuckin' sense at all.

We were in a newish restaurant on the Clontarf Road, close to the Wooden Bridge. It was six months since the last time we'd met. We emailed each other occasionally, or texted, usually about music or football or dead friends and neighbours. We didn't crawl the pubs in town, the old places, like we used to when I came home. I'd always added an extra day's recovery before I went back – home – to England. I didn't drink now. I'd stopped. A glass of wine, the occasional bottle of craft beer at home – that was me. I stayed out of pubs. I don't think he drank much either. It was Monday night, this time. The restaurant was half empty. We weren't loud men. There was no one sitting too near

12

us. The waiter was young but old-school. He stayed away between courses and didn't keep passing, to ask us how we were getting on or if everything was perfect.

—Well, that was how it felt, he said. —Like we'd never been apart.

—But –.

—I know, he said. —I know. We'd never been much together. But I'm talking about feelings here, not facts. Feelings. The feel of the thing.

It sounded like something he'd said before. More than once.

He looked different, I decided. He looked bad – torn. In crisis. He was picking at his food. There wasn't much left on the plate – he must have been eating. But he looked too thin. The skin under his neck had become loose, wattled. I'd told him he was looking well, when we'd met an hour before, and I'd meant it. But now I was actually looking at him. He was scratching the palm of one of his hands. He'd been doing it since we sat down. He kept putting his fork down to do it. He'd been scratching his neck too. There were pink tracks under his ear. I'd almost been enjoying the car crash – man meets old flame and ruins his life. He'd been helping me. It was almost like he'd been sitting back, relating his misadventures, an arm resting on the back of the chair. But I saw it now, he wasn't like that. He was leaning forward, looking down at the table – examining what had happened.

He was sweating. But so was I. It was late May, and hot. The grass outside was brown. I'd cut my father's grass and the bucket behind the mower had filled with dust. The sweat on Joe was like a mask a footballer might have worn to protect a facial injury. He ran an arm, a sleeve, across his face and became Joe again, just Joe; the mask was gone.

I copied him. I rubbed my forehead with my napkin.

—The heat.

—It's not too bad in here, he said. —But we're not built for this, are we?

—No, I said. —There are forest fires – I saw it – inside the Arctic Circle. In Sweden.

—There you go, he said. —The end of the world.

—Bring it on.

—Yeah – fuck it.

He scooped some rice onto his fork.

—Look, he said. —Davy. I know it sounds a bit mad. What I'm telling you.

—Well –

—No, I know. It's okay. But it wasn't – it isn't. Mad. It felt normal. Perfectly – yeah. Normal. Not the event itself, I mean. The way it felt. At the time. It felt normal. Do you understand?

—Kind of.

—Is it boring?

—No.

—Trish said it was.

—You told Trish? What you've been telling me?

—I didn't get the chance, he said. —I didn't get far with Trish, I'm afraid.

—That's understandable, I suppose. Is it?

—Absolutely, he said. —No – I understand. Her position, like. I'm guessing I'd feel the same.

It was what I wanted to hear, Joe explaining what had happened with Trish. How he'd met this timeless beauty while Trish was on the next corridor, in the queue outside home economics.

14

He put the fork to his mouth. I watched him chew, then swallow. He picked up his glass.

—The food's good.

—Yeah.

—We'll come here again.

—Yeah.

—Anyway –.

They stood beside each other in the queue outside the maths room. He didn't ask her if it was a daughter or a son she had in Transition Year. It didn't feel like they had to catch up, rattle off the list of kids, and he didn't want to waste the time they had until he was called in to meet the teacher.

—So you did feel it was a bit unique, I said.

—No, he said. —No. But the queue was getting shorter. I was there to hear what the teacher had to say. That was why I was there – I hadn't forgotten that. And I'd have to go in.

—Okay.

They talked about the school, about the weather. The everyday stuff. It was raining out there and the shoulders of her jumper – a big, baggy thing – were wet. Her hair was wet too, a bit. The hair was long, unusually long for a woman of her age. It was the length it had been when we'd first seen her, he told me, maybe just an inch or two shorter. It was the same colour – he thought. She was the same woman. He asked her nothing and she asked him nothing. They just talked. Two parents ahead of him, a couple with matching runners, went in. He was next. The time was running out. She took her phone from her jeans pocket.

—I'm 087 –, she started.

—You knew something was up.

—What?

15

—Something was happening, I said.

—Of course something was happening, he said. —Have I been denying anything?

—Well, look, I said.

I felt like I was leaning forward, inviting him to thump me, pushing my face at him. But I wasn't. I was sitting back and I knew I was making him angry. Goading him – because I wanted to.

—A woman takes her phone out, I said. —And starts reciting her number to the man beside her. She's not married to him, he's not married to her.

—Come here, he said. —Do you have to watch the end of a film before you decide if you'll watch the rest of it? Is that how it works in your house?

—No.

—Do you get my point?

—Do you get mine? I said. —She took out her phone. She wanted your number. She wanted to give you hers. She wanted to see you again. You knew that – you must have. And you're saying it was all perfectly normal?

—What's abnormal about falling in love? he said.

—At a parent–teacher meeting?

He smiled. He was looking at it, looking at himself in it, what had happened a year before, and it suddenly made him happy.

—For the first time in the history of mankind, he said. —In the history of the Irish education system. What do you think, Davy? A man and a woman in a queue and they end up falling for each other. Has it happened before?

—I'd say so, yeah.

—I agree with you, he said. —One broken marriage for every parent–teacher meeting is my estimate. I don't have the statistics to back that up, mind you. Will I go on?

—Yeah.

—It *is* different, he said. —I promise you that.

—Okay.

—So anyway, I took my phone out.

He went to Contacts and tapped as she recited the rest of her number. Then he gave her his. He put the phone back into his pocket. There was no deal; neither of them said they'd be in touch.

—Then I couldn't remember her name, he said.

—Ah, Jesus.

—Blank, he said. —Fuckin' blank. Nothing.

—For fuck sake.

—Do you remember it? he asked me. —Now?

—No, I said. —What is it?

—Wait, he said.

He wasn't even sure if he'd ever known her name – when he was outside the classroom.

—I could've asked her, I suppose.

—That might have been a bit strange, I said.

—True, he said. —But, anyway.

—Did she know yours?

—She did.

—Are you sure?

—I think she did.

—Was the maths teacher happy with Holly? I asked.

—Very, he said. —Holly's great.

He had her number but not her name. He decided she'd have to phone or text him first. If it was going to happen, it was up to her. What *it* was, he didn't know.

—Some sort of hole to be filled, he said. —No – that sounds wrong. I don't mean it crudely.

—Okay.

—An emptiness or something, he said. —Four wasted decades.

—You're joking.

He shook his head. The grin – the fun in his eyes as he looked over his lenses – was gone.

—Just because you saw her?

I watched his face as he pushed back words that wouldn't do.

—No, he said, finally. —Not just that.

He was trying to put the words together, the right words in good order; I could see him doing it. He wanted to hear himself say exactly what had happened, what he'd thought – how he'd felt.

—If –, he started. —If I'd seen her – just seen her. It would have been nothing. Just nice – or –. Nice to have seen that she was still around and looking so well, you know. But that's all. I think. I'd have texted you – for example. That kind of reaction. If I'd seen her from the car, say. Or if she was in here and we saw her leaving. A bit of a buzz – but nothing. I wouldn't have dashed after her. Or, even if she saw us and came over to say hello, that would have been it. But.

He picked up his knife and fork and cut at a piece of his peri peri chicken.

—That wasn't how it was, he said.

I expected him to fill his mouth and keep me waiting while he chewed. But he didn't. He wasn't entertaining himself now, or me. He was trying to understand. He was trying to be me, on the other side of the table, listening to his story, his version of events – the only version – for the first time. I'd been over for a few days between Christmas and New Year's, six months before – but he hadn't mentioned anything then. When I'd asked him how things were – and I'm sure I did ask him – he'd answered, 'Grand.' And nothing more. It was the response I always had ready too when I came over to Dublin. *I'm grand. We're grand. Everything's grand.* He must have left Trish by then; he must have walked out of the house.

He was listening, examining his own words.

—She expected me to be there, he said. —And I was expecting her.

—Is that true? I asked.

I believed what he was telling me. I could see that he was pushing aside other possibilities, resisting the urge to add or amuse.

—Which? he asked back.

This time he put the chicken into his mouth.

—That you expected her, I said. —Is that actually true? Is that how you felt?

He swallowed.

—Yeah.

—Then, I said. —There? In the school.

—Yes, he said. —Definitely.

—Your long lost love suddenly appeared in front of you, I said.

—No, he said.

I was there to listen, not to cross-examine him. I was there so he could see me listening. He hadn't noticed my sarcasm, or he hadn't cared. And, immediately, I was glad. I didn't want to hear it either.

—That wasn't it, he said. —It wasn't like that. I'd imagine that would be huge. A heart thing, you know. Thump, thump. Like terror. When you think there's someone following you. To mug you. Did that ever happen you?

I nodded.

—You were mugged?

—No, I said. —I thought you meant the feeling, when you know you've a heart in your chest. Pumping away. It happened to us, remember?

—I do, yeah, he said. —Near Fairview.

—Yep.

—I'll never forget it.

—No.

—The fuckers.

—Yep.

—But, anyway, he said. —This wasn't that – when I met her. It wasn't like that at all.

There is a reason why men don't talk about their feelings. It's not just that it's difficult, or embarrassing. It's almost impossible. The words aren't really there.

—That – you know – that 'Oh Jaysis' feeling, he said. —It wasn't like that. It was calm.

—Calm?

—Yeah, he said. —I think. It's a year ago. But, yeah – I think that's how it was.

—Well, it hasn't been that calm since, I said. —Judging by what you've been telling me.

—No, he agreed. —That's true.

He cut more chicken.

—It's not a mid-life thing either, he said. —So don't even mention it. I'm fuckin' sick of it.

—I don't go in for that shite, I told him.

'Shite', 'grand', 'Jaysis' – I packed the words with my clothes and toothbrush when I was coming to Dublin for a few days.

—I didn't fall for some young one, he said.

—I know that, I said. —I was there when she was a young one, remember.

—Yeah, sorry. I think –. I don't know.

—Don't know what?

—I think it might have been easier if she had been a young one. If I'd made an eejit of myself running after someone half my age.

20

—With your dick in your hand.

—That's exactly –, he started.

He was whispering now, leaning over his plate.

—You've no idea how many times I've had to listen to that phrase in the last twelve fuckin' months.

He gave me four different voices.

—With your dick in your hand, with your *dick* in your hand, with your *dick* in your *hand*, with your fucking *dick in your hands*.

—Was Trish the last one? I asked.

—No, he said. —No. That was my son. Gareth. Trish was the first. And the second.

He laughed first, and I followed.

—Hang on, he said.

He put the chicken into his mouth. He looked at me, raised his eyebrows as he chewed. He was pale – a mid-winter face in very hot weather. He looked like he was starving. My own plate was empty. I remember looking down at it and being surprised. I'd eaten the salmon, the broccoli – I must have; I remember ordering them – but I'd tasted nothing.

He rested his fork on the side of his plate.

—I think they'd have understood, he said. —It would have made sense. If I'd been caught with a younger woman. Or even a neighbour, you know. The mad one next door.

I nodded.

—A bit of stupidity through the garden hedge, he said. —They'd have got that.

He sighed, smiled.

—But –, he said.

—But what?

—I'm – I don't know. Here we are and I'm still trying to explain it. I looked at her and it was like

21

nothing much had happened since the last time I'd seen her.

—And again, I said. —I'm going to ask you. Is that actually true?

He looked down at his plate. He looked up.

—I don't know.

She was the girl with the cello. But we didn't know that until later, in a different place. We sat at the bar that first day and felt accepted. One of my children is the age I was then – he's older – and I look at him when he lets me and I see a child, a kid trying to be an adult. He has a beard and a boyfriend; he lives in London, in Peckham. He's up and running, as they say. But he looks so young. The beard is a disguise.

We must have looked like that. We were working and twenty-one but we must have looked like two boys chancing their arms, hoping to get served in a real pub, in daylight. Served by a grown-up. That was how I felt, even though we'd already been drunk once that day and had had no problem being served in any pub in Dublin; I hadn't been refused service since my second-last year in school. But this one was different. This one felt like a club. Its lack – no radio, no television, music, no framed Doors of Dublin poster – seemed like more.

It was quiet.

—I love this, Joe said – he whispered.

—Me too, yeah.

I hadn't read a newspaper in a pub before but this was where I was going to do it. I hadn't sat by myself and drunk a slow pint; I'd never had a pint alone. I would now, here. I'd sit and look in front of me. I wouldn't shift on my stool or look over my shoulder. I'd be a man.

I didn't say this. I didn't think this. I felt it. For a while, I noticed no one else. I didn't see the women and the man pick up their instrument cases and leave. I must have heard them, I suppose, and I probably turned and looked at them as they left. It's not that I don't remember; I didn't care – that was what mattered. I remember how I felt. I'd entered a new state. I'd put on a man's jacket. I was a man. Because I'd walked into this particular pub. The boys who'd pissed in the bucket across in Mercer's Hospital were gone.

The place emptied and filled, and emptied again. The man with the magazine – it was *Private Eye* – stayed. But after the musicians had left, the place quickly filled again, this time with people with shopping bags. Previously, even earlier that day, we'd have sneered. Fuckin' shopping. Now we smiled. These were adults. Having a drink like us. It was women with shopping bags, and men with women. They were damp – it was raining out there – and happy. There were bursts of quiet laughter. There was no one trying to lasso the room. They all knew the barman. He was the landlord and, that afternoon, he ruled alone; he'd no help behind the bar. He beamed at the customers, greeted them all like they were fresh off the mailboat. And they beamed back. They'd known him for years, and he'd known them. He served them drink but it seemed incidental. They'd come in for a chat and approval, and he gave it. He really knew who they were. He liked them and they loved him.

He was called George. The name was in the air, never out of it. *George?* It was in the smoke. *George.* It was never a demand, always a greeting. He never rushed but he was always there. He smiled at us whenever he passed.

—Gentlemen, he said.

He wasn't being sarcastic, or snide. This was the thing: he respected us. And this is true: no adult male – no man older than me – had ever respected me before. Except, perhaps, my father. But he was my father, and a widower. There were just the two of us in the house and we got on fine without having to try too hard; I loved my father and I hated him. George didn't know us but he gave us the time he gave everyone else. There were generations of his customers there, in that hour between five and six. Some came in earlier, and some stayed longer. But they were all there in that hour, every Saturday. It became my favourite time of the week. There was no television or radio to give us the football results but I didn't miss them. We were going to become those people; we already were those people. There was a handsome man who hadn't shaved for a few days, with a bit of good grey in his hair. He was with a great-looking woman with a Switzer's bag. I'd be that man in ten years, maybe fifteen. I'd be here at teatime every Saturday. It would never be teatime in this world.

—How long've we been here? Joe asked me, that first afternoon.

—Don't know, I said.

I looked at my watch.

—Two hours? More? Three, maybe.

—How many pints have we had? he asked.

I had to think about it.

—Two, I said.

I looked at my pint. I wasn't ready for a fresh one.

—One an' a half.

—Jesus, said Joe. —That's fuckin' amazin'.

24

Ordinarily, we'd have been on our fifth, becoming just us, closing off the world around us. Protecting and building ourselves. We'd been drunk already that day, so we were just topping up what was already there. But it was different. We were here. We didn't need to cower or snarl, turn our backs on people who wouldn't have noticed. We didn't have to make our own noise. It was a dream; it had all the qualities of a good one. It was the drink, I know, the holes and fuzz it could give to the surroundings. Nothing was sudden or unwanted; there was nothing beyond the afternoon. It was the perfect state and I know now, decades later, it was only possible on a Saturday afternoon, in George's. I don't think I'm being sentimental, or *just* sentimental.

I smiled at George.

—Two, please, George, I said.

I don't recall smiling but I must have. I was twenty-one. In the ten years before that afternoon I'd smiled only when I'd decided to. This, again – *here* – was different. I watched George fill the glasses and leave them on the towel, beside four other waiting pints. He smiled at the line of six, then turned to fill glasses with gin and vodka. I looked at Joe. He was smiling, so I must have been too. It wasn't a grin. It wasn't because I'd been cheeky, because I'd called a middle-aged man I didn't know George. I hadn't been cheeky. Cheek was a thing of the past, as were anger and resentment, stupidity, exclusion. That was why Joe was smiling. We were in a new, unexpected life and we were at home in it. Adulthood wasn't too bad at all.

There was another thing too, another ingredient. We were being shown a new life; we were observing the middle-class world, an ease, a grace we'd never seen before. It could be ours if we wanted it.

—Gentlemen, said George when he put the pints down in front of us.

—Thanking you, George, said Joe.

It was his turn to call a grown man George.

—They look the business, he said.

George chuckled and accepted the money. He brought back the change – 'Now, sir' – and left it beside my pint.

—Thanks, George.

We were pissed, of course. Rat-arsed. I knew that when I stood up and went downstairs to the Gents. I was counting the steps down. I heard myself and stopped. But even that, the trip to the jacks, was different. My feet on the wood gave back the self-assured taps of a man who knew where he was going. I even looked back to see who was coming down behind me. There was no one; it was me who owned the self-assurance.

I came back up from the toilet and the place was emptying. The shoppers were heading home, and so was the man with the *Private Eye* and ponytail. For a minute – a minute – it was just us and George. It was thrilling.

—It's quiet now, said Joe.

—Yes, said George.

He was gathering the empty and half empty glasses and bottles from the three tables behind us. He put them on the counter.

—The calm before the storm, he said.

He was still smiling. He loved the storm, he loved the calm.

I looked around. It was a black and white world. White walls, black window frames, black counter, the white shirt on George.

—The jacks, I said quietly.

—Wha'? said Joe.

—You should see it.

—I will.

—It's clean, I said.

—Fuck off.

—It's well lit, I said. —There's a fuckin' bulb.

—My God.

—I'm tellin' yeh now, I said. —You'd eat your fuckin' dinner off the floor.

The room was warm and the cold that rushed in when the door opened was dramatic and welcome. But the intruder wasn't. We'd had George to ourselves and now we didn't. It was a small young man who'd come in – he wasn't a man at all; he was just a boy, a Dickensian kind of kid – and he took off his anorak while the door was still swinging shut. He was wearing a white shirt. He was staff, the apprentice.

—William, said George.

—George, said William.

—Did you have your dinner? George asked him.

—Liver, said William.

George clapped his hands and rubbed them.

—Lovely, he said. —With onions.

—I don't like onions, said William.

He'd disappeared behind a door and he came back out without the anorak. He looked at us and nodded. I didn't like it. He was seventeen, maybe eighteen, and he was nodding at his peers, two lads from across the river. He didn't see what he should have been seeing. George would look at us now and see kids.

—Did your mother put the onions on your plate? George asked William.

—She did, yeah, said William.

—Then I hope you ate them, said George, and he winked at us.

And that was it. We were still adults. William absorbed the lesson and George put the last of the glasses and bottles onto the counter. Then he went back behind the bar and started to wash them. George washed, William dried. He dropped the bottles that George rinsed into a crate and carried the crate away, downstairs. I expected George to look at us again, and smile. But he didn't. I was yearning – dying – to say something softly cruel about the kid. But I didn't. It wouldn't have been welcome; I knew that. It would have been childish.

—Good man, George, said Joe. —The lad should know his onions.

George laughed. He dried the last glass and put it on a shelf below him. His laughter wasn't loud or con-spiratorial, or diplomatic or forced. He'd heard something amusing and he'd laughed. Joe wasn't asking him to betray his apprentice, or to give us permission to tear into him when he came back upstairs. He'd said something funny – onions were always good for a laugh – and, while he was at it, he'd asserted our right to a vote in the land of the grown-ups. And George's response had affirmed that right.

—Two more, please, George.

The door swung open, and open, and open, and a new population slid in and took over the room, younger than the shoppers from earlier but two or three signifi-cant years older than us. We were at the back, near the coat hooks and the two flights of stairs, down to the Gents and up to the Ladies. People flowed in so quickly, it was as if one big gang of friends was arriving at once. They occupied the area near the door, then seemed to send out scouts to the remaining corners. Passages opened and two or three stepped in and took the remaining stools at the bar and the tables and benches along the walls. They were all at home, all of them linked, somehow. Although I could see now, it wasn't just one polite mob. There were men in twos and threes, there were two men alone, there were couples, and couples with couples, and two bigger, looser groups of friends. But there was something about them. Confidence, perhaps. Physical ease – they stood and leaned and sat, crossed their legs like they'd been trained to do it properly. It wasn't Christmas or coming up to Christmas but they all seemed like returned emigrants who'd picked up ways, notions, a body language that they could never have learnt in Ireland.

They were gorgeous.

William topped up our pints and placed them in front of us.

—Did you get the results? I asked him.

I needed a blast of familiarity and William was the nearest thing to us in the shop.

—Which do you want? he asked.

—Leeds.

He smiled.

—Lost.

—Liverpool, said Joe.

—Won.

He gave Joe his change.

—Now, sir.

That was enough; it steadied us. I'd felt the urge to leave or get plastered. I'd been panicking a bit and Joe, I knew, had too. But we said nothing. We sat and watched, and listened. It wasn't the fact that most of these people had a few years on us. I wasn't sure about that now, either. I was looking at young faces around me, and in the long mirror behind the bar. I reminded myself: I'd be twenty-two before the end of the year. I was educated; I had a degree. Joe had been working for more than three years. These people were at home; that was it. At home here, with George. At home everywhere, I suspected. We'd just arrived. We were only in the door. We'd none of their blood.

Joe was better at it than I was. I was good in my head; I was debonair, polished, ready to talk. But – I see it now; I see myself – I sat there. I looked at them all in the mirror. I didn't feel excluded. That was the big advance. But I was shy.

Joe wasn't. Or, I don't think he was. He didn't turn on his stool, to join in with the group of men and women behind us. He didn't offer anything on Ronald Reagan or the state of Irish rugby. He didn't, as my father would have put it, butt in. But he was lighter, somehow – looser. He sat on his stool side-saddle and helped pass back pints and change. He joked with people he'd never seen before. He smiled at women. He was *there*, much more than I was or could be. I loved him for it, and I didn't.

She was there. The woman we'd noticed earlier, the girl we'd find out played the cello – she was back. I saw her properly now. I realised first that I'd seen her before and I was a bit slow grabbing the fact that I'd seen her here, once, just three hours before. She – the sighting of her – seemed much more important. She felt long lost and suddenly found. I even thought I'd know her name.

She was beautiful. Something about her was beautiful. Gorgeous was our usual word but there was something about her: she wasn't real; she was more than real, or less – *too* real.

She'd changed her clothes and done something with her hair. It had been in a ponytail earlier – I think – maybe even a bun. Now it was free and long, like a veil or a scarf. She was wearing a black leather jacket, a biker's jacket. I hoped she'd look at me; she'd see me in the mirror, over her friend's shoulder, and she'd smile. I'd smile back at her reflection. I'd turn in my stool and smile at her. Then something magic would happen. She'd come to me or I'd get off the stool without deciding to; I'd go over there and I'd make her laugh. I'd stop being drunk but the courage would stay with me. She just had to look. To smile.

But she didn't do either. I remember nothing else. But we were there again the following Saturday.

—So she phoned you, I said.

He looked at me. He hesitated.

—Yes.

He seemed happy with the answer. We were back to facts, events.

—Not immediately, he said. —Not, like, that night or the next day.

—How long after?

—End of the week, he said.

—Friday?

—Thursday.

—I'd have guessed that, I said.

—Why – how?

—She'd phone you on Thursday, arrange something for Friday. End of the week. TGIF. That kind of shite.

—Don't get fuckin' snide, he said.

31

He meant it. He was hurt.

—Sorry, I said. —I was just imagining the start of something – an affair, I suppose. A fling.

—And have you ever had an oul' fling, yourself, Davy? he asked.

The anger was gone. For the first time that evening he was curious. The question was defensive but he wanted to know the answer.

—No, I said. —I haven't.

—Okay.

—What about you? I said. —Have you? Before –.

—Yeah, he said. —Yeah. Once – one. A woman in work. The Christmas party, believe it or not. All the fuckin' clichés. A good while ago though – ten years. More. It was stupid.

—Did Trish find out?

—No, he said. —No, she didn't. Thank God. It was –. Ah, Christ. She was unhappy.

—The woman?

—The woman – yeah. She was getting married.

—Jesus. And did she?

—Yeah, she did, he said. —But, no, it didn't last long.

—The marriage?

—No, the fling, he said. —The whatever. I don't know about the marriage – I'd have my doubts. But it was just, really – we needed some sort of a justification for the sex. I think. We couldn't admit that we did it because we were drunk. Too old for that or something. So we met up again twice after Christmas. Three times – yeah, three. And we were drunk then as well. It was fuckin' terrible, really. Jesus, when I think about it.

—Did she invite you to the wedding?

—No, he said. —God, no.

—Anyway.

—Yeah.

—She phoned you, I reminded him. —Your woman. After the parent–teacher meeting.

—Yeah. Yeah – she did.

He smiled now.

—She did.

—What's her name? I asked. —She must have said it when she called – when you answered.

—Jessica.

Nothing happened. Nothing rolled in my head, clicked into place. I couldn't remember her being called Jessica.

—How long did it take? I asked.

—What?

—To find out her name.

—You're asking strange questions, he said.

The wrong questions, he meant. Her name didn't matter.

—Just curious, I said. —These things can be awkward, I suppose. And you said it, yourself – you didn't know her name. I'm always forgetting people's names. Especially these days.

Six months before, the last time we met, we'd have had a laugh about the indignities of ageing, the list of daily humiliations. *Especially these days.* What I'd half intended telling him about this time was the sheer scale, the limitless variety of the surnames I had to deal with at work, and the first names too – never the *Christian* names, how the names accompanying the English accents had changed, or been added to, since I'd moved to England. I was good at it, in fact. I made sure I knew the names – Okeke, Igbinedion, Anikulapo-Kuti, Sargsyan, Dewab, Ali, Smith, Bautista, Chan.

I enjoyed it. I made sure there was never the hesitation before the name, or a little question mark after it – Mr ... *Okeke*? More important things, vital things I forgot – completely. But not at work, not the names. I made lists. I conquered the names and voted Remain. I'd intended – half intended – telling him that.

—Same here, he said. —It's shocking. Head like a fuckin' sieve. But yeah – she said, Hi, it's Jessica.

—And you knew it was her.

—Yeah, he said. —I'd put *George* into the address book. Temporarily. Till I found out her name. If she phoned.

—And she did.

—She did.

—Where were you?

—At home, he said.

—What time?

—Nine? he said. —A bit later – half-nine. We were watching – actually.

He sat up straight. He smiled – he grinned. He became himself.

—D'you know what we were watching? he said.

—What?

—*The Affair.*

—Really?

—Can you fuckin' believe it? You've seen it, yeah?

—No.

—Watch it, he said. —It's brilliant. Filthy. The first series, anyway. We were watching the second series.

—What episode?

He laughed.

—Four.

He shrugged.

—I don't know, he said. —But it might have been four.

34

—And she was Jessica.

—Yeah.

—Did the name ring a bell?

—Yeah, he said. —It did.

—You remembered she was called Jessica?

—Are we in a police station again, Davy? he said.

—Sorry, I said. —It's just, I've no recollection of her name at all.

—But you remember it now, he said.

—Yes, I said. —Yeah, I do. At least –.

—What?

—I don't know. I think I do. Yeah, yeah – I do remember it.

But I didn't. Not then.

George smiled as if he'd been expecting us. William came out of the room in the back and gave us the half time scores. The man with the ponytail looked up from his copy of the *New Statesman* and stared at us.

She wasn't there – and that was when I remembered her. I hadn't thought of her all week but now I missed her so much I wanted to go home. There were two women and a man, three violin cases. I didn't know if they were the same women and the same violins, but they were at the same table and under the same window. Three violins, two women, no cello.

We parked ourselves on our stools and watched George put the glasses under the Guinness taps. He put the pints on the towel to settle.

—Gentlemen, he said.

—Thanks, George.

The door swung open and he went down to meet the men who'd just walked in.

—No cello today, I said.

—No, said Joe.

I knew then that he'd noticed her too and that, like me, he was happily suffering.

—She might be in later, I said.

—Yeah.

We were sober. We hadn't seen each other during the week. We'd met at the bus stop down from Joe's house. We hadn't bothered with the Dandelion Market; we'd gone straight to George's. We hadn't said much. We were afraid to talk, I think, afraid that we'd find the place altered, or ordinary. Not once, though, did I think of her. It was the stool, the counter, the pint in front of me, my friend beside me, the night ahead of us. But then she was there, or her absence was there, and I was devastated and so was Joe. The other women didn't interest us. There could be no compensation. We watched them leave with their instruments. We watched the arrival of the shoppers, and the departure of the shoppers and the man with the ponytail. We got the final scores from William. We watched George at work. Joe went out to the phone box at the foot of the stairs to the Ladies, to tell his mother that he wouldn't be home for his tea.

—Why d'you do tha'? I asked him when he got back.

—Wha'?

—Phone home.

—Just to tell her.

—Tha' you won't be home?

—Yeah.

—You're never home.

This was for George. He was at the taps, filling glasses. Listening – not listening – smiling, taking orders.

—Yes, I am.

—On Saturdays, I said. —When was the last time you went home for your tea?

—A while ago.

—Months ago.

—Okay. She just likes me to phone. She likes answerin' the phone. We've only had it a couple o' years.

We were waiting. Holding our breath. Waiting for her. Praying for her. The woman I now know was called Jessica. *Is* called Jessica.

—Wha' d'you think? he asked me.

I knew exactly what – who – he meant. The place was filling again. The day was over; we were sitting in the night. We were looking at women. There was always the ideal woman but there were all the other women too. We were recovering. Starting to feel the buzz of the previous week. These would be our people now and this was still our future, with or without the woman. We were laughing again, chatting. Soaking it in, soaking in it. I could feel myself melting – it was good – flowing slowly into the noise, the accents, the jokes, the stories, the geography. Listening. Hoping someone would say something to me. Male, female – a way in. The start. It was why we'd been coming into town. To make the break. To live up, somehow, to the music we loved, the books we read. To walk streets instead of roads, cross a real river, sit in the pubs that Behan and Flann O'Brien had sat in, find the women who'd see, who'd understand, who'd hold us, who'd do things to us. Who'd come up to us and start it. Let us in. Let us soar.

She was there.

I think I knew it before I saw her. But I've no idea why I think that. It's a long time ago; I'm a different man. I'd forgotten she existed. Her sudden resurrection – Joe pushing back the stone – was unsettling.

She was there.

Over at the door, behind a group of men and women at the other end of the bar. She'd asked for a pint of Harp and I watched George carry it from the tap to that group and I saw her hand, her arm, her shoulder, her face, as the bodies made way and she leaned in and paid for the pint, took it and smiled at George. Then the curtain closed and she was back behind the gang. But I knew she was there before I saw that. I knew the pint that George was pouring was for her. I might have heard her voice through the other voices – although I hadn't heard her speak the week before. But I knew the hand was hers, the arm, the shoulder. I saw the curtain open, I saw the curtain close.

We were at the wrong end of the bar.

That was what we were, it was what we did. We anticipated rejection, we guaranteed it. Outsiders – and we made sure it stayed that way. Honest, vital, yearning, pure. One woman – that woman – would see it. She'd come and take my hand.

My hand.

Our hand.

—What did you tell Trish?

—What?

—When she phoned – when Jessica phoned you. When you were watching *The Affair*. What did you say to Trish?

I wanted it to fall apart. I wanted to delay it – their second meeting.

—Nothing, he said.

—Nothing?

He shrugged.

—Work, he said. —Something like that.

—Were you sitting beside each other? I asked him.

—I think so.

—Hang on, I said. —Joe.

—What?

—So far, like – so far. You've been really precise. Seeing her in the school. Watching *The Affair*.

—I don't remember which episode.

—Don't start, I said. —You know what I mean. You know exactly where you were sitting. You know exactly what happened. You might regret starting to tell me, okay. But it's too late for that.

I think he'd heard himself and he didn't like it. He was belittling Trish – inevitably. He was being cruel. His kids were in the house, somewhere near. He was about to destroy his family and, in the telling, he'd laughed.

He looked at me.

—I don't –, he said. —I actually don't know why I'm telling you.

I didn't respond. He was talking to himself. He knew exactly why he was telling me.

—I was sitting beside her, he said.

I said nothing but he heard the next question, anyway.

—Close, he said. —We watch – watched, fuck it – a lot of box sets. Sky Atlantic and Netflix, you know. Some great stuff. We –.

He stopped. He put down his fork. He picked it up.

—We always went to bed early after *The Affair*.

He sighed.

—It's a bit shit, isn't it?

I didn't answer. I didn't nod or shake my head.

—So, yeah, he said. —The phone went. It was in my pocket.

He smiled, slightly.

—I had it on vibrate, you know. Trish felt it before I did. She nudged me – that's your phone. And –

—It was Jessica.

—Yeah. So. I – well – I put the phone to my ear.

—You knew who it was.

—Yeah. I told you. I'd put *George* in the address book. I don't know any other Georges, except George from the pub. So – and yeah, I looked at the screen before I accepted the call. And, anyway – yeah. It was short.

—Did you go out into the hall or anything?

—What? No – no. Trish put the telly on pause. And it was very short, you know – the call. She asked me how I was. I said fine or grand. She said she'd like to meet up.

—Did you ask her how she was?

—No. I just said I'd phone her in the morning.

—You made it sound like work.

—Well – yeah. Yeah. But I didn't plan it, like. It's – what? – it's sneaky or something. I know – I *knew*. But I didn't have lines prepared in case she phoned me when I was with Trish – or at work. Or anywhere. It just seemed the easiest thing to do. But really, I could've just told Trish that it was someone I used to know and we'd met at the parent–teacher meeting, and we'd swapped numbers.

—As it had happened.

—Yeah – exactly. As it happened.

—Why didn't you tell Trish then?

—Honestly? he said. —I'm not sure. And honestly – I didn't want to.

—You could have told her that day – the day you met. On your way home together.

—That's true, he said. —And I didn't. I never even thought about telling her. That's not true, though. I didn't want to tell her. So, there you go. It's all out, Davy. I told Trish it was a woman from an ad agency. A pain in the arse, I said. I showed her the screen – George – the name, you know. And we laughed. Trish thought it was a bit hilarious, a woman called George. Like Enid Blyton.

—What?

—There was a girl called George in the Enid Blyton books. The Famous Five, or the something Seven. D'you remember?

—Think so.

—So, he said. —She was supposed to be a lesbian.

—What?

—George in the Enid Blyton books. I heard that, or read it somewhere. I think it was Trish told me. Yeah, she was gay, apparently. Or maybe it was the actor who played her on the telly – doesn't matter.

He looked at me. He wanted me to take over, to ask him. But I didn't.

—We watched the rest of the episode, he said. —And went up to bed.

He looked out a window, at the road and the bay and Bull Island. He had to turn to do this. I was the one facing the windows. He spoke as I looked at the side of his head. I half expected to see Trish's face on the other side of the glass, staring in at us.

—Same as always, he said.

He turned back to face me, although he looked down at his plate.

—Yeah, he said, as if answering a question. —Same as always.

—Really?

41

—Yeah, he said. —Yeah – no. I knew –. At least I think I knew. I felt –. I felt it was the last time we'd have sex. I felt – it's hard to – I don't know. Be honest, I suppose. Candid – is that the word? I imagined it was going to be the last time.

—Was it?

—No, he said. —Like I said – the same as always. There was nothing sudden or anything.

He looked at me.

—Okay.

—Life went on, he said.

—And that was –. Was that a good thing?

—What?

—Life, I said. —The sex. You weren't suffering, pretending? Feeling violated.

—No, he said. —Not at all. God, no.

He'd missed my sarcasm and I was glad now that he had. We rarely spoke about sex in any kind of detail, especially since we'd got married. We wouldn't be starting now. I didn't want the details. I didn't want to hear myself making up moments to match his.

—But, he said. —I definitely felt something was happening. And I don't just mean I'd be phoning Jessica in the morning and whatever might have come from that. The possibility of cheating – the idea. I don't mean that. It was like I'd remembered something.

—What?

—Something, he said. —Something important that I'd forgotten I'd needed.

—Your keys.

—Don't start, he said, and smiled. —I've thought about this. To try and explain it to the kids some time. If they ever want to hear it. And to myself, to be honest.

—Do they talk to you?

—The kids? he said. —No. No, they don't. It's shite.

—Must be.

—Yeah.

—Sorry, I said. —Go on.

—I think, he said. —The easiest way – the clearest way. Say you suffer from amnesia.

—A blow to the head.

—That'll work, he said.

I checked my phone. I took it from my pocket, had a quick look. The screen was blank – no missed calls or messages.

—You forget everything, said Joe. —Absolutely everything. But bit by bit things come back. Colours, say. The names of the colours of things that you can see from your bed in the hospital. It's a gradual thing, day by day. The names of things come back to you at random. You realise you're lying on a bed, you're looking out a window.

—You've thought about this.

He ignored that.

—There's a seagull out there, he said. —And a plane. You're slowly filling up with words. And the images that come with them. But there's still a huge hole. You don't know why, but you know there's something missing. And it – the hole, I mean – the knowledge, the lack of it. It becomes more important than the other discoveries. Your son comes in and you know him – you *know* him. He's not just the moody kid who comes in to see you. You know his name because you've always known it, not just because you were told it. You gave him his name – you know that. And you know what a son is – really is. And what a father is. And what it feels like. It's like your life, all your living, your

43

experiences, are filling you, pouring through you again. Your wife, your other kids, your mother. Your job. Everything's becoming sharper. Feelings are making sense. You wake up with an erection and you know why. The word erection is there for you. And it's great – although maybe not in a hospital bed. But it's great. You hold the thing in your hand and you know what it's there for and you know you remember what women are like and why they excite you. And skin. And breasts and all the other things you've loved – skirts, hair, laughter. And babies and birth, and you're beginning to feel complete. But not. You're certain there's something important missing. Something's still lost and you haven't a clue what it is. You just know it's there – and it's not. And say you get out of the hospital and things stop being fresh and new and life is normal again, and it's as if you never had the accident or whatever it was in the first place. It's as if you never lost your memory. Day to day, everything seems back in place. Like footballers' names, say, when you see them on the telly. And knowing exactly where to put your hand, how far you have to lean across, so that it lands exactly on your wife's hip when you're both in bed and falling asleep. Your day to day life smothers the ache, the sense that there's something missing. You're back in your life. And then bang.

   —Jessica.

He blinked.

   —You understand, he said.

   —I think so, I said. —Yeah, I think so.

I'd forgotten he spoke like that, that he'd once been capable of speaking like that. That I'd sit back while he rolled out the story. I'd forgotten, completely. I'd often wondered – I'd just been wondering – why I kept in touch with this man. I'd forgotten who he was. I understood exactly what he meant.

—What about Trish? I said.

—What?

He looked annoyed, and a bit stupid. For a second.

—Sorry, he said. —What about Trish?

—Jessica filled the gap, so to speak. Like you just said. And I'm not trivialising what you said, by the way. I *do* know what you mean. I think I do. But what about Trish? Did she – I don't know – did she just stop being there? Jessica arrives and –

—Are you serious? he said. —Davy – are you fuckin' serious? Trish?

He was alive again, glad to be speaking.

—Did she stop being there? he said. —Did, she, stop? You don't know Trish.

—No, I agreed. —I don't know her.

—You do.

—Not really, no, I said. —I don't. And you don't know Faye.

—Okay, he said. —You don't know her well, we'll say. But Trish is a force of nature. That sounds like shite but it's true. She's amazing, Davy. Believe me. Like, to be clear here. Davy? To be clear. I love Trish.

—Okay.

—I love her. The fuckin' ground she walks on.

—Okay, I said. —I hear you. But when you followed her up to bed. After *The Affair* and the phone call.

—Davy, he said. —This isn't about sex.

—You had sex with Trish.

—Yes.

—You'd just spoken on the phone with Jessica.

—Yes.

—You brought that upstairs with you. You must have, surely.

—Okay, he said. —Yes.

—And this isn't about sex – you said.

—Now, he said. —Now it isn't. Now. It's misleading.

—Well, I'm feeling misled.

—We're jumping the gun, he said. —That's the problem. It's my fault, I think. So – being blunt. I had sex with Trish that night.

—But you were thinking about Jessica.

—No, he said. —No. Honestly, though – a bit. But Trish is Trish. Trish –. I'm not going into detail – it'd be wrong.

—Yes.

—I'll just say. Actually – two things. I'll say two things. One is that, with Trish. There was only the two of us in the bed – really. Okay? And the other thing is, and I only thought of this later. I think she knew.

—Trish knew?

—I think so, he said. —I think she did.

I watched him. He was looking at a corner of the room, above me, to my left. Then he looked at me.

—It was like she was doing her driving test, he said.

He burst out laughing. He did – the noise charged out of him. A woman sitting near the front, at a window, turned and looked our way, squinted at Joe's back, then turned back to her plate. It was the first time we'd been loud. I was laughing too.

—Sorry, said Joe. —Fuck – that sounds terrible. But it came into my head. Remember when you were doing your test and you were told – well, I was, anyway. By my da. Not just to remember to look in the rear mirror and the side mirrors but to make sure the inspector

46

saw you doing it. The inspector or the instructor or whatever his job description is. Make sure he saw you doing all the correct things.

I was still laughing.

—Well, Trish was doing her driving test that night, he said. —If she heard me, Davy – fuckin' hell. I can hear her. *At least I fuckin' passed it.* But anyway – yeah. I think she knew. At some level she knew. And now that I think of it, I was probably the one who was doing the test. And Trish was the inspector.

—Did you pass?

—Probably not. No.

—She'll have to go to the jacks, said Joe. —And this is fuckin' Thermopylae.

We were sitting right at the doors, down to the Gents and up to the Ladies.

—She's drinkin' pints, he said.

—Harp.

—She'll have to pass this way.

And she did. Jessica, or the woman – the girl – I know was called Jessica. Her hair passed us. And her back. And we saw her legs for a second from the knees down, her jeans, as she went up the stairs.

I waited for Joe. He didn't let me down.

—God, Davy, I wish I was a toilet seat.

—Tha' particular toilet seat.

—Yeah – Christ. Only tha' one. Or the jacks itself, I'd prefer tha'. The fuckin' flush – the whole shebang.

—I'm not so sure.

—I fuckin' am, he said. —She'll be done by now.

—Washin' the hands.

—Always, he said. —Here we go, she's comin' back.

47

Even when the place was full, you could hear the feet, you could feel them, on the stairs as the women came down from the loo. But never going up – a different journey, a different kind of weight. We heard her, then saw her feet, her legs, and we turned away just as she got to the foot of the stairs and opened the door, back in.

At least, I turned away. Joe didn't.

—She smiled at me, he said, and we watched the back of her head as she pushed her way – and she did push; I remember that – back to her friends at the front of the shop.

—Did she?

—Yeah.

—Have you witnesses?

—Myself, he said. —An' her.

—That's not enough, I said.

—It fuckin' is.

—Did you phone her back? I asked him.

—She phoned me, he said.

—Before you did.

—Yeah.

—I mean the second time, I said. —The day after.

—I know, he said. —No, I was going to but then I wondered about it, you know. What was I letting myself in for. I wasn't sure if –. I was perfectly happy, Davy, you know. That's true – really. I don't know –. I kind of decided. I'd wait till lunch time, or whatever. I'd wait.

—Put it off.

—Or forget about it – yeah. But –.

He sat back, then sat back up. He put his elbows on the table. He looked down as he did it, made sure he was well clear of his plate.

—I love her, he said. —I always loved her.

—What?

I waited for him to grin, become Joe.

—I loved her, he said.

He nodded, slightly. He was listening to himself, and answering himself.

—Yeah, he said. —So –

—Sorry, Joe, I said. —I'm being stupid here. You loved who?

He looked at me.

—Jessica, he said.

He looked around, like he was looking for a waiter; he wanted to get the bill and go. But he didn't. He settled down again, looked back at me.

—It sounds mad. I know.

He was still listening, talking to himself.

The waiter was beside the table.

—More beers, gentlemen?

—Yes, please, I said. —Thanks.

—It's true, said Joe.

He was looking at me again. He sounded different, more convinced. Less pale. I didn't want to say anything now. I didn't know why I'd let the waiter go off for the beers. I wanted to go. Back to my father. Back to something I understood. I half hoped I'd feel the phone in my pocket, a text or a call. But I couldn't resist.

—How can you say that? I asked him.

—What?

—You loved her.

—Because it's true, he said.

—For fuck sake, Joe, I said. —Thirty years. Thirty-five years – no, thirty-six.

—Asbestos can incubate for forty years, he said.

—Sorry?

—Inhale asbestos, he said. —It can still get you forty years later. It happened a friend of mine – you didn't know him. Jim Cahill – a carpenter.

—Are you saying she's asbestos?

I was hoping he'd sit up and glare at me, laugh, hit me or the table.

—No, he said. —I'm only saying.

—What? I said.

I was furious now. I wasn't sure why. What he was saying was ridiculous. That was fine; I don't think I minded that. But he expected me to follow him, to nod and believe. So I kept going. My own elbows were on the table.

—You're saying – what? Your love was incubating? Fuckin' hibernating, in your fuckin' heart? Is it a song? My love is incubating.

The waiter arrived back and put the bottles on the table, picked them up again one at a time, took the tops off them, and put them back down. He picked up my glass.

—That's grand, I said. —Thanks. We'll pour them ourselves.

—No better men, said the waiter.

He smiled and was gone.

—Go on, I said to Joe.

—You go on, he said.

—Well, I said. —This. You see the woman for the first time in – we'll say thirty-five years.

—It's thirty-seven years.

—Grand, I said. —And you can't remember her name. You might not ever have known her name.

—I did.

—Okay, I said. —And – it's not that you fell for her. I could understand that. Not that it matters if I

50

understand anything. But I'd understand it. She's well-preserved. The ageing beauty – and she sails down the corridor at you. You're feeling low, unloved.

He was looking straight back at me. He nodded slightly.

—Redundant, I said.

—Are you? he said. —Do you feel redundant?

—God, yeah, I said. —So. Yeah. I can imagine being excited. And a bit smitten. There's nothing in me that wouldn't understand that. If it was me. If she asked me for my number or whatever. If she kissed me and stayed close to me, so I'd feel her breath on my face. I'd go home imagining being with the younger version, half hoping she'll phone me. Half hoping she won't. And seriously – Joe. Joe. I *can* imagine phoning her back and falling in love. If I saw her doing the same. Or I thought I did. Falling for me – even enjoying my company. If we met for lunch or a drink and the chat wasn't too awkward. It would be great, I'd say. Brilliant. The same age, like. None of the guilt – calculating that she's nearer your daughter's age than your own. You'd have plenty to talk about. Especially if the years have been kind to her. She'd be a bit of an upgrade – I don't know.

I'd run out of words; I didn't want to be crude. *A bit of an upgrade.* I wished I hadn't said it. His expression hadn't changed. He looked like a man who was interested in what he was hearing.

—But, I said. —Saying you've always loved her. That I don't get. I don't understand it. Sorry.

I poured the beer into my glass.

—That living a lie thing, I said.

—What?

—All these years I've been living a lie.

51

—Did I say that?

—No.

—Did I suggest it?

—Yeah.

—How?

—Of course you did.

—How?

—You said it there. You always loved her.

—I did.

—But you hadn't seen the girl for most of your life.

I could feel myself wanting to shake, wanting to get up and go, or just move.

—It's like what I said about it incubating, he said.

—That's fuckin' idiotic.

—Fuck you, Davy.

—You can't take asbestos – or anything else, right. And compare it to human emotion, and expect to go unchallenged. No fuckin' way, Joe. The argument, if it's even an argument, has no validity at all. It explains absolutely nothing – sorry.

—Okay.

He shrugged.

—Maybe that's the problem with honesty.

—What?

—No one really believes it, he said.

—Jesus, Joe.

I'd give it another five minutes.

—What's happened to you? I asked him.

—Nothing.

—Joe.

—Nothing, he said again. —A lot – obviously. If you look at it one way. My life has changed completely. Fuckin' completely – Jesus, Davy.

He picked up his bottle.

—But I'm still the same, he said. —Same man.

—You're not.

—Oh, I am.

—Okay.

I watched him fill his glass. It was easier than watching him.

—But, I said. —Tell me.

—What?

—Your amnesia theory.

—It beats the asbestos theory, he said. —Or, so it seems.

He smiled. He was going to laugh; I hoped he was. He'd been having me on. He'd met a good-looking woman. They'd been having a fling. It had gone past that, too far. He was a fuckin' eejit – it would be a boast. He was where he was. For fuck sake.

I decided to give him a nudge.

—What's the sex like? I asked.

—There isn't any.

He smiled again. He should have shrugged. But he didn't.

—I told you already, he said.

—You didn't. When?

—I told you it wasn't about sex, he said. —Will we stay here or move on?

—We can finish these first, I said.

I held up my glass.

—Okay, he said. —Grand.

I wasn't a drinker. I dreaded having to drink two or three pints. I'd tell him I had to get back to my father. It wouldn't be a lie.

—You met her, I said.

It seemed like days since this had started.

—Yeah, he said. —So, anyway, she phoned me. Again, like. The day after.

—Where were you?

—The toilet, he said. —In work. I swear to God, the glamour. I was washing my hands, drying them. A Dyson, or one of those jet engine ones.

—Give me a towel any day.

—Or the sides of my trousers, yeah. Anyway. I felt the phone in my pocket, just in time. I nearly dropped it.

—You knew it was her.

—No – yeah. No. It could have been anyone – any one of dozens of people. I've got the thing stuck to the side of my head half the day. And non-stop in the car.

—You'd said you'd phone her back.

—What?

—The night before, I said. —When she phoned you the first time. When you were watching *The Affair*. You told me you told her you'd phone her in the morning. You showed Trish your phone. *George*.

—Yeah.

—But you didn't.

—Because she phoned me first, he said. —Are you trying to catch me out here?

—No.

—Okay, he said. —But I told you already. Like – I had serious fuckin' misgivings, Davy. I told you.

—Did it not worry you? I asked him.

—What?

—That she phoned you again, I said. —That she couldn't wait.

—Are you serious?

His face was back; he was Joe again.

—When was the last time you felt that a woman couldn't wait to meet you? he asked. —Never mind everything else? When?

—Never, I said. —If I'm being honest.

54

I wasn't. Being honest.

My wife decided I was going to be her husband three minutes after she met me. Or so she's always said.

She was someone's daughter, some old friend of my girlfriend's mother. We were sitting beside each other at a wedding. At my girlfriend's brother's wedding. The friend, the mother's old friend, had recently died.

—I'm sorry.

—Ah, thanks.

—It's hard, I said.

I was about to tell her that my own mother was dead.

—Oh, good, she said. —Let's see if we can keep it that way.

She looked up from her prawn cocktail. She stared at me, and smiled, and changed her fork from her right to her left hand, and put her hand right under the table, on my leg. She walked her fingers backwards, up my thigh, and she leaned out, in front of me, against me, so she could chat to my girlfriend.

—You've a fab boyfriend here, Cathy, so you do.

—You watch yourself now, said Cathy.

She said it cheerfully, for the table. But she didn't like Faye. That was very clear.

—Don't worry, said Faye. —I'm only here for the grub, so I am.

She patted my leg goodbye and put her fork back in her right hand.

—First time I've ever eaten these yokes, she said.

—Prawns?

—Yeah.

—D'you like them?

—They'll do, she said. —I like the pink stuff. The sauce, like.

I watched her eat.

—Actually, I said. —Now that I think of it. Faye.

I gave Joe time to remember that Faye was my wife.

—What?

—She was all over me, I told him. —When we met each other the first time.

He smiled.

I wanted to talk to him for a change, and not have to listen. I wanted to entertain him.

—She terrified me, I said.

He laughed.

—It was at a wedding, I said. —Do you remember Cathy?

—No, he said. —Do I?

—We went with each other for a while.

—Hang on, he said. —The garda.

—That's right.

—She was nice.

—Yeah, she was, I said. —I really liked her.

—What happened?

—Well, I said. —Faye.

—Do I know this? he asked. —Did you tell me before?

—Don't think so, I said. —I don't think I'd have been able to tell anyone back then.

—Great, he said.

—It was too fuckin' –.

—Embarrassing.

—No, I said. —Unimaginable.

—Great – go on.

He was glad we'd swapped places, and so was I. And I told him about the wedding, why I was there, why Faye was there, what she'd said when I started to offer my condolences.

—She said that?

—Yeah.

—With Cathy right beside you?

—The other side of me, yeah.

—And did you? he asked.

—What?

—Stay hard.

—More or less, I said.

It wasn't right, what I was doing. I knew it, and felt it. It was crude and possibly cruel. And treacherous. But I knew this too: I wanted to hear myself talking about Faye. I wanted Joe to witness her. I was tired of his no-sex fling.

—Love at first sight, said Joe. —Jesus.

—I didn't even have to see her, I said.

That was true, somehow. The day after the wedding I couldn't have described her. I could have recited every word she'd said but I didn't know what colour her hair was, or her eyes. She overpowered me.

—I didn't have time to drink, I said.

He laughed again.

—Let's go and get one now while we're at it, he said. —A drink in a pub. Can we cope with the excitement?

—If we're careful, I said.

We paid the bill, gave the waiter two credit cards, left him a real fiver each for the tip, and went outside. It was still hot, shockingly hot.

—It's like we're stepping into a different country, said Joe.

—Yeah.

—I'm a bit sick of it.

—Yeah – same here. A bit.

—No more weather talk.

—Grand, yeah. Where'll we go?

There were two pubs we could walk to, the Sheds and the Pebble Beach.

—I was in the Sheds a while back, said Joe. —A funeral – the afters. It was fine.

—Grand.

We headed that way.

—Or we could go in to George's, said Joe.

—No.

—Come on.

He'd turned around, and I looked back too. There was a taxi coming towards us, heading towards town.

—We'll have one in the Sheds, I said. —And then decide.

He looked at his watch. It was more than three hours to closing time.

—Okay, he said. —That'll work.

I'd have the one in the Sheds, then head back to my father. I'd tell that to Joe when we were there with the pints in front of us.

—Go on, anyway, he said, as we walked through the heat, as we got used to it again. —What happened then?

—I'm not sure if I can tell it that way, I said. — Chronologically – blow by blow. So to speak.

—Did she?

—What?

—Blow you.

—No. No – shut up.

His Jessica was some sort of ghost of Saturdays past but Faye was to be the slut who crawled under the table at a wedding and opened my zip.

It was my fault.

—When she put her hand on my leg, I told him.
—She was joking.

—What?

—She wasn't really – I don't know. She wasn't trying
to seduce me.

—But, said Joe. —Her hand was still on your fuckin'
leg. Was it?

—Yeah.

There were times when I could still feel the fingers
marching up my thigh.

—But she wasn't –. Like I said, trying to seduce me
– or tease me. In the conventional sense. It wasn't like
that.

—Then what –?

—Shut up and listen, I said. —I shouldn't have told
you about her hand.

—But you did.

—I know – shut up. It was everything about her.

I wanted to go home. I wanted to go now to the
airport, get home and see Faye. Ask her to forgive me.
For forgetting, being stupid, a coward. For being here.
Away from her. For keeping her away.

—More than anything else, I said. —It was her voice.
No, not her voice. Her words.

—Her words?

—The way she spoke, I said. —Yeah. She commen-
tated on everything.

—Jesus, he said. —I'd hate that – no offence.

—You weren't there, I said. —It was incredible. The
best thing ever. That sounds crumby, but it was. It was
the sexiest fuckin' thing.

—Sexy?

—Ah, man, I'm telling you –.

I came from a silent house. My father and I passed each other and smiled. We spoke when we needed to, when we sat together at the kitchen table. My mother's death destroyed him. I remember laughter – his, hers. I remember long trips in the car, a black Ford Anglia, the two of them chatting while I stood between their seats. I was twelve when she died, and the radiators went cold. The bedroom was cold, the hall and the landing were cold. I used a can opener for the first time. I taught myself to make tea properly. I filled the washing machine and got it right. He put money in a cup and told me to take it when I needed food. Or anything. I wasn't unhappy. Once the shock of my mother's death passed. Although I'm not sure now that it ever did. Her voice still wakes me sometimes – I think. I took money from the cup and bought a shirt, a record, ten Silk Cut, and a packet of coconut creams. I watched television till the programmes stopped. He discovered me when I was fifteen – that was what it felt like. He stopped in the hall and asked me how I was. He booked a holiday for us, in Italy, a week in Rimini. We both flew in a plane for the first time. He asked me about school, my favourite subjects, what I wanted to do. One day, we passed a church.

—Do you go to mass? he asked me.
—No.
—Ever?
—Not really.
—Okay, he said. —Do you think about your mother?
—Yes.
—So do I, he said. —All the time. Literally all the time.

Neither of us had eaten pizza before.
—Do you like it? he asked me.

—It's brilliant, I said.

—You're right, he said. —I wonder can you get these things in Dublin.

—Don't know.

—Worth investigating.

He held his wine glass out to me.

—Give this stuff a go, he said.

He watched me, he smiled, as I took a sip. It was a big thing, his smile; it took over his face. It changed him.

—D'you like it?

—No, I said. —A bit.

—Oh, the slippery slope, he said.

He laughed, and so did I.

—She'd have liked you, he said.

I didn't know what he meant.

—She'd have liked the boy you are now, he said. —The man.

His eyes watered.

—Sorry.

I often lie awake and think of that week. I never saw him cry again. He never saw me cry. But I came home knowing he loved me. I've never forgotten the solidity of that. It's what kills me, sometimes.

We never became talkative. He left me alone. He checked on me.

—How are things?

—Fine.

—Alright for money?

—Yeah.

—How's the study going?

—Good.

—Grand.

★　★　★

61

Faye overwhelmed me. I'd never known a funny woman. Faye was funny and knew it, and she knew she was often hated for it. She was a smart alec, a bitch, too big for her boots. I saw that around the table at the wedding, before I really saw Faye. She spoke like a man, like she was entitled to speak. I saw eyes raised to heaven, elbows discreetly nudging ribs. I saw affection, envy, lust, hatred. I saw no one yawn.

I heard Cathy.

—For fuck sake. This one.

It wasn't cruel. It was an adult quietly assessing a precocious child, expressing an opinion she knew I'd share. But I wasn't sharing anything.

We were half the length of the banquet room away from the top table, our backs to the bride and groom. When the speeches started, we – myself, Cathy, Faye – turned our chairs to face the speakers and clap. It was the first wedding I'd been to.

—Is it yours? I asked Faye.

I was apprehensive asking her. I knew it wouldn't be a simple Yes or No, and she was going to attract attention. But I wanted to hear her; it was all I wanted.

—Jesus, no, she said. —I was at my parents' wedding, so I was.

This was 1986. Faye was nineteen.

I laughed. No one else did.

—How was it? I asked her.

—Oh, romantic as fuck.

—She was like Mícheál O'Hehir, I told Joe.

We'd reached the Sheds. We stood outside.

—You fell in love with a woman who looked like a racing commentator?

—You know what I mean.

—Not really, he said. —No. Did she sound like Mícheál O'Hehir? I'm puzzled here a bit, Davy. I don't think I remember what Faye looks like. Do you have a photo?

—No.

I wasn't lying.

—Let me be absolutely clear, I said. —Faye was nothing like – looked nothing like Mícheál O'Hehir. Or sounded like him.

—Grand.

—But she leaned against me and talked into my ear, non-stop, right through the speeches.

—Christ.

Joe pulled open the lounge door and I followed him in.

—That would do my head in, he said back to me.

We stood at the door.

—So, go on, he said. —Mícheál O'Hehir was trying to get off with you.

—Fuck off, I said. —And just listen.

—I am.

—Just fuckin' listen, I said. —Say – Jennifer Lawrence, let's say. Jennifer Lawrence sat beside you at a wedding. And she leaned right up against you, just as – like – it was dawning on you that it was her. And you're much younger than you are now.

—Why? he said. —Why does that matter?

—It just makes it a bit less unfeasible, I suppose. Slightly less. And it's more comfortable that way. And anyway, I was only twenty-seven when this happened, remember.

—Okay.

—So, she starts talking – Jennifer Lawrence. She starts talking – whispering into your ear, and you can feel each word. Like the tip of her tongue.

I was surprising myself.

—Right through all the speeches. And you're surrounded by people. Including your girlfriend, by the way. Would you object?

—Well –.

—Would you object?

—I was only going to ask – fuck off. Which one is Jennifer Lawrence? What's she been in? D'you want a pint?

I wasn't sure if I did. I don't drink Guinness, not since I moved to England. But there was something – a feeling, something behind my eyes. This might be the last time I'd spend with Joe. We both knew it.

—Okay, I said.

—Two pints, please, said Joe to a barman who stood behind his counter, waiting for us.

We sat at the bar. The place wasn't busy; we had a stretch of the counter to ourselves. The television above us was on – some sort of panel discussion on Sky Sports. But the sound was down – mute.

I was trying to think of a Jennifer Lawrence film.

—*The Hunger Games*, said Joe. —That's her, isn't it?

—Yes – yeah.

—I didn't see it, he said. —Hang on, though. *American Hustle*. She was hilarious in that one.

—There you go, I said. —A hilarious, gorgeous woman keeps talking into your ear. For what seemed like hours. And, actually, mightn't have been much less than an hour. Because the fuckin' speeches went on for ever.

—I'm beginning to get you, he said. —I can see how that might distract you, alright.

—Captivated me, I said.

I'd found the word I wanted.

—Good man, he said. —And was Faye gorgeous? Like Jennifer Lawrence?

I wanted to go. I wanted to stand up off the stool, turn my back, stop looking at him. Go.

—I thought so, I said.

—Good.

—He rides his housekeeper, so he does. And her sister.

She was talking about the priest holding the microphone at the top table.

—And he's been in the bride's mammy as well. Sure, there isn't a lady up there at that table that he hasn't serviced at some time or another. Usually in the morning, mind you. After mass and before confessions. A quick bang and the holy rosary, a drop of tea and a couple of Jaffa Cakes. He eats them off their arses, so he does.

I knew my life had changed when I noticed that I was leaning into her; I was the one doing the leaning. I still had a girlfriend and we had plans, hinted at, half formed. I was holding her hand. And she was holding mine. Cathy. But she got there ahead of me, a few days later. She phoned my father's house; she left a message. I'd a flat of my own but there was no phone there. I stayed with my father a few nights a week. I used the washing machine. I took food he left for me in the freezer. Cathy normally phoned me at work.

—She won't be around this weekend, my father told me. —She told me to tell you.

—Okay.

I liked Cathy. I liked being with her. I liked waiting to meet her, especially when she was coming off duty. She raced at me. I thought I'd loved her.

65

—I don't want to interfere, said my father.

I'd forgotten he was there; I'd forgotten where I was. I was surrounded by Faye, swallowed by her.

—What? I asked my father.

—I'm not sure you'll be seeing her any weekend, he said.

—Who?

—Cathy, son.

—Okay.

—The way she spoke.

—Okay.

—Is that for the best?

—Probably.

—She was brusque, he said. —On the phone.

—Okay.

He'd met Cathy. I'd brought her home to meet him. They'd chatted; they'd liked one another. But it seemed so far away. In another country, another life.

—I liked her, he said.

—Yeah, I said. —So did I. *Do.*

—You're not too heartbroken, anyway?

I didn't answer. I didn't know how to. I was sad, relieved. I wondered if he could smell Faye. Because I could.

I looked at Joe as he accepted the pints and handed a ten-euro note to the barman. He placed each glass on a beermat. He seemed to be measuring distance, making sure he got the calculation exactly right. I could tell: he'd forgotten what we'd been talking about, what I'd been telling him outside. What he'd said.

—Where are you living? I asked him.

He looked at me. He moved sideways on his stool so he could do it.

—At home, he said.

—Where's that?

And was Faye gorgeous?

—Jessica's, he said.

—Is that home now? I asked him.

—Yep.

He nodded, like he was examining what he'd said for truth, and found it.

—Yeah, he said. —I kind of think of it as home.

—What about the other one?

—Well, there you go, he said. —Fuckin' hell.

—What happened?

—We'll get there, Davy. Don't worry.

We made love, myself and Faye, the night before I went to see my father, the night he gave me Cathy's message. Faye clung to me. We were in my flat, a room without pictures except for the record covers stacked along the wall, beneath the window. Faye grabbed me tight to her. Her mouth was at my ear.

—Sanity, sanity, sanity, sanity.

I didn't know what she was saying. Whispering. Gasping. The word formed itself later, while I watched her sleeping. She was fast asleep, out for the count. I remember thinking that – *out for the count*. I'd fucked her to sleep. She'd fucked herself to sleep. Her face was deep in the pillow, under her hair. Her mouth was slightly open. Her breath lifted some strands of hair. They dropped, and shot up again. She was a cartoon, I thought, one of Disney's perfect females. She was the girl at the end of *The Jungle Book*, but she had all of Baloo's lines, and King Louie's lines, and some of Shere Khan's. I was afraid to sleep. I was afraid she'd stop being there. The light would come up and she'd be gone.

—What're you fuckin' looking at, David?

She was awake. I could see her eyes shining. She hadn't moved.

—You.

—Grand.

That was what I loved. She wouldn't let me fantasise, make more than was there. She was real. Everything – she did, she said, she didn't – was real.

They'd met.

—Where?

He looked annoyed. I'd interrupted him. It was like he'd been composing his story, alone, writing it. A minute ago, he'd been chatting to me. With her, with the idea of her, he didn't want me there. It surprised me. I thought he'd been showing her off earlier, in the restaurant. And I'd expected a bit of triumph, the bit of crack. I don't think I wanted it but it was what I'd been anticipating.

They'd met in a café in town, Wigwam, on Middle Abbey Street.

—Why there?

I wanted to irritate him now. To wake him up.

—Distance, he said. —And proximity.

—To what? I asked. —Who?

—Work, he said. —People in work. Wigwam's near to, and a safe distance from. I wasn't hiding anything, though.

—You were, I said. —You lied to Trish.

—Not really, he said. —I withheld information.

—Withheld the truth.

—Okay – fuck it, he said. —It was simpler that way. It wasn't malicious, or dishonest – I don't think. Although Trish might disagree. She'd tear my fuckin' eyes out. But look, I didn't want anybody seeing me. From work, I mean. Or anyone else. And as well, I didn't want it to seem like I was hiding. Seem to myself, I mean. Because I wasn't. I don't know –. It was near enough to work but not too near. And I needed the car after – after I met her, like. I don't know why I'm going into all of this.

He met her in Wigwam. One of his sons – I can't remember the name – had worked there before he'd moved to Cork, and that was why Joe had thought of it. No one he knew would be there and he'd never met any of his son's more recent friends. He wasn't worried about anything getting back to the son or to Trish.

—It's a hipster spot, he said. —The beardy lads.

—Tattoos.

—Tasteful ones, yeah, he said. —Middle-class tattoos. Art. Do any of your kids have tattoos?

—Yeah, I said.

—Same here. Does Faye?

I looked at him.

—No, I said. —Does Trish?

He shook his head.

—No, he said. —But you never know. She might have had *Joe Is a Cunt* tattooed to the back of her neck or something. In Mandarin or Latin.

—She was there, anyway, I said. —Jessica.

—She was, he said. —She got there before me. She was sitting at one of the tables, with a pot of tea.

—Did she stand up when you got there?

—What?

69

—Did she stand up?

—Why?

—Politeness, I said. —Tradition – formality. Although it's usually the man who does that – is it?

—No, he said. —She didn't. There was none of the formal stuff.

That was what he'd been trying to say.

—It was like we'd never been apart, he said.

—You were never together, I told him.

—Okay, he said. —And that's not strictly true either. And anyway, the woman doesn't have to stand, does she? It's the man's job – I think you're right. Holding the door open and stuff like that. Used to be, anyway. It might cause offence these days, though. Opening a fuckin' door.

It was a good place, Wigwam, a cool place. But they were easily the oldest people there; they had decades on everyone else. He noticed it; she said nothing. He ordered a coffee, an Americano, paid for it, and sat. He sat beside her. The table was too wide, so he wasn't going to sit opposite her. It would have been like a job interview.

—Or a parent–teacher meeting, I said.

—There you go, he said. —Love stories begin.

He got in behind the table and sat beside her. She kissed him. On the cheek.

—Now this sounds mad, he said.

—Go on.

He felt he was living his real life.

—Like, the minute I sat down, he said.

It wasn't that he was suddenly waking up. It was nothing as dramatic as that, nothing that made him angry or giddy. It was just that: he sat down. It was her weight beside him, and her warmth, beside him and against him. It felt familiar and right. It was an

70

emptiness filled; it had always been this way. This was how he felt. He was in the rest of his life.

I was looking at him. There was no twitching. He wasn't shredding a beermat. He looked well in the pub light.

—But, he said. —This is the gas bit.

—What?

—I couldn't remember her name.

—She told it to you – when she phoned you.

—Yeah, but I put George into my phone. I told you that. And I didn't change it. I never have. But – there – I couldn't remember her fuckin' name.

—That *is* weird.

—I know, he said. —In a way.

He had a theory: he didn't remember her name because he didn't have to. He was fairly certain he knew it all the way to the café. He'd parked in the Arnotts car park.

—I thought you said it was near where you work?

I'd no real idea what Joe did for a living. 'In the bank'. That job description described nothing any more. I knew he'd done a degree at night, ten years or so after we'd left school, and that he had a master's too. I knew he'd been 'in the bank' since 1977 but I didn't know what, or where, that meant. Or which bank, or what type of bank.

—What was near where I work? he asked.

—Wigwam.

—Yeah – true. But I needed the car. Immediately – immediately after. I was going to see Holly. She'd a match over in Booterstown. I can do a lot in the car – work, like. It's all talk – the phone. Anyway, let's not get bogged down in the car park. It doesn't matter.

That was one life. The job, the car, the daughter. He'd been in that life as he crossed Abbey Street and

71

watched the Luas approach from the Jervis stop, as he walked into the café. He knew her name, the woman he was meeting. He knew her first name; he remembered it. Then he didn't. Because he didn't have to remember it. He was where he was supposed to be, beside this woman. This was his life.

Jessica.

The name was there. A few minutes later.

—But it didn't pop up in my head, he said. —Do you know what I mean?

—Yeah, I said. —I do.

—It was like my own name, he said. —Just there.

—Okay. Did you get to the match?

—Yes – yeah. Yeah. Of course.

He smiled.

—I was late. But I was always going to be. I was aiming for the second half.

—Did she win?

—You're a terrible bitch, Davy, he said. —Yeah, she did. She scored two goals. In the second half. So I got to see both of them.

They'd stayed in the café for an hour and a half. She had to get home.

—Is she married?

—No.

—Was she?

—Yeah. But years ago. Back around our time. That era, like.

—So she was young when she got married.

—Yeah, he said. —That wasn't unusual, though. Back then.

She'd lived with a man for years, after the marriage. Or, he'd lived with her; it was her house. She had a daughter.

—Is he the father?

—No, he isn't. That was a different guy, again.

—Okay.

—It's not as – what? – as frantic as it sounds, he said.
—I don't think it was. We're talking about decades.

—Okay, I said. —And she's in Holly's class, is that
right? The girl.

—Same year, he said. —Not the same class. Except
for one or two subjects.

—And how's that?

—Not too good, he said.

—Hardly surprising.

—No, he agreed. —Holly refused to go to school for
a while. And she wouldn't talk to me. It wasn't great.

—How is it now?

—Still not great. A bit better. I texted her a while
back – last week, I think. And she answered. *Fuck off x*.
But that's Holly – all over. She answered, that was the
thing. First time in – Jesus. Months. Anyway, I look at
the *x* a couple of times a day. Only one *x*, mind. It
used to be two.

He wasn't joking. I wanted to ask him about Jessica's
daughter. I wanted to dig away at him. But I didn't; I
restrained myself.

—What did you talk about? I asked him.

—That's the thing, he said.

—What?

—We didn't, he said. —Talk. I mean, we did. But
we didn't catch up, if you know what I mean. We didn't
fill in the years. Kids, partners, jobs – there was nothing like that. Or the school – the girls' school, like. We
didn't mention the place at all.

—What did you talk about then?

I wasn't believing him. This strolling in and out of different lives – I wasn't having it. He was sitting beside me and there was only one of him. He'd been having an affair, he'd been caught, and he was trying to make something mystical or inevitable out of it. It was boring.

—Like I told you, he said. —It was just like we'd always been together. I don't really remember what we talked about. Just – stuff.

—Fuckin' stuff?

I came back to Dublin to see my father but I knew I'd keep doing it after he died, a couple of times a year. I loved speaking like a Dubliner. It felt like physical exercise.

—I honestly don't remember, he said. —She was reading a book – when I came in.

—And you spoke about that?

—I think so, he said. —Although she said she'd got it in Eason's for her kid – the daughter.

—What's her name?

—Hanoi.

—Are you serious?

—Yep.

He shrugged; he grinned.

—The kid hates it, he said. —She tells everyone it's the Irish for brilliance.

—Bright kid.

—Yeah.

—Do you get on with her?

—I do, yeah, he said. —We –. I suppose we kind of keep a distance. But I like her.

—What was the book?

—What?

—The book Jessica was reading.

—A school book. Chemistry, I think.

—She was reading a fuckin' chemistry book?

—Flicking through it, he said. —Killing the time.

—Were you late?

—No, I wasn't, he said. —I was bang-on. I'm never late. Ever. Anyway, she said she'd been in Eason's and she'd bought a pen as well, and she showed it to me.

—For fuck sake.

—That's my fuckin' point, he said. —It was like we'd seen each other earlier and there wasn't much filling in to do. Somehow, like – I knew she'd have the book.

—Come on –

—Just calm down, he said. —I'm telling you, that was what it felt like. *Felt*, not facts. But there now – she knew what I do for a living.

—Facebook.

—I'm not on Facebook.

—You've always worked in the bank.

—Yeah, but she never knew that – I don't think. But she did. In Wigwam.

I told him what I was thinking.

—It's kind of boring, Joe.

—I know, he said. —That's my point as well. I think. It's boring if you're looking in the window at it but not when you're inside.

—So you swapped one kitchen for another one.

—You don't understand.

—No, I agreed. —Is she better looking?

—Ah, stop, for fuck sake.

—I don't fuckin' understand.

—She is, by the way.

He shut his eyes like he wished he hadn't spoken.

—It felt –, he said.

He picked up his pint, and put it back down.

—It felt like I'd come home, he said.

—In Wigwam?

—Fuck off, Davy, he said. —I'm wasting my fuckin' time. It's impossible.

He picked up the pint again and brought it to his mouth.

It was my round – I needed something to do, to get away from Joe's face and the urge to whack it. I was looking at the barman, waiting for him to look my way. He was in the passage between the lounge and the bar, hiding there, looking down at his phone. I wasn't a local; I didn't want to interrupt him.

The barman was standing to my left. Joe was on the other side of me and he took advantage of the back of my head; I wasn't looking at him as he spoke.

—I'd always been with her, he said.

The barman looked up. I lifted my glass. He nodded and took two empty pint glasses from under the counter.

—Okay, I said.

I didn't care. I knew Joe – or, I thought I knew Joe. We'd end the night with his story, not mine. I didn't care about either of his homes, the new or the old. Or him. I was here, listening, because I used to know him. Old times' sake. But it wasn't enough; I knew that. I looked at the barman filling our glasses. I took my phone from my pocket and checked it. I had it on vibrate but I was worried I'd miss a call or a message. There was nothing on the screen.

—There were two things she told me that kind of caught me on the hop, said Joe.

I put the phone away, leaned back to get it deep into my pocket, and looked at him.

—What were they?

—She's dyslexic, he said.

—Really?

—Yeah, he said. —She was flicking through the book, like, and she mentioned it.

—How? Should you not've known that already, if you'd been with her all along? Like you said.

—I didn't mean that literally.

—Okay.

—You know that.

—Okay.

—So, anyway, he said. —She said she envied Hanoi and I asked her why.

—That was brave.

—What d'you mean?

—Middle-aged women hate younger women, I told him.

—Their daughters, though?

—Oh, yeah.

He shrugged.

—Okay, he said. —But, no. It was the reading she envied. She can't really read.

—Faye can read, I told him.

—Yeah, he said. —So can Trish.

We laughed. It felt like the first time we'd laughed that evening; I thought it might have been. It was like a new sound, a new feeling.

—What was the other thing? I asked him.

The barman was approaching with the pints. I was rooting in my jacket for my wallet. It was stupid, bringing a jacket. The heat – the last thing I'd needed was a jacket. But I hadn't been thinking when I'd gone back to the house to shower, to change, after I'd phoned Joe earlier. I'd been given permission: I was escaping for a while, a couple of hours.

I'd stopped carrying cash in my trousers pockets. Some years back – maybe ten – I'd noticed that I was hitching my trousers every time I stood up, and often as I walked. I'd seen a woman at work looking at me, and looking away. I'd blamed the coins and the keys. So I'd banished them from my trousers, everything except the phone. Now, as I put my hand into the inside pocket of my jacket and found it empty, I was anxious enough to assume that the wallet was gone. Drink had never made me relax; it had never made a different man of me.

The wallet was in the second inside pocket. Joe waited while I took out a twenty. A bookshop loyalty card and a couple of petrol station receipts slipped out with the money. He tried to catch them but they fell onto the tiles. I gave the twenty to the barman.

I was drunk.

—Thanks.

Joe handed me the receipts and the loyalty card and sat back up on the stool.

—She has a son as well, he said.

—Jessica has?

—Yeah.

—Older, younger?

—What?

—Than the girl.

—Older.

—And what's his name? I asked. —Bangkok, Rangoon?

—He has a daughter, said Joe. —His name's Peter.

—Peter? I said. —That's a bit fuckin' conventional –.

There was something he'd just said; it had slipped away but it rolled back.

—He has a daughter – you said.

78

—Right.

—So, I said. —Your girlfriend's son has a child.

—Yeah.

—She's a grandmother.

He nodded.

—You left your wife and kids for a glamorous granny.

He nodded again; he was pleased. I'd been bored; I'd told him. He knew I wasn't bored now.

—Looks like it, he said.

—Same father?

—Sorry?

—Is what's-his-name's –

—Peter.

—Peter – is Peter's father the same as Hanoi's?

—No, he said. —There's a big age gap. He's much older.

He put his new pint on the beermat. He drew a line with a finger, down through the condensation on the glass.

—I think I might be, he said.

I knew what was coming. I'd known it – somehow – all night. I'd slipped into his new life too.

—Might be what? I asked.

—His father.

—Are you?

—I think so, he said. —I might be.

—For fuck sake.

—I will never, ever give you a grandchild, my daughter, Róisín, told me a few years ago.

She was eighteen, and joking. I'd just told her I wouldn't give her the money to go to Berlin for the weekend. I laughed – I always laughed when Róisín wanted me to laugh. But I believed her. I felt no loss; there was nothing being whipped out of my arms. I looked at Faye but I wasn't sure she'd heard.

—Your lovey-dovey thing with Róisín, she'd said once, a few years before. —What's that about?

—It isn't about anything, I'd said. —I don't even know what you mean.

—It gives me the sick, she said.

—I'm her father.

—You are.

—Fuck off, Faye.

—Nice.

—Well, yeah – fuck off. What are you even saying?

—Nothing, she said. —Me? Nothing. You're spoiling her.

Róisín was, I think, fifteen. We'd been watching *Mean Girls* together. She'd been watching; I'd been watching her watching. She leaned against an arm of the sofa and draped her legs across mine. She wouldn't let me look at my phone or iPad. I watched her getting ready to laugh; I watched her silently recite lines that were about to be delivered.

—How many times have you watched this thing?

—More times than I care to remember, she said.

Róisín is English, born here, in Wantage. She had only one living grandparent in Ireland, my father. But she liked the Irish phrases. She collected them. She liked her name – she liked the *fada*s, the accents on the 'o' and the 'i'. She liked the trouble they caused in school and elsewhere.

—The lady asked if I was an Arab, she told me one evening when I picked her up after swimming.

—What lady?

—The lady at the swimming pool. When she asked me to spell my name.

—The swimming teacher?

—The lady behind the glass.

—Why did she want to know your name?

—I had to give her the envelope.

—The swimming money.

—Yes.

—She thought your name was Arabic? Syrian or something.

—Yes.

She giggled.

—The fucking eejit, she said.

—Now now.

There was a rule: she was allowed to say 'fuckin' eejit' now and again, but only when she was alone with one of us and only when the situation – the fuckin' eejit – warranted it.

We laughed.

She made me laugh. Just as her mother had – and did. Although they were very different. Their senses of humour couldn't sit in the same room. It had been like that since Róisín had started talking, probably before. But I might be making that up. I *am* making that up.

—I love her when she's asleep, said Faye.

Róisín was the baby in the cot, beside our bed.

I thought Faye was joking. And she was. But she wasn't. That was Faye.

—It's when they're awake, she said. —Fuckin' Jesus.

—They're work, I said.

We had two children – a toddler and this baby.

—Do you have a photocopier in work, Dave, do you?

—We do, I said.

—Do you love it?

I laughed quietly.

She nodded at the sleeping baby.

—Then why should I love these yokes?

We lay back on the bed, still dressed.

—No squeaking now, David, she said. —She'll wake up on us.

I looked at Joe. I'm his father, he'd said. I might be. I was a character in his box set but I'd slept through a couple of episodes. I'd missed something – I hadn't heard something, when I'd been concentrating on grabbing the barman's attention.

He'd had sex with her, long ago. Or, he thought he had. He'd had a son he'd known nothing about. Or hadn't told me about. 'I might be'. The way he spoke, the way I'd heard him – it sounded like a decision he was thinking about making. I wanted to rush in. I wanted to pulverise the possibility. The betrayal. I wanted to leave, to get away from anything else I might hear.

And I didn't.

—Have you met him? I asked.

—No.

—How come?

—He lives in Perth, he said.

—Australia.

—Yeah.

That was handy, I thought. Borneo might have been better. Or way up the Limpopo. Away from Skype and Qantas. He wasn't confessing anything. I'm his father – I might be. It wasn't a statement. He was listening, testing the words – not on me, on himself.

I don't drink any more. I've given up, more or less. There was one night, I was having a fight, wanting a fight, with Faye and the phrase – that's the drink talking – introduced itself, nudged me, and I believed it.

—I'm sorry, I said.

—Are you?

—Yeah. I am. I – Christ – I don't even know how we started. It's me – I'm sorry.

—So, she said. —Just to be clear. In future, if there's going to be a row between us – unlikely as that might seem now – I'll be the sole instigator. Is that right?

—If you want.

—I do.

—Okay.

—Grand, she said. —And what do you want back, David? Let's play treaty negotiations. What are your proposals, tell us? What would you like?

—Nothing, I said.

—Ah, go on, spoilsport, she said. —Would you not like to ride Alison up the road? I've seen you looking at her.

—I didn't realise that was something you could organise, I said.

—I'm the queen of the madams in this town, so I am. And that one's a right hoor. Isn't she?

—Yes.

—A hoor. So, is that what you want, Kofi Annan, is it?

—No, Faye, it isn't.

—What, so?

—Nothing.

—Ah, go on, she said. —Not even me?

—I always want you.

—My eye, you do.

83

—I do.

—That's definitely the fuckin' drink talking.

—I want you now.

—I'm fuckin' here, look.

I didn't make a declaration. I didn't tell Faye or anyone else that I wouldn't drink again. I didn't go to AA; I'm not an alcoholic. I just stopped drinking once the fridge and the wine rack were empty. Faye buys a bottle of wine whenever she wants one. She's always said it: wine looks stupid lying on its side. I don't go to the pub; I don't have a local in Wantage. I drink very occasionally. I feel it – I feel it in my head, almost immediately. I can go months without a pint, yet feel drunk after a couple of gulps, like I'm topping it up, carrying on where I'd left off the night before.

I don't drink. But I was drinking with Joe. And the drink was going to talk. It already had; there'd been a nastiness in some of the things I'd said. I saw it – I'd heard it. I was being a prick. A prickless prick, Faye once called me, after I'd had a go at her, fooled myself into thinking that I could be as quick as she was.

I was never violent. Just stupid.

There was something I knew, or felt: this was the last time I was going to speak to Joe. He wasn't going to contact me again, and I wouldn't be contacting him. There wouldn't be a fight; nothing would come to a head. The pub would shut, and we'd leave – we'd go. I'd have one more pint and I'd leave. I wouldn't go into town with him, to George's. I wasn't going to let that happen. We'd go outside and talk for a few more minutes. We'd shake hands, probably hug, and go. Our separate ways. My father would die and I wouldn't come back to Dublin. Staying away wouldn't be too difficult.

84

I'd be careful now.

—How does that feel?

—What? he asked.

—Having a son you didn't know you had, I said. —A man. He must be – what? – mid-thirties.

—Yeah, he said. —Mad, isn't it?

—He's not far off middle age, I said. —When you work it out. You'll get to know him when his life is half over.

I wasn't being careful enough.

I wanted to kill Joe. I wanted to obliterate Joe. I just wanted to fuckin' kill him.

But I didn't. The fog opened – it wasn't me talking. I could hear Faye. That'll be the drink, will it?

I knew how he was going to answer.

—I wasn't –. I don't know, Davy – I wasn't that surprised. When she told me.

I was right.

—Does nothing surprise you, Joe?

—Good question, he said. —But no. No, I don't think so.

—I have a free house, she told me.

—Is that right? I said.

—It is.

She'd phoned me in work four days after the wedding.

—How did you know I worked here?

I needed to speak softly but I wanted to shout. I wanted the lads and girls around me to know that I was being chased by a woman – by this nineteen-year-old woman.

—I phoned every office in Dublin, she said. —And I told them, I need to talk to the ride with the hair.

She'd phoned Cathy's brother, on his honeymoon, and she'd asked him where I worked. She told me about it months later. Cathy never told me.

My boss was standing at his door, looking my way. I was chuffed. All eyes were on me.

—And the house, I said. —Could you tell me where it is, please?

—Gorey.

—Really? That's fine, yes.

—Not all the girls give a flying fuck about living in Dublin, she said. —Some of us can function perfectly well away from the bright lights.

—I'm sure you're right, I said. —Could I get your number, please, and I could phone you back later?

—No.

—No?

—I'm in a fuckin' phone box, she said. —Did you think I was lying back in bed or something, in my negligee? Are you holding your pen?

—Eh – yes, I am.

—I'm going to give you the address. I'll be expecting you on Friday night. What time do you finish work?

—Five – that's right.

—See you at eight and don't dare be fuckin' late.

—Thank you –.

She was gone.

—I'll get back to you when I have the details – bye bye.

I put the phone down and took the applause and the slagging.

—We're telling Cah-tee! We're telling Cah-tee!

I borrowed my father's car.

He looked at me. It was the day after Cathy had left the message; she wouldn't be meeting me at the weekend. We'd just been talking about her. He took the key off his keyring.

—I liked Cathy, he said.

I'd asked him for the car and told him I'd have it back on Sunday – or Saturday if he needed it. I hadn't told him I was meeting someone else.

He held out the key. Like he didn't want to do it, like it was going against his better judgement.

I was tempted not to take it.

He rarely spoke about my mother. He was younger than I am now. I don't think he saw other women; I never met any. There'd been none in the house. I used to dream of that – awake, and sometimes when I slept. I'd find a woman in the kitchen. She'd be lovely, when I was in charge of the dream. A bit too old to be gorgeous – she'd be handsome. One of the great-looking mothers. I'd sit in school thinking of her. When I slept she was warm; she was warmth – that was all.

I made it to Gorey with thirteen minutes to spare. The drive through Arklow nearly killed me. I didn't have a driving licence. I'd driven with my father on Dollymount Strand and, once, to Howth and back. Alone, I'd driven to Northside Shopping Centre, and home to my flat with a gas canister. The crawl through Arklow – my legs ached, the car cut out twice, I was afraid I'd go into the bumper in front of me. I was starving. I missed Cathy. I could feel the pint in my hand; I could feel her beside me as we found a bit of free wall and leaned back together in the full, Friday-night pub.

I couldn't remember what Faye looked like.

That's still the case. Her eyes are brown but I might be wrong. I'd be surprised if they aren't, but not that surprised. I could go downstairs now and check. But she'd see me looking and she'd want to know why. Or, much more likely, she'd know why.

—You're sticking me into your book.

I haven't told her I'm writing. I don't need to.

She wasn't exactly beautiful. There was nothing striking about her; I think that's accurate – except her eyes. Her eyes came from a silent movie – maybe that's why I can never be sure of their colour. They were huge and they moved so precisely, when she told them to. Always, to make me laugh. And she moved, she walked, like she was going to come straight at me. She touched everything, rubbed her fingers along walls as she went, tapped fragile things, pressed buttons, picked up phones, tried on coats and hats – women's, men's, children's. Stared at me, not smiling – but smiling. Not just her eyes – all of Faye was in a silent movie. But then there was her voice, her Wexford accent – the words, the stream of brilliantly managed madness. I don't think I ever fell in love with Faye. I don't think I had time to. I knew, when I sat with her at the wedding, she was dangerous. She'd have said anything – she didn't care, and she gave all of herself so you'd know that. Nothing she said or did was predictable. I don't think I ever successfully anticipated what Faye was going to say – I think that's true. There were two types of men. There were the men who encountered Faye, and backed away. Then there were the men who met Faye, and fell over. The latter outnumbered the former. Faye became the only woman in the room, on the train, at the table.

Her house was at the top of the town. I was in a town that had a bottom and a top. It stood alone – the doctor or the priest's house. It had its own wide gate and high stone wall. And a tree that leaned out over the street. I didn't know if I should drive right up to the front door; I didn't know if I was allowed to, if it was done.

I chanced it.

There were no lights on in the front of the house. The front door was deep inside a porch. There was no bell – I couldn't see one – just a brass knocker, a fox's head.

I gave it a tap.

And another.

The door opened. The hall light hadn't come on.

Her top teeth had trapped her bottom lip, like she was trying not to laugh – I could see that.

—Well, it's David, she said. —You're a bit early, aren't you?

—Will I wait?

I was pleased with myself; I'd managed to talk.

—You will in your hole, she said. —In you get. What's that yoke you have there?

I looked down at the thing she was looking at.

—My bag, I said.

—Oh, she said. —How's Cathy, tell us? She's not in the fuckin' bag, is she?

I was still outside the house.

—Hope not, I said.

—I like Cathy, she said.

—So does my father.

—Grand, so. They have each other.

She walked away from the door. I stepped into the dark of the hall and followed her.

—Shut the door, for fuck sake. I hope you love cats.

—I don't mind them.

—Grand.

I was there a night and most of a day before it occurred to me that I hadn't seen a cat. There was a dog sitting on my lap, licking my chin. I laughed.

—What?

She was sitting beside me.

—You don't have any cats, I said.

She sat up and turned, so she was looking straight at me.

—I will never be a cat lady, she said. —I swear to fuckin' God.

—Was your mother a cat lady?

—Are you fuckin' suggesting I got rid of the cats when my poor mammy died, are you? I threw them in after her, into the cold, cold grave – they bounced off the fuckin' coffin. Is that what you're suggesting?

She was naked under her father's dressing gown. He'd been wearing it when he died, she told me.

—Look, she said.

She took twenty Sweet Afton from a pocket.

—His fags, she said. —Exactly where he left them.

She put them back.

—There was a cat, actually, she said.

—Yeah?

—It disappeared after she died.

—Seriously?

—Just fucked off, so it did.

She leaned over me, and the dog; she was on her knees now. She was inspecting the arm of the sofa.

—Aha.

She picked up something.

—Exhibit A.

—What is it?

I couldn't see anything. She was pretending to hold something right in front of my eyes.

—Moggy hair, she said.

I could see something now.

—Could be a dog hair, I said.

There were three dogs in the room. There were more, out behind the house.

—I'm allergic to cats, she said. —If I put this anywhere near my face, my eyes will explode.

Her face was right up to mine. She'd shoved the dog off my lap. There was a fight going on now, down on the floor, with the other two. But I didn't look. I couldn't, and I didn't want to. I could see the hair now, clearly; it stood up between her fingernails like a pin. She held it right under her left eye.

—Cat or dog?

Her left eye was all I could see.

—Go on, she said.

I gave her the answer I thought she'd want.

—Cat.

The white hair divided the eye in half. Then I saw it move, slide, down the eye. She didn't blink.

The hair was gone.

—Anything happening?

—No.

She sighed.

—Ah, well – must only be a dog's.

She sat back.

—Next time maybe.

She pulled the dressing gown around her.

—I like being an orphan, she said. —It's kind of cool, isn't it?

—Yeah, I said.

I thought about it.

—It is.

—Men like riding orphans, she said. —Did anyone ever tell you that now?

—No.

—An orphan with a house and a shop and a vagina, she said. —Do you know what that makes me in the town?

—What?

—The catch with the snatch.

Neither of us laughed. The words sounded vicious – like she was hurting herself.

Faye didn't often laugh.

—Do you own a shop? I asked.

—I do, she said. —The name over the door and all. You have no idea how many mammies have called in to me since my own mammy went to her maker. Women, now, whose husbands slept with my mammy – or stayed awake while they gave her a seeing to. But the wives – they're more than willing to let bygones be bygones. Because they want me for their sons.

—Do they bring the sons?

—They've more sense, said Faye. —They bring cakes. Flans. And shepherd's pie and flowers. And they ask me how I'm holding up and how I'm managing, rattling around in this old place all on my own, and who do I have to look after the shop for me till I sell it, which would be a crying shame because – now – the town needs that shop, that shop, they tell me, was the making of the town.

—What's in the shop?

—Garments for the peasantry, she said.

—Clothes.

—Well done. Clothes. My mother was mad.

—What did she die of?

—Ah, sure. Well –. She kind of killed herself – accidentally, of course. But that's for another day. Cathy.

I couldn't keep up. (I still can't.) She seemed to be telling me that Cathy had been involved in her mother's suicide. I'd never heard of a woman killing herself before. It had always been men and boys – and not many of them.

—What about Cathy? I asked.

—Did you ever meet her dad?

—Well, yeah, I said. —He was at the wedding last Saturday, remember?

—But, I mean, you've met him. You've had a chat with him, have you?

—Yeah – a short one. When he was up in Dublin for a match. What about it?

—He's a nice man. He'd be number one on my list of the nice dads who've been in this house.

—Did your mother –?

—She did.

—I didn't know Cathy was from around here.

—You never met my mother, she said. —You wouldn't have just crossed the street to have a look at her. You'd have driven the length of the county and further. Can you think of one spectacular thing in Ireland? Name it – quick, quick.

—The Cliffs of Moher.

—My mammy was the Cliffs of Moher. I'm not like her.

—You're the Giant's Causeway, are you?

It was like she hadn't heard me. Nothing crossed her face.

—I will never be like her, she said.

—Okay.

—Listen, she said. —Listen to this. Listen.

—I am.

—I will only ever know the one man, she said. —Do you read your bible, do you?

—Not really, I said.

I was trying to understand what she'd just said.

—That's the *know* I mean, anyway, she said. —The biblical know.

We'd made love the night before. We'd made love half an hour before.

The eyes – they had me pinned. They were waiting for me to say something.

—Okay.

—She cried when they were late, she said. —And she cried when they left. She gave them the bum's rush if they were on time, she laughed at them if they wanted to stay. She threw all the little statues at them. Look at the mantelpiece, sure – there's nothing left on it.

—Were you here?

—I was only ten when Daddy died.

—Okay. Who managed the shop?

—She did.

—Did she?

—She reinvented the place. One of the shepherd's pie ladies told me. She said it was the best thing that ever happened the town. You could go shopping without having to go up to Dublin. She converted a big shop into a fuckin' department store.

—Well worth her husband's infidelity.

—Whose husband?

—The shepherd's pie lady.

—Well, God, she said. —Yeah, well worth it. All the major brands for the loan of the husband's mickey? Well worth it, boy. Cathy's mother tried to persuade the brother to start courting me.

—The brother that got married?

—That's him.

—You're messing.

—I don't think I am.

—When he was already engaged to your woman that he married?

—This was business, she said. —To be fair to her. I own a fuckin' department store and the fiancée's only an oul' nurse. His wife she is now, God fuckin' love her.

I waited a second.

—Did he call you? I asked.

—No, he did not.

—Then how do you know his mother was going to loose him on you, so?

I didn't know where the language – *loose him on you, so* – had come from.

—I turned on a lamp, she said. —When she was here, like. His mammy – in here. It was getting dark. But it didn't turn on. But she said, 'Cathal will fix that for you.'

—It was probably the bulb.

—I knew that. It was only the fuckin' bulb. And that's what I told her – it's only the bulb.

—And was it?

—No, she said. —It was banjaxed.

I looked around, at the three or four lights in the room.

—Where is it?

—You won't be fixing it either.

—I know.

—I flung it out the scullery door, she said. —That's where all the broken shite is going from now on – from here on fuckin' in.

It was quiet now. There was something about the air; I thought she was going to cry – was already crying. But she wasn't, she didn't. The dogs had gone off,

95

wandering. I thought I heard them on the stairs. It was dark now, and cold.

—Are you an only child? I asked her.

—D'you think I'm a fuckin' child?

—No.

—I did the Leaving last year, she said. —I was a schoolgirl less than a year ago. Does that make you feel guilty?

—Not in the least.

—Or the opposite, she said. —Does it give you a horn?

—No.

—Grand, she said.

She sang a song I didn't recognise.

—I ain't got no sister, I ain't got a brother, I ain't got a father, not even a mother.

—How did you do in the Leaving?

—I'm a lonely girl, I ain't got a home. All honours. The genuine articles.

—College?

—Fuck it, she said. —I'm grand. I'm up past my fuckin' gills in expertise. Did you ever hear a stupider word than 'sibling'?

—No – I don't think so.

—Have you any of the sib-illings, yourself, David?

—No.

—Interesting, she said.

—Why is it?

—We're both only children – *only* children. With dead mammies.

—Why is that interesting, though?

—It just is, she said. —Things happen for a reason. Says I.

She looked straight at me.

—You'll do me, she said.

She wasn't smiling.

—Thanks, I said.

I was. Smiling.

We watched as she pushed her way to the front of the pub, to her friends.

—Did yeh get a good look at her arse?

—Perfect.

—Yeah.

—Fuckin' perfect.

—What'll we do?

We did nothing. We stayed where we were. We kept an eye out, in case the wall of shoulders and heads opened. We glimpsed her, we nudged each other.

—Did yeh see the way she leaned out there, to get her pint?

—The tit – the shape of it under her jumper.

—Ah, man.

—A hand on tha' thing.

—Ah, man.

—The weight of it – can you imagine?

—Ah, fuckin' man.

—Look, said Joe. —Your man up there is goin'. Will we grab his stool?

We'd get in there, closer to her. We'd start chatting to the lads on the edge of her crowd. We'd find something in common – there'd have to be something. Joe would get us started. Someone would shift, leave, go for his coat, and she'd be in front of us. Me. I'd talk – I'd think of something, something would happen.

—Is he goin' or wha'? He's sittin' down again, the cunt.

—Fuckin' arsehole – make your fuckin' mind up, for fuck sake.

—What'll we do?

Joe stood up. He picked up his pint and he grabbed his jacket.

—Come on, he said.

I watched him as he politely battled his way up the room. He smiled at the people he was pushing. I couldn't see his face but that was what he was doing. I knew Joe. I knew what was in him, and I knew I held him back.

I stood up and grabbed my own pint and jacket, and I went after him. He'd found room for his pint on the counter. He'd thrown his jacket onto a pile near the door. He was listening to two men and a woman. He was getting ready to speak when I got there.

That might be what happened, or something like it. I can see it happening; I've no problem describing it. Joe made the move, and I'd have followed him. I wouldn't have waited.

—The Ramones, he said later that night. —They never let yeh down, sure they don't?

We were walking home along the North Strand, towards Fairview. We had to walk that far every weekend before a taxi, going back into town, would stop for us.

The Ramones were what the two lads and the girl had been talking about when Joe had arrived and parked his pint. The two lads were thinking about going to see *Rock 'n' Roll High School*, later, after closing time.

—The best music film ever, said Joe.

They said nothing back. They didn't know him; they'd never seen him. They didn't turn away but they didn't really look at him.

—Better than *The Last Waltz*, even, said Joe.

It was the girl who spoke. —Really?

—I think so, said Joe.

I knew this: he hadn't seen *Rock 'n' Roll High School*.

—How did yeh know? I asked him on the way home.

—Know wha'?

—Tha' she liked *The Last Waltz*.

—I guessed, he said. —She'd hair like Emmylou Harris.

—No, she didn't.

—She used to, he said.

—How d'you know tha'?

—I just do.

—Fuck off, Joe, I said. —What're you on abou'?

—I could tell, he said. —She'd got her hair cut recently – a whole change o' style. She kept puttin' her hand up to it. Pattin' where it ended. An' it was black, like Emmylou Harris's.

—You're a spoofer, I told him.

—You really should've had a few sisters, Davy, he said. —The things you'd've learnt, I'm not jokin' yeh.

—Like?

—Like – tonigh'. One o' me sisters got her hair done a while back an' she cried for fuckin' days after it. She wouldn't come ou' o' their bedroom. An' when she did – when she started actually fuckin' starvin' – she kept touchin' her hair. Where her hair used to be. Like your woman tonigh'. I could tell. She was anxious about it. More, she was grievin' for it. Kind of. Even though she likes the new look. She's missin' the hair. Like me sister did. Panickin'. It must be a huge decision for a bird with long hair. When her hair is the most spectacular thing abou' her. I'd say, anyway. The fairy tales are full o' women's hair.

—Which sister?

—Paula. I think. I can't remember. But I'd say Paula.

I wondered then, as I'd wondered before, why he hadn't had more success with women. He knew all about them, it seemed to me. How they worked, what they thought. What was important, what made them laugh. I remember once, when we were still in school, he'd stopped the life in the classroom with just two words.

—Girls wank.

No one doubted him. No one said 'No way' or 'Fuck off, Joe.' But what did they wank with? It was a question no one was going to ask. What did they pull or stroke? The teacher – I can't remember who it was; I can't remember the names of most of our teachers – he couldn't believe the silence, couldn't quite accept it, when he walked into the room and shut the door.

—What's going on? Out with it.

He opened the door again, in case he had to escape; that was what it was like. Hostile, anxious. A lad at the back, behind us, whispered.

—He's right.

The mothers liked Joe. The sisters liked Joe. The women and girls in the shops liked Joe. Or, they didn't dislike him. They were civil, sometimes even patient. They didn't see him as the enemy. And there'd been regular messages from other girls. *Mary wants to go with you. Tell your friend Joe that Jackie Salmon says he's a ride. I do not, you – fuck off.* I wondered why he hadn't gone from girl to girl to woman, why he hadn't lived a different life. Maybe he had – he was claiming children now that I'd known nothing about, *he'd* known nothing about.

—You're still a spoofer, I said that night, on the North Strand. —Emmylou Harris, me hole.

—Well, you fuckin' explain it then, he said. —G'wan ahead. Give us the benefit of your hard-earned fuckin' expertise.

—She liked us, I said.

—Us?

—Me.

—Fuckin' you?

—Both of us, I said. —Doesn't matter.

—Hang on, he said. —This is Emmylou the skinhead we're still talkin' about, yeah?

—She wasn't a skinhead.

—Grand, he said. —But she fancied us, you're sayin'. Us.

—Yeah, I said. —Me, anyway.

—She fuckin' hid it well, he said.

He was never going to let her fancy me. He wasn't going to let me think it.

We'd gone to *Rock 'n' Roll High School*. We'd tagged along, not exactly welcome, but not unwelcome either. We'd stood outside George's while they – we didn't know who they were – convened, decided, left, stayed. Our girl was there, moving among them. There were ten or eleven going on to the film. We were in there with them, and we got going; we set off. We moved down South William Street, on the path, off the path, onto the street, past the Hideout, past Grogan's.

She wasn't there. She'd gone; she'd left – she was going somewhere else, with someone else.

—She's not with them.

101

—Doesn't matter, said Joe. —This is a long-term investment.

—What d'you mean?

—We're in the gang, he said.

It's how I remember it. This is what we said and did.

We lost them somewhere before College Green but caught up with them on O'Connell Bridge. I don't remember any names. I'm not sure I ever knew any. But I must have known some – there were parties later, conversations, sex. I can see faces. I can see a woman's hip, a smile, eyes. I can almost feel skin, and breath. I remember the Emmylou Harris girl. I think her name was Alice. But that was later; I learnt it later, another time. I didn't know Jessica's. I'm sure of that. But her name is there now, in the story. I remember things, events, and now she's become a woman I knew much better than I know I actually did.

O'Connell Street was wild. There was a fight at the rank outside the Gresham. There was blood on the ground, and a tooth. There was a screaming girlfriend and another girl who was trying to get at her hair. She was being held off by more girls and a man who was threatening to hit her.

We made it to Findlater Place, and into The Regent. The Emmylou girl was sitting in front of us. She turned and smiled, at Joe – then me.

—This better be good, she said.

—Wait an' see, said Joe. —It's great.

That seemed to be it: Joe had organised this adventure, even though she'd been looking at me as she spoke.

—It's brilliant, I said.

She smiled, and turned back to face the screen.

We were out of the seats the minute we heard 'Sheena Is a Punk Rocker'. We got into the narrow lane between

102

the wall and the seats. We were still at it, pogoing and bashing into one another, long after Joey Ramone had stopped singing. Joe had his hand on Emmylou's back; they were gasping together, laughing. I'd be going home alone, I thought. The routes out of town at two in the morning – Summerhill, Seán McDermott Street, the North Strand – they terrified me.

But here we were an hour later, walking home, the two of us.

We'd convened again outside the cinema. They gathered, and moved. Emmylou was there, near Joe, then not. She moved – he didn't.

He was with me.

I was happy.

—Great fuckin' film, I said.

—A load o' shite, said Joe.

—You said it was the best music film ever.

—Tha' was before I saw it.

—It wasn't tha' bad.

—It served its purpose, he said.

We were in the gang – we hoped we were. Like Joe had said, as he'd predicted. But we'd have to wait and see. We never spoke about why we were doing this. Was it to know the girl, to sleep with her, to fall in love with her? Both of us – or Joe? I remember thinking – or, feeling: it was about acceptance. I remember wanting something more.

We were coming up to Newcomen Bridge and the blocks of flats. There was a gang of lads on the other side of the street. Seven or eight of them – they seemed too chaotic to be interested in us. Still, passing them, waiting for the footsteps, the shouts – I knew it would happen, I felt it, expected, almost wanted it. The need to stay quiet, the urge to speak. To run, and draw attention to ourselves. I'm almost sixty now, but I can still feel the pain in my chest – the exhilaration – when I ran as if my life depended on it. Because it did.

We were over the canal bridge when we heard the voice behind us.

—Here, lads, d'yis have a light?

It was too early to run.

Joe looked over his shoulder.

—No.

—Come here – what's your fuckin' hurry?

Now it was time to run.

—Fuckin' queers!

I thought we'd be okay. If they'd been waiting for us, they'd have been ready for the ambush, dispersed across the street. We ran under the railway bridge. We were close to the widest section of the street, and the fire station. (I don't remember if the station was there, if it had been built when we ran past where I know it is now.) We'd been drinking all night but we were fast and they weren't that fussed about catching us – that was the hope. There was Fairview Park now, to the right. A gay lad had been battered, murdered in there, for £4 and a watch. A few months before – for being gay. It might have been these guys – they might have done the kicking. I couldn't hear their steps now – I wasn't sure. I didn't look back and I wasn't going to. They'd kicked the poor guy to death – they'd been waiting for him. I could hear Joe beside me; his breath was mine. My legs were hurting, my chest was torn. I could hear them behind us, still there, still chasing. A taxi – a fuckin' taxi! Crawling back into town. On the opposite side of the road. Joe saw it too. We got out onto the road and dashed across to the park side. We stopped running – the taxi was coming up to us. If the driver saw us running he'd keep going. I tried not to bend over, to get my breath, to vomit. I didn't look behind me. Joe lifted his arm, his hand. The taxi approached – we were fucked if he didn't stop. They'd push us over the railings, drag us into the park. Kick us to death. The papers would suggest that we were gay. Last chance, the last second, the taxi halted just behind us. Back door open – Joe got it open. We were in. Safe, saved. Joe told the driver where we were going. He did a U-turn – the street was empty. The park was dark. We saw shapes back at the fire station. The lads, the queer-bashers. They'd given up before we'd stopped the taxi. It didn't matter.

The sweat was cold.

The taxi turned on to the Howth Road.

—The things we do for love, said Joe.

He started laughing.

—Next week, he said. —Wait an' see. It'll all have been worth it.

It made no real sense.

But it was great.

—Does he look like you? I asked Joe.

—Do your kids look like you? he asked.

I've been told that my children look like me. I've been told they look like Faye.

—A bit, I said. —People say it. Faye says it.

—A bit, said Joe. —That's the thing. We all look a bit like everybody. Seriously. Get a picture of Whitney Houston up on your phone there. And we'll find something that makes her look a bit like the barman. Go on.

He was trying to escape. But I did it. I googled Whitney Houston and chose an early photo, pre-*The Bodyguard*.

—God, she was lovely.

—And the barman fuckin' isn't.

We were close now, shoulder to shoulder; we leaned into each other to share the phone.

—His forehead, look.

—Okay, I said. —That's Whitney's.

—Look at the way he's standing – look. He's definitely one of the Houstons.

—It's weird, that, isn't it? I said. —How we inherit the way we walk or something like that. My Róisín walks exactly like my mother did. According to my father.

Joe nodded at the barman.

—Maybe he sings like Whitney, he said.

—It's not impossible.

—We could start singing 'I Wanna Dance With Somebody' and see if he joins in.

—And get ourselves barred.

—Maybe she never died, he said. —She's a barman in the Sheds.

—Does Peter look like you? I asked.

—Don't be a cunt, Davy.

—I'm not being a cunt, I said. —I'm trying to remember.

—What?

I shrugged. I sat up, away from his shoulder, from him. I tried to straighten my back – stay straight.

—Some of it's so vague, I said.

—What?

—Back then, I said. —There are things that are like yesterday.

He nodded.

—Same here – yeah.

—And other stuff, I said. —That must have happened at about the same time. But –. Like, for example. Faye says we did something and I haven't a clue. No recollection of it. Say, some place we went to. She'll talk about food we had, maybe – where and what. I can't remember it but I don't doubt it happened. Then she'll mention something else that happened on the same day, same place, and I'll be there – every detail.

I wanted him to see us both back then, back in George's, back on the stools – stools like the ones we were sitting on now. I wanted to be there. It was my story too. We'd adored the same woman. It had been a joint decision. A thing we'd made up together. In the space of an evening – food and a few drinks – he'd gone from reminding me of the existence of a woman we'd never got to know to telling me that he might have been the father of her grown-up son. I'd been there at the beginning and this ending wasn't acceptable.

There was a question I hadn't asked, a question so obvious I almost burst out laughing.

—Does she say you're the father?

—Not in so many words, he said. —No. She doesn't insist on it.

—So –.

He sighed, and I heard him inhale.

—It's tricky, Davy. Look – just tricky. I'm not doing it justice. The words are letting me down.

I understood what he meant – I think I did. I could feel the solidity of my marriage to Faye, although I couldn't have explained it. But my children were mine

– it was very straightforward. There were events I attended, events I took part in. I fucked my wife and she fucked me. We have two children. She's the mother; I'm the father. There were miscarriages and an abortion. I ache when I think of my children; they are beyond anything I could put words to. I think of their weight when I first held them, their cheeks, their first laughs, the fat little hands clutching my finger. But there was also blood and shit. My children are facts and Joe's phantom, middle-aged baby made me fuckin' furious.

—I have to go for a piss.

We walked down Main Street that first weekend. We weren't going anywhere in particular – I didn't think we were. We'd no goal, no destination. Gorey then wasn't Gorey now. Gorey today is windows full of wedding dresses. Gorey then was fewer and smaller windows, a country town in Wexford trying to be a bit more. Gorey today seems like a suburb of Southside Dublin, somehow cut off from the mainland.

—Just showing you the roots, said Faye as she shut the back door.

She didn't lock it.

—What'll you do with the dogs? I asked.

—They can go for their own fuckin' walk, she said.

—I meant, when you leave.

—Who says I'm leaving?

—You do, I said.

—Do I now?

—Yeah, I said. —You said as much.

—Said as much. Did I say I was leaving this place – in actual words?

—You implied it.

—And tell us, she said.

We were out on the street now.

—Did Gladys Knight sing, 'I'm *implying* on that midnight train to Georgia' – did she?

—Not really.

I loved being with her.

—No, she fuckin' did not. I never implied on a train in my life and neither did Gladys. Or any of the Pips. It's downhill all the way, this place, look.

She was right. We were walking down a hill, towards a crossroads.

—Even coming back up, it's fuckin' downhill.

—You're not happy here, I said.

She snorted.

She stopped.

—And do you think now, David, that if I leave – *if* I leave, pack a case and actually leave – it'll be because of you, and this will make me a happy girl?

—Yeah.

—God love you.

The town – this end of town – was quiet, although there were cars and vans passing us, slowly. I could see people down the hill, below us. It was late afternoon, getting dark, already cold. We were outside a shop that had a pyramid of jars of blackcurrant jam in its window.

She moved again. I went with her. She found my hand. That thrilled me.

—Where's your shop? I asked.

—Wait now – wait. Till you see.

She stopped again.

—I'm making a prediction, she said. —One day – one day – there'll be traffic lights at this crossroads. Watch out for the tractors now.

We ran across the street, although we didn't have to. The traffic wasn't moving.

She let go of my hand.

—Look now, she said. —There.

She pointed across the street. The shop was twice the width of the other shops, to the left and right. The name was big and red, above – across – both window displays.

—Your surname's Devereux, I said.

—There now, she said. —You've had your hand on my arse and only now you find out that the arse is called Devereux. It's shocking, so it is. What's the country coming to?

She took my hand again.

—What happened your mother? I asked.

—What d'you mean, like?

—How did she die?

She let go of my hand and pointed across the street again.

—The shop?

—It's not a shop, she said. —I told you. It's a department store.

—And it killed your mother?

—I'm blaming it, anyway, she said. —It's more interesting than cancer, sure, isn't it? A woman in a man's world, David. A woman takes over the man's world. She was made for the job – and she wasn't. It killed her – they killed her. She wasn't wired for it, so she wasn't.

She was holding my hand again.

—The cancer only came skipping along behind it, she said. —I could blame my dad for dying, I suppose. And leaving her with the fuckin' thing. Come on.

—We're not going in?

—I'll never go in, she said. —Which, now, is a pity. Cos I loved it in there. Being in there with Mammy. In under everything. Watching her. I loved it. But, sure.

—Will you sell it?

We were heading back up through the town.

—When the probate's sorted, I will, she said. —Sounds medical, doesn't it?

—Probate?

—Like something with veins.

I stood at the urinal, then at the sink. No one else came in. The toilet was near the back of the pub. There was a smoking area a bit further back; I'd seen the sign for it. I could go out there – there might be a gate, a way to escape without going back in and past him. I'd leave my jacket – and my wallet; I didn't care.

But I'd just needed the time. The minute alone. I hated what Joe was at, but it was intriguing, perplexing – familiar. The things we say and don't say, the things we tell and don't – I knew what he was doing.

I checked my phone. There was nothing.

I went back out – back in.

I separate us. I sit alone in George's. Joe isn't beside me. I watch her at the table. I see the cello case, leaning against the wall, under the window. I decide it's hers. She's beautiful. She shines. I don't know why I think that – *she shines*. It could be that there's nothing physically outstanding about her, except, perhaps, her hair. The words about her arse and tits – banter, bravado – frightened lads. I'm alone now. I'm not in competition. I'm not reining back jealousy or

111

desperation. But she *is* beautiful. She *does* shine. She has a pint of lager in her hand. Her fingers are long. She puts the pint down. She stretches – I want to shout. Her head goes back, her hands reach for the ceiling. I can see an inch of white tummy – it's not a stomach. Her head is back, she's not listening to her friends. She lowers her arms – she changes shape, becomes smaller, fuller. She smiles at her friends – she's back. *Sorry.* She grins. I see her teeth. And I've already heard her voice. Southside Dublin.

This didn't happen.

Nothing like this happened.

She sat at the table with her friends, the other musicians – the music students, whatever they were. She had her back to the window. She wasn't beautiful. She was gorgeous. And she didn't shine. She was human – she was gorgeous. I remember that. Flesh and blood – legs, arms, neck. I remember her lifting her arms to stretch. I remember groaning. It was theatrical but it was real. Joe was beside me – *Oh, for fuck sake.* He can fuck off; he's not there. I'm alone. I was alone. I was looking across at her; there was no running commentary. Thirty-seven years ago. She was gorgeous. I was in love with her. In love with what I made her. She stood – she wasn't tall – and came over to me. She stood beside me while she ordered her drink – *Point of Horp, George, please.*

—Point of Horp, Joe whispers beside me. —For fuck sake.

I push him away again – he's not there.

She was real. A great-looking woman. I wouldn't have called her a woman back then – a girl is what she'd have been, back when I was still a boy. She was one of a line of girls and women that myself and Joe

112

declared ours in the years we hung around together. Gorgeous, real, but not for us – impossible. And that was the point – the impossibility. We invented them. We had the raw material, safely on the other side of the bar, the window glass, the road. We'd make them up, give them traits, habits, urges. We even gave them names. We'd been doing it for years.

After the girl in George's, we never did it again.

But my point is: I was there. I was there *too*. I saw her too. I fell for her too. I never even got to know her name – too.

—What happened after Wigwam? I asked him.

—More Wigwams, he said.

—You met her again.

—Yeah, he said. —Yeah. I did.

I was calm again; it didn't matter. I'd be going home soon, to England. I'd tell Faye all that had happened. She'd put down her book, she'd look at me over her reading glasses; she'd take them off, put them on her head. She hadn't really known Joe. But this was a story. She'd love it.

They'd met again.

—Four days after.

A pub this time – he couldn't remember which.

—How come?

—I just don't.

—You remember everything else, I said.

—Let's say it was Harry Byrne's, he said.

—Was it?

—Let's say it was, he said. —It probably was. It was, once – definitely.

—Does she still drink Harp? I asked.

—What?

—She used to drink Harp, I said.

—That's right, he said.

He laughed.

—I'd forgotten that, he said. —Jesus.

He looked down the bar, to the line of taps.

—Does Harp still exist? he said.

—They still drink it in the North, I think.

—Do they?

—I think so – yeah.

—That's gas, he said. —But anyway, no. She had a glass of Merlot. I think. Red – some sort of red. I don't think she drank it. She just had it in front of her.

—A point of Horp, I said.

—What?

—That was how she used to pronounce it.

—Is that right?

—Yeah.

—Okay, he said. —I can't remember that.

It was late afternoon, the second time, on his way home from work.

—I know what you're thinking, he said.

—You don't.

—Okay, he said. —But I think I do.

—Okay.

—You think we had a couple of drinks – for the Dutch courage. And then we went somewhere. Howth summit or somewhere – for a smooch. In the back of the car.

Earlier in the evening I'd thought exactly that. Or a hotel room – that was more likely. He'd slept with the woman of our dreams thirty-seven years after we'd put the thought into our heads. Now, before he spoke, I knew I was wrong. It hadn't happened – the hotel, the

114

back of the car. But I didn't know what *had* happened. Nothing had happened. But that, I knew, wasn't it either. This was a different kind of story.

And that was it, I thought. It was a story. Not an account, or a long boast. Joe was telling me a story.

—How come I do it all? Faye said once, after she'd moved to Dublin.

—What d'you mean? I asked her.

We'd been living together for two months. We were lying on the bed. It wasn't housework and it wasn't money – I didn't know what she meant.

—I do most of the talking, she said.

—Yeah, I agreed. —You do.

She said nothing. I wasn't worried.

—If we were in a film, I said. —You'd get up on your elbow now. You'd make sure your tits were covered by the sheet and you'd stare at me before you said your next thing.

She laughed.

Faye rarely laughed. It was another thing I loved about her. It was always a surprise. And a victory.

—That's what I mean, she said.

—What?

—I'm the one who'd normally have said something like that, she said.

—True, I said.

—Why, though?

—It's you, I said.

—It's me?

—Yeah.

—So, then – what's you?

—I'm the one who loves you for it, I said.

—Is that right?

—Yeah.

—I like that, she said. —Oh, I do like that.

And she did. For a long time. Maybe she still does.

—I'll marry you now for saying that, David, she said.

—Will you?

—I will, she said.

—Good.

—And we'll see how it goes.

—Grand.

—You can kiss the bride now, David, she said. — Anywhere you want.

They met twice a week at first. She didn't ask about his family. Joe asked her nothing. He thought – the way she sat, the way she looked at him, and didn't look at him – he thought she thought, he already knew. There was nothing to ask, no years to fill in. He thought.

—She was a cheap date, so, I said.

The drink was talking. It was the night's second energy. I was enjoying myself again.

—Hang on, said Joe. —Hang on. Listen – I looked up the word salacious – a while ago there. I googled it. I've been hearin' the word all me life and I knew what it meant, and I didn't – exactly. If you know what I mean.

—I do.

—So I googled it and read the definitions and the synonyms and all that. And this isn't salacious or crude or prurient or indecent. Or anythin'. What I'm tellin' you. And it won't be.

—Great word, though.

—Granted. Brilliant word. Gives me the horn.

He burst out laughing.

—Why did you look it up? I asked him.

—Somethin' Trish said.

—You're still talking to Trish?

—Listenin' to her.

I saw his face. He regretted what he'd just said, he wanted to take it back.

—There's nothing necessarily salacious about having sex with a woman you're not married to, I said. —Or talking about it – more to the point. Is there?

—Not at all, he said. —Not at all.

The drink was talking for him too.

—Not at all. But what I'm sayin' is, it wasn't like that. We didn't – I don't know – paw each other.

—Did you want to?

—What?

—You said it, not me – paw her. I don't know – put your hands where you'd wanted to put them back in the day.

—No.

Where you'd wanted to, was what I'd said. Where *we'd* wanted to, was what I'd meant.

—Not really, he said.

—Not really?

—Stop it, Davy.

—Stop what, Joe?

—Just fuckin' stop it. You're not listenin'. You're like fuckin' Trish.

—I'm sorry?

—Lookin' for muck where there isn't any. Wantin' it to be about body parts.

I knew now why he'd been googling. I could hardly remember what Trish looked like but I could hear her saying salacious. And body parts.

—Okay, I said. —Sorry. I'm interrupting you. Go on.

—Well, he said. —What?

—Go on with what you were saying.

—Well, all I was sayin' – all I wanted to clarify –. Was that it wasn't about – like – the biology. Or just biology.

—Okay.

—Just that. It was like we were friends. Lifelong friends, I mean.

—Like you and Trish.

—Okay, he said. —Yeah.

—How did Trish take it? I asked.

—Oh, for fuck sake.

He seemed to be grateful. He was off the hook. He'd have no problem relating this part.

—God, he said. —Jesus.

—Did you tell her?

—What d'you mean?

—Did you tell her? I repeated. —I mean, did you get to tell her, yourself, or did she find out?

—Oh, he said. —No, no. I told her. I plucked up the fuckin' stupidity. Jesus.

He laughed.

—I made sure the house was empty, he said. —But I don't know, Davy. I didn't –. I thought it would be grand.

—You didn't.

—I did.

—You can't have.

—I fuckin' did, he said. —We were gettin' on great, me and Trish. We always have. But, I can see why that might seem like a ridiculous thing to say, and I agree – it's fuckin' daft. But I'll tell you what happened. The

118

way the unconscious works or whatever – fuckin' hell. I decided I'd better put me shoes on. Before, you know, I told her – don't ask me why.

I started laughing.

—I know, he said. —I thought I'd have to escape – I don't know.

—Probably.

—Yeah – but I don't know. It made sense – if anythin' made fuckin' sense. But they were in under the coffee table. I'd taken them off earlier. We were watchin' –

—*The Affair.*

—No – fuck off. Somethin' else – I can't remember now. But, anyway, here goes, I said to myself. Get it out there. It was Friday, the kids were all out. And I started puttin' one of me fuckin' shoes on. Why are you doin' that? she asks. And d'you know what I said? I'm just goin' to put the bins out. It was the first thing I thought of – instead of what I'd actually been goin' to tell her. Puttin' the fuckin' bins out. It's Friday, she says. I'd put the bins out the night before. And I'm still puttin' my other shoe on. I should've stopped – I don't know – and waited for another time. But she was lookin' at me like she might be witnessing early-onset Alzheimer's or somethin'.

He was loving this. He was telling a different, much easier story.

—I should've taken the fuckin' things off – the shoes, like. But –. This is where the madness kicks in or somethin'. I actually told her. I decided to go ahead and tell her. To reassure her, nearly. That I wasn't losin' the marbles.

—You told Trish you were seeing another woman so she wouldn't think you had dementia?

—Basically, he said. —Yeah.

—How did you word it?

He ignored my question, or he seemed to.

—The shoes were fuckin' awkward, he said. —I'll tell you that.

He looked down at his feet – he stuck a foot out.

—These aren't the same ones, he said. —They were more like boots, the ones I was wearin'. It was a bit of a fight gettin' them on – especially the way we were sittin' – back on the couch, you know. And so, anyway, I was puttin' the other one on – doin' the lace – and I said, I met someone I used to know, by the way.

—Like that?

—Yeah.

—And?

—Hiroshima, Davy. Fuckin' Hiroshima. She was straight in there, no warnin'. I knew it! I fuckin' knew it! You fuckin' bastard!

He looked around, to make sure he wasn't being heard. He looked at me.

—I expected her to say, Who?, or somethin' like that. I don't know – ease my way into tellin' her. But she went straight to the end. D'you know what she said?

—What?

He'd lowered his voice.

—I knew you weren't ridin' me.

—Jesus, I said. —That's brilliant.

—It is in a way, he said. —Isn't it? Not accurate. But deep – or somethin'. Astute. Would we ever guess that?

—Men?

—Yeah, he said. —Would we? That our partner was thinkin' of another man while –

—Or a woman.

—Better yet. But a man – keep it simple. A different man. While she's with you.

—Would we notice – is that what you mean?

—Yeah. Or care. Anyway, I wasn't. Ridin' a different woman.

—But you were thinking of her.

—No, he said. —No. I wasn't.

The fun was out of his voice, suddenly. He was remembering: he had something he'd been trying to tell me.

—It wasn't about sex, he said. —Jessica.

—Really?

—Yeah. Really.

—Is that an age thing? I asked him.

—What?

—Well, I said. —If you'd met her, say, twenty years ago – even ten. Would it have made a difference?

—She's a beautiful woman.

—I don't doubt you, I said. —I didn't say different. Just to be clear. I'm not saying that you weren't all over her because her tits have sagged or she has a couple of chins that she didn't have before.

I didn't like talking this way – but I was enjoying myself, now that Joe wasn't.

—And so do we, by the way, I said. —We all age, is what I'm saying. The urge mightn't be there – or it's different. Or subtle. Not based on erections.

—Take it easy, Davy, for fuck sake.

—No, listen, I said. —You see a middle-aged woman. Almost elderly, really. Statistically. You meet her again after years apart. But – here's the thing. She's contemplating an elderly man – almost. You. Late middle-age – very late middle-age. It has to – I don't know – influence how we behave. Somehow. Doesn't it?

I was denying him the integrity of his story. But I wasn't. I was with him. Still with him. Trying to stay with him. For old times' sake.

—I don't think so, he said. —Not the way you mean.

—What do I mean?

—We get older, we slow down, he said. —I'm with you there. I agree with you. We calm down. We're less impetuous. Unless –. But, okay, I see what you mean. Two people – man, woman – both of them nearly sixty. There'd be a different pace. The energy levels are different – it's only natural. But.

—But?

—I don't want to be – well – salacious. I already have been, just there, I know. But that was what Trish said. I was only quoting her. But. Me and Trish made love every night, for weeks. Months – before I left. Nearly every night now. Twice a fuckin' night, occasionally. Now and again.

He'd lowered his voice again. I was leaning over to him again, to hear.

—I couldn't get enough of her, he said. —And she was the same – just as bad.

—She didn't know you were leaving. Presumably.

—You're missin' the point, Davy, he said. —I think you are. And, actually, I think she did know. She sensed it. That's what she was sayin', anyway. And I wouldn't be disagreein' with her. Although I hadn't made the decision. And I never did. She threw me out, basically.

—Did she?

—I couldn't stay, he said. —It was fuckin' unbearable. But she knew all the time – so she said. But that's a different story – kind of. The point is, the sex was never better. Old and all as I am – we are. She is. She'd kill me if she heard me but it was fuckin' incredible.

I could see it again: regret.

—So, you're right, he said. —But you're wrong.

—Go on, I said.

—Well, he said. —I think I'm too drunk now. I've lost me thread. Or somethin'.

—Not really, I said. —It's my fault. I've been interrupting you. Distracting you. Go on.

—Okay, he said. —But I am drunk – a bit. I'm out o' practice. You're the same, I'd say – you must be.

—A bit, I said.

—We should have gone into trainin', said Joe.

—Go on, anyway, I said.

—Where was I?

—Sex or the lack, I said. —Trish versus Jessica.

—Fuck off, Davy.

—Sorry, I said. —I'm only jogging your memory.

—Right, he said. —Like –. Okay. This sounds –. This is what I've wanted to say all night. But it feels too late. I've missed the opportunity.

—You haven't.

—All the talk about sex. It wrecks everythin'. Always has. Tryin' to do your exams – back in the day. And all you could think about was tits. D'you remember that?

—I don't need to, I said. —But we're falling into the trap again.

—The tits trap.

—There are worse traps.

—There are. But Jesus. There now – did Jesus think about tits?

—Definitely.

—Up on the cross?

—Especially up on the cross, I said. —He was looking out over the crowd. Scoping the talent. Your woman at the back looks pleasant.

—There we go again.

—Go on.

—Avoidin' the issue.

—Go on then.

—Yeah – okay. But I'm goin' to ask your man for a glass of water. I'm not used to drinkin' any more, Davy.

—Same here.

—We're up for the sex but down on the drink, he said. —Excuse me?

The place was still quiet; the barman heard him.

—Could you give us a glass of tap water, please? said Joe.

The barman nodded.

—No problem.

—And two more pints, said Joe.

He sat back.

—While he's at it.

He sat up again, put a hand on his back.

—So, he said.

He waited until the barman had brought him the water.

—Thanks very much.

The pints would be another few minutes.

—So.

He knocked back half the water. He placed the glass behind his pint glass.

—This is –. I have to be careful here, Davy. How I express it. I'm not bein' cagey or whatever. But first of all – goin' back to Trish an' that. She was wrong. There was never another woman in the bed with us.

—Okay.

—I don't know why I'm tellin' you all this, by the way. Maybe cos Trish wouldn't listen to me. You're Trish for the night, Davy. How does tha' feel?

—I'll get back to you, I said.

We laughed.

124

—You were puttin' your shoes on, I reminded him.

—I was goin' to tell you about the other thing, he said.

—What other thing?

—How I felt about Jessica.

—Finish the Trish story first.

—It's not a story, he said.

—Oh, it is, I said. —It definitely is.

—Well, it's a true one, he said. —She caught me on the hop, anyway. And that's puttin' it mildly. What was I doin', puttin' my fuckin' shoes on, though?

—You knew you were going to have to leave, I said.

—But I didn't.

—Didn't know?

—Didn't leave.

—Oh.

—Not then, he said.

—But she attacked you.

—Well, yeah, she did, he said. —I told you what she said – I knew you weren't riding me. An' God, Davy – I hadn't been anticipatin' anythin' like that. Like I said, she skipped loads of pages an' went straight to the fuckin' conclusion. An' I think now, actually –. I think puttin' the shoes on, continuin' that – it helped. It gave me somethin' to do, if that makes sense. Does it?

—Yeah.

—I could kind o' stay calm, he said. —Because I was doin' somethin' else. She was standin' up over me. She'd stood up – that was the problem. Part of it. And another thing went through my mind. The things we think of – Jesus. In moments o' crisis. We've a stove in the room, a gas stove. We got it put in, it must be fifteen years ago – longer. But I was thinkin', thank Christ we did. Because we'd the coal fire up to that, you know.

125

So there would've been the poker there an' the coal tongs and she'd have fuckin' skulled me with the poker.

—Has she hit you before? I asked him.

—Trish? No, never – no. But this was kind of exceptional, in fairness. An' the way she exploded –. But, like I said, I stayed calm. Not calm – numb. Numb's better. I stayed where I was – sittin', I mean. An' I kept putting the shoe on. What're you on about? I said. It was only someone I used to know. But she wasn't havin' it. No way. Who is she, she wanted to know. An' I said, Who said it was a woman? An' she definitely wasn't havin' that. Did I take her for a complete eejit? And I probably had. An' the only eejit in the room was me.

He stopped. I watched him, thinking. I said nothing – I made sure I said nothing.

—I'm fallin' for it again, he said.

—What?

—I'm pretendin' it's about me bein' caught doin' the dirty on me wife. But it isn't. But Trish, I suppose, thought I was, so I got dragged into tha' – that interpretation, I suppose. But tha' wasn't what I'd intended at all. But I was back-pedallin' from the outset, so to speak, an' I never got the chance to say what I'd wanted to say.

—What did you tell her, though? I asked.

—Oh, he said. —Just, she's a girl I used to know, ages back.

—That's true.

—But it's not, he said. —It's not true. She's not just anythin'. But I told Trish it was – she was; Jessica – before her time an' I'd hardly known her then either. I dismissed it – her. Jessica. But funnily –.

—What?

126

—Trish didn't.

—Wha'?

—Dismiss it, he said. —She wanted to know everythin'. Her name. An' I was blessed there. I didn't know her name – her surname. It's true. An' I must've looked honest when I said I didn't, because I didn't. But then she grabbed my fuckin' phone.

—Oh, Christ.

—Exactly. But then I thought, it's not too bad because I didn't have Jessica's name in the phone book.

—George.

—There you go – you remember. But Trish is racing through my phone – the fingers, you know – the way women can do it. An' I don't stop her. I don't try to get it back. But I'm lookin' at her an' I'm thinkin' she's done this before, she's searched through my phone before. I mean, she knew my password already. And that's grand – I know hers. Do you know Faye's?

It took me a second to realise he'd asked me a question.

—Yeah, I said. —I do.

—I'd have thought so, he said. —It's the same with most couples is my bet. But the way Trish was doin' it, scrollin' through whatever she was scrollin' through. I knew she'd done it before. When I wasn't there. An' I knew I was fucked. She'd been ready for me all along. You phone this George item a lot, don't you? she says. An' she phones you as well, look it. And she phones her.

—Trish phoned Jessica?

—Yep.

—On your phone.

—Yep.

—Fuckin' hell, Joe.

—Go on, he said. —Laugh. Get it over with.

He was laughing before I was.

—Jesus, Joe.

—I know.

—Your two worlds collided.

—Oh, they did, he said.

—What happened?

—Well, he said. —She phoned her. An' she answered. Is that George? she says – Trish – an' she doesn't wait to hear wha' Jessica is goin' to say. Is that George the lezzer from Enid Blyton? she says. I couldn't believe it – I nearly laughed. But then she says, Stay away from my husband, bitch, I know where you live. An' fuckin' hell, I wondered if she did.

—She said it with conviction.

—She fuckin' did, man, he said. —Then Jessica must've been talkin', because all Trish did was go, Yeah, yeah, yeah, yeah – drownin' her out, you know. Just you mark my words, she said. Stay away from him or I'll improve your face for you. I'd never heard her talk like tha' before – so brutally, like. An' then she deleted the number. She held it up to show me she was doin' it – Look.

—What did you do?

—Nothin', he said. —I just sat there. But then she was scrollin' through my photographs. Do you take many photographs, Davy?

—Not really – no.

—Same here, he said. —I don't think many of us do, men our age. It doesn't come natural. So all she found, really, was pictures she'd sent me, herself. The kids, an' sometimes somethin' she was thinkin' of getting' an' she was askin' what I thought, d'you know the way?

—Yeah.

—Curtains or a fridge, or whatever.

Faye had once sent me a photo of a single Weetabix, and the message: Will I buy the pack? I'd been telling her earlier about the busy day I had ahead of me, before I went to work.

—At least you haven't been sendin' her pictures of your penis, said Joe.

—Trish said that?

—Yeah, he said. —An' that gave me a chance to speak. Why the fuck would I do somethin' like that? To give the girl a laugh, she says. The poor miserable bitch. She wasn't lookin' at me – she didn't look at me the whole time. She was like Carrie from *Homeland*, totally concentratin' on the phone. An' the way she spoke – it was like she knew Jessica. Like she'd met her an' didn't like her.

He was running out of steam. He'd finished telling the story he hadn't wanted to tell, the event that was – he thought – beside the point. Jessica definitely existed; I knew that now. Trish had made her more real than Joe had been able to manage.

—What happened then? I asked.

—Nothin'.

—Nothin'?

—Nothin' much, he said. —Then. But, yeah.

—Yeah what?

—We had sex again, he said. —Me an' Trish.

—But not that night.

—Says who?

—Really?

—No, he said. —Not tha' night. But listen, Davy. I was sayin' earlier. Like, this isn't about two women fightin' over me or anythin' like tha'. Or me havin' the midlife crisis or somethin'.

129

—Midlife?

—Late midlife, he said. —Fuck off. It isn't. When I saw Jessica, when I met her again. I thought – I felt. It felt like I'd been livin' two lives. That's it, really. I've been livin' two lives. There was my life – the family, Trish, the job an' tha'. The – I suppose – the official life. An' there was a shadow life I've been livin' as well – that I've only become aware of. Since, like. Since I met her. Because I didn't really meet her, Davy. I'd been with her all the time. Tha' was how it felt. What I've been tryin' to say. Honest to God. I wasn't cheatin'.

—What did she think about Trish calling her?

—She didn't mention it.

—Did you?

—No.

—Come here, I said. —Did you ever tell Trish?

—Wha'?

—About Jessica, I said. —Did you ever manage to tell her what happened?

—Not in one sittin', he said. —No. Not really.

There were no other customers at the bar when we got there, at half-three, immediately after the holy hour. George was lifting the window blind in the far corner.

—Gentlemen.

We sat at our end of the bar, and looked whenever we heard the doors – pushed open by shoulders and shopping bags but not by instrument cases. She didn't come in. And no one arrived with a violin or cello, an advance party from the college around the corner.

—D'you get many comin' in from the College of Music, George? I asked.

—Oh, we do, said George.

—Especially on a Saturday.

—Not especially, no, said George. —But when there's an orchestra around in the Gaiety, they'd come in, a lot of them, between the matinee and the evening performance on the Saturdays.

—With their instruments?

—No, no.

George laughed – he chuckled.

—You'd never get a piano through that door.

He rubbed his hands and walked down to meet two lads who'd just come in. One of them was carrying a record bag.

—Spandau Ballet is my guess, I said.

—Duran Duran, said Joe.

—Fuckin' dopes.

—She might be in the orchestra in the Gaiety, said Joe.

—In the pit.

—But listen, he said. —There's no way she's playin' in a panto. I'm not havin' it.

—There wouldn't be a cello in a panto, would there? I said. —An orchestra.

—No, said Joe. —Probably not.

I'd never been to a pantomime. I've been to quite a few since then. There were seven or eight years when our kids loved going to the panto at Christmas, the trip to the Wyvern Theatre in Swindon, the dinner before, ice-cream during the interval. Faye loved it too.

—Timmy Mallett, she said once.

We were just home, in bed, after going to *Aladdin*.

—You wouldn't know whether to bring him home or kill him, she said.

She sighed, and put her hand on my back.

—Kill him for me, David, she said.

—Is that an order?

—I think it is.

—Now?

—No rush, no. Just, before next Christmas.

—Opera, maybe, I said to Joe.

—That'd make more sense.

—I've never been to an opera, I said.

—Same here.

—Will we go?

—What's the point? said Joe. —The best part of it will be under the stage.

—Our girl.

—Sawin' away in the dark.

—It can't be dark, I said. —They'd have to be able to read the music. Wouldn't they?

—Would they not just know it off by heart, like the singers?

—Don't think so.

—Our bird would.

—I kind of like the idea of her readin' the music, I said. —And turnin' the page.

—Okay.

—Maybe even wearin' reading glasses.

—Ah, no, said Joe. —Fuck that.

—No?

—Well, maybe. Okay – black ones.

—No lenses.

—Cool.

—Would she be smiling as she plays? I asked.

—No, he said. —No. Geniuses don't smile.

—She's a genius?

—Definitely.

—She's mad then.

—Grand, said Joe. —But she's not drinkin' this afternoon, so she can't be that fuckin' mad.

There was a short period, a few minutes at about
half-four, when there were no women at all in the room,
just men.

—What's the story?

—Don't know.

—Maybe it's the future, said Joe.

—Wha'?

—A world withou' women.

—Bleak.

—Uncomplicated.

—Fuckin' bleak.

We could pretend that women complicated our lives.
There was no one there to sneer.

We'd started our second pints when I realised
something.

—I haven't eaten since Thursday.

—Serious?

—Yeah, I said. —No breakfast yesterday. An' no
lunch. I forgot me sandwiches an' I went to buy the
Joe Jackson album, an' I had to leg it back to work by
the time I'd stopped talkin' to your man in the Sound
Cellar. Then a few pints after work an' I fell asleep in
front o' the gas fire at home. An' then we came straight
into town. An' no fuckin' breakfast.

I didn't tell him about the girl from work, the girl
who'd smiled at me earlier in the day, or how I'd stood
beside her in the pub – Hartigan's – and hoped she'd
talk to me, say something and then I'd be able to talk
to her; how I'd left after seven pints, five pints after
she'd left.

—You slept in front o' the gas?

—Till abou' two. I woke up sweatin' – Jesus. Wringin'. Then –

—Did your da not wake yeh?

—He never goes into the front room if I'm in there.

I'd often seen him – the darkness made by his feet – on the other side of the door. The feet would stay there a minute, then go.

—Does he think you're with a bird or something? Joe asked.

—Don't think so, I said. —But anyway, I'm fuckin' starvin'.

We left.

—Back in a bit, George.

—Ah, now.

We went to the Coffee Inn on South Anne Street, for spaghetti bolognese. Food always felt like a waste of money. But I liked the place – packed with more of the people I wanted to be. We had two pints in Kehoe's, two in Neary's, two more in Sheehan's. It was a different part of the day, a different life, when we got back to George's.

I was alone, outside. Joe had been with me, beside me, on Chatham Street. Then there'd been no room on the path. I'd gone out on the road, back onto the path. I'd lost Joe, but hadn't noticed.

I stood outside. I looked in the window. The door glass – both doors, both panes – was frosted, with a clear, round section just below eye level, a porthole. I had to bend slightly to look in.

She was in there, among the friends. I looked at the men around her. If I'd had a marker, I could have drawn on the window, followed their eyes, mapped them, circled where their gazes intersected. On her face, all of them on her face. And – somehow – on my face, my eyes reflected in the glass watching her.

She scratched her neck. She pulled the neck of her jumper down, slightly. She scratched a point above her collarbone with just one finger, then patted the jumper back into place. She looked at no one in particular – no man or woman. She was alone. She didn't see the map.

Joe was beside me. Looking through the other porthole. Seeing what I saw. We stayed out there. For minutes.

—Does she still play the cello? I asked.

His answer surprised me.

—Yeah.

—Does she?

—Yeah, he said. —Every day.

All women were mad. Faye told me that. And I believed her.

The sun was bright outside; the curtains seemed to have disintegrated. My father was downstairs, in the kitchen. He was making no noise. I pictured him sitting at the kitchen table, tea and Saturday's *Independent* in front of him, looking at the door to the hall or at the ceiling. He was smiling, shaking his head.

We were in my old bedroom because we hadn't been able to stop a taxi the night before and the house had been nearer than our flat, and I wanted him – I didn't tell Faye this – to see her. I think now too: I wanted to provoke him. To be difficult. To amuse him. I wanted to give him something to tell other men, if he spoke to other men. Give him the chance to smile and raise his eyes to heaven.

—A lot of the men are too, she said.

—Mad?

—That's what I'm fuckin' talking about, David.

She slapped my chest.

—You should be bloody listening.

—I am.

—Yes, she said. —Mad. A fair few men are. But not necessarily in a good way. Almost never.

Faye was at her funniest, her most interesting, most entertaining, before sex and after sex. I don't think I ever correctly anticipated what she'd say. But when she spoke, when she started giving it the full Faye, I knew there was going to be sex. I wanted it and she wanted it.

—Mad men are bad men, she said.

—Am I mad?

—No, she said. —But I'm working on it. But not really. I like you kind of sane, so I do.

Women were mad.

She'd point them out. The hints, the clues – the eyes, the clothes. The walk, the hair, the gaze. There was madness in them and on them all.

—And you're mad, I said.

—I'm the fuckin' Queen of the madness, boy, she said. —Or I will be, by the time I've finished.

It was mascara, or a pair of tights, or dark eyes behind a curtain of hair. The attempts to stand out or fit in. Madness was the destiny of all women, she said, so it was best to claim it before it claimed you.

—My mother tried not to be mad, she said as we lay in bed in my old bedroom. —She tried so hard, she ended up being some kind of a man. She beat the men at their own game. When Daddy died, they thought my Uncle Jim would step in. Daddy's little brother, a real

Devereux, like. It was in the blood and all that fuckin' nonsense. But Mammy wasn't having it. She'd always thought the shop was a bit shite and she wanted to give it a go. Make a proper place out of it. And she did. Uncle Jim and the rest could all fuck off.

I was listening for sound from downstairs. I wanted my father to know that I wasn't alone, that there was a naked girl beside me. That I was fine. That I was happy.

—Cathy isn't mad, I said.

—Oh, she fuckin' well is, said Faye. —And I haven't finished telling you about Mammy.

—Go on.

—The good's gone out of it now.

—Go on.

—Well, said Faye. —You know about ladies' men?

—Yeah, I said. —Kind of.

—You wish you were one.

—I don't.

—Liar, she said. —You're a big fuckin' liar. You do so.

—Am I not one already?

—You'll do me, David, she said. —Mammy became a man's lady.

I'd no idea what my mother had been like, if men had liked her or if she'd enjoyed the company of men. I had nothing to help me. Just her with me. I couldn't recall her out in the world.

—What d'you mean? I asked Faye.

—She was one of the lads, she said. —She really took to it. And they let her – they loved it. She drank with them, she went to the race meetings. She'd have seduced their wives if she could've. And maybe she did once or twice, I don't know. When I was out at school. But no, not really – I don't think that. That wouldn't

137

have been on. So, she seduced the lads instead. And she lost it, somewhere.

—Lost what?

—The sanity.

—Oh.

—But, said Faye. —When was the last time you changed these sheets, by the way?

—Well, I don't live here.

—Ah, Jesus, she said. —It could be years.

—No, I said. —I don't think so – I don't know. A few months.

—They look worse.

—I slept here at Christmas.

—Fuckin' Christmas? That's nearly a year ago – Jesus. She slapped the bedclothes.

—Fuckin' dust, she said. —My God. But there's no girl smell off them anyway. So there's that, at least. You're the lady's man elsewhere, David, but not in this *leaba*. But Mammy. There was a time, a point, when she was happy mad.

—What's happy mad?

—In control of her own madness. She decided, I'll ride him – for the crack. Before he decides he's been riding me.

—Are you serious?

—I am, David.

—How d'you know this?

—I'm an observant lassie, so I am. And there was only the two of us in the house. After he died – Daddy. And she was happy.

—Because he died?

—No, she said. —Not really that. She cried a lot – I remember that. I'd hear her just before I'd walk into the kitchen or something. And she'd stop when she saw me.

She'd wipe her eyes, and smile, call herself an eejit. She was fuckin' devastated. I'm pretty sure she loved him.

—I never heard my father cry, when my mother died.

—Ah, sure, that's only natural, she said. —I could never like a blubbery man.

—I'll remember that.

—You'd better.

—I will.

—And it doesn't mean he didn't, she said.

—I don't think he did.

—Nevertheless. Mammy tried to hide it – kind of. Your dad might have succeeded.

—Okay.

—Anyway, I think it caught up with her or something, she said. —And she died, God love her.

—Was it not cancer?

—That's just the official version, she said. —She thought she was beating them at their own game – the lads. The best of Wexford's economic fuckin' wonders. But really, all she was doing was riding. It disappointed her, David. And then some.

She sat up.

—Let's go meet him, so.

She dropped off the end of the bed and found my jumper on the floor.

—Will he like me? she asked.

I watched her pull the jumper over her head.

—I like your stink, David, she said. —It's nice and manly.

—Thanks.

—Now get up, she said.

—He'll love you, I said.

★   ★   ★

—Is she any good? I asked Joe.

—I think so, he said. —Yeah, she is. It's one of those instruments though, isn't it?

—What?

—The cello, he said. —It's hard to tell if it's bein' played well or not.

—Is it?

—When it's alone, he said. —By itself. No violins or flutes or whatever.

—Is that right?

—Ah, yeah, he said. —Definitely. Like a bass guitar or somethin'. At a gig. Did you ever enjoy a bass solo?

—No.

—Same here. If he's good, grand. Just don't play a fuckin' solo to prove it.

—I'm that way with guitar solos too now, I said.

I hadn't been to a gig in years. I'd suggested to Róisín that we go to Arcade Fire together, in London, a few years ago. She didn't even laugh at me. Although she let me buy two tickets, for herself and a friend of hers who I never met.

—Fuckin' unbearable, said Joe. —Are solos even a thing any more?

—Good question.

—An' we don't know the answer, he said. —Which, in itself now, is a fuckin' answer.

The pints had arrived. I'd paid for them and the barman had gone back to his hiding place. The stools on either side of us were empty. We were still alone.

—But it sounds like music, he said. —When she plays. It's good. Not bad at all.

—I interrupted you, I said.

—Yeah, he said. —Again.

—Sorry.

—I don't blame you, he said. —It must seem a bit bizarre. What I'm tellin' you. I can hear tha' – I understand it.

—Did you tell Trish?

—Tell her wha'?

—What you just said. About livin' a shadow life.

—Well, I did, he said. —Or I tried to. But – not the night I was tellin' you about.

He picked up his new pint.

—She said somethin' about my shadow cock an' where it had been all these years.

I laughed.

—Fair enough, I said.

—I suppose so, he said. —I don't know if I want this pint.

I picked up my own.

—Has to be done, I said, although I didn't want mine either.

I tapped his glass with mine.

—The shadow life.

—Don't get fuckin' nasty, he said.

—I'm not.

—Okay.

—Sorry, I said. —Go on.

—Will we go in to George's after these?

—No, I said. —We won't. Tell me – go on.

—Right, he said. —Okay.

He brought his pint closer to him. He looked at it.

—Like, I felt that way when I saw her in the school – Jessica. The time when I saw her comin' down the corridor. I wasn't surprised – like there'd been no gap, no years in between. An' listen, I'm not addin' a gloss to it, significance or somethin', after the fact. But I know as well. It happens. It's happened to me.

—Me too.

—The head playin' tricks. The light in a room, or somethin'.

—Or a piece of music.

—Sometimes, yeah – I don't know, though. I don't mean nostalgia. Or the other one. Déjà vu.

—I know what you mean – go on. It's like wakin' up – a bit. As if your real livin' has been the dream.

—That's it, he said. —To an extent. But I'd sometimes feel tha' way if I was at a meetin' an' I'd only been half listenin' to what was goin' on.

—That's my normal state, I lied.

—Yeah, he said. —Yeah. But this wasn't daydreamin' or dozin' off.

—I know.

—It was much –. It wasn't that at all.

—I remember once, I said. —We were away for a week, me and Faye. About five years ago. Portugal. Just the two of us. In Lisbon.

—Nice.

—It was. But I woke up and the light – at the edge of the curtains, around the edges. It wasn't that I knew I was somewhere different – the hotel room. I actually thought that it was my bedroom – that I always woke up to this light.

—Yeah –

—Hang on. When I turned in the bed, I didn't expect to see Faye. Faye was a shock. For a second – just a split second. I didn't know who she was. My real wife wasn't there. It felt like somethin' was pulled out o' me.

I heard it: my accent was changing, reverting. I was becoming the Dublin boy I'd been when we'd first seen Jessica. And so was Joe; he was well ahead of me. The drink was letting us pretend. The drink was making it easy, and honest.

—Did you know your real wife? Joe asked. —If you know what I mean. In the dream.

—No, I said. —No, I didn't. I wouldn't go tha' far. But it lingered – for days. I even resented Faye. Although I knew tha' was daft. I'm not sayin' the experience is the same as yours, by the way. But there are similarities. Aren't there?

—Absolutely, he said.

I had him going again. He wanted to shove both of my wives out of the way. He wanted to hear himself telling me his story.

—But I didn't reject Trish, he said.

—I didn't reject Faye, I told him.

—You forgot about her.

—Only because I was half asleep, and only for a couple o' seconds.

—I didn't forget Trish.

—Good man, I said. —Look, Joe – for fuck sake.

—I know, he said.

He grinned – gave me the old Joe.

—What're we fuckin' like? he said.

—It's the drink, I said. —Makes us fuzzy.

—It always did.

—We were better at it, though – back then.

—That applies to everythin', but – doesn't it?

—Except cookin'.

—Exactly, he said. —The shite tha' doesn't matter. D'you cook?

—A bit, yeah.

—Same here. It's messin', really, but, isn't it? Playin'.

—An excuse to drink.

—That as well, yeah.

143

An excuse to turn my back and hide, I could have said. An excuse to avoid talking.

—Go on, I said. —We'll be thrown out before you're finished.

—Right, he said. —So – anyway. I dismissed it. The feelin'. I kind o' did. I kept sayin' to myself, she's just a great-lookin' girl from your past – cop on. A well-preserved woman, as they say. We liked them, even when we were kids.

—True.

—D'you remember Missis Early?

—She was probably only thirty.

—Forty.

—A kid.

—Okay. But anyway, I kind of insisted tha' that was it. Tha' was what I was up to. Messin', really. The bit of excitement. I have the number but I won't be phonin' her, but I can if I want. An' it worked.

—Wha' d'you mean?

—Well – Trish. Jesus. I won't be salacious, Davy. But I was rock fuckin' hard. An' Trish –

—Can I stop you there? I said.

—Wha'?

He looked like a man who'd been delivering a very good TED Talk.

—Did you not do it, swap phone numbers and meet her, just to add spice to your life? That's what I'm hearin'.

—I thought so, he said. —That's what I'm tryin' to say. At the start I did. I was open to tha' theory.

—It wasn't conscious, no?

—Well, okay, yeah – it was. It *was* my fuckin' theory. To an extent. But I wasn't just actin' the bollix. I wasn't actin' the bollix at all.

144

—But it was workin' out well.

—Ah, man, he said. —D'you remember what it was like, when you'd fall for a girl. Like, after the first time you'd been with her. After the sex, I mean. The feelin' – how full you'd feel.

—Spunk eyes, we called it.

—I know, yeah – I remember.

He laughed.

—Spunk eyes, he said, and laughed again. —A head full o' spunk. But it was like tha'. Like there was milk behind your eyes. You'd drift through the day with an erection an' a sponge for a brain.

—Overwhelmed.

—Fuckin' literally. You couldn't think of anythin' except the woman. The smell of her – Jesus. Everythin'. You didn't even count the hours till the next time – it was too fuckin' mathematical. You were too stupid. There was just – yeh know, like. The cunt.

—Okay.

—It's funny how we use tha' word so casually these days, isn't it?

—I don't like it.

—Same here, he said. —But anyway, that's where I was. With Trish. Back in my glory days. I was in love with me wife, for fuck sake.

—Gas.

—Well –. It was brilliant. But it's exhaustin', man, I'll tell you that for nothin'. We were neglectin' the kids.

He thought about what he'd said – I saw him – and he burst out laughing.

—Jesus –.

He slapped my shoulder. It was a new one, a gesture – an act – that wasn't his. Or, it hadn't been.

145

The barman was looking across at us.

—Anyway, said Joe. —Back on track. Tha' was the drink talkin' again.

He took a breath, held it, let it go.

—But, he said. —I believed in it. The feelin'. I expected somethin' to happen.

—Wha'?

—I didn't know, he said. —Somethin'. I wasn't actin' the maggot – is what I'm sayin'. But, all the same, I felt I was cheatin'. When I was makin' love to Trish.

—Cheatin' on who?

—Trish, he said. —Jessica. Me, even.

—It didn't stop you, though.

—No, he said. —No, it didn't. I thought –. I think I thought. It was becomin' the new normal – or somethin'.

He wasn't smiling. He wasn't a rogue.

—I wish I'd agreed with Trish, he said.

—What d'you mean?

—When she said she knew I was ridin' someone else, he said. —I mean, it wasn't true. Wha' she said – it wasn't. But I wish I'd been brave. I denied every-thin'. An' here I am. If I hadn't denied it, where would I be?

—D'you know?

—No, he said. —But I shut the door too quickly.

—D'you think Trish wanted another woman in the bed?

—It's not about beds.

—I'm lost, so, I said.

I sounded like Róisín pretending to be Irish.

—What is it abou'?

—I don't know, he said. —Souls?

—Ah, for fuck sake.

He stepped down off his stool.

—I've to go to the jacks, he said. —Back in a minute. Stay there, Davy.

—Your bladder's the same age as the rest of you, at least.

—Fuck off.

He smiled at Faye – I thought he was smiling at her.

—I've heard all about you, he said.

He hadn't. I'd said nothing to him. I know now: he hadn't needed to hear anything. He'd have seen me, gazing at nothing, the times I'd been to see him. Looking at my watch, dying to get away.

I'd never been upstairs – in my childhood bedroom – with Cathy. I'd brought her home to meet him but we'd never sneaked in, shoes off, half pissed and giggling. I'd liked Cathy but I'd never had what Joe and myself called the spunk eyes. I'd gone through none of the time in a white daze. She'd needed a boyfriend and I'd do her. I thought that then – I think I did – and it had suited me too. I'd have married her; we'd been well on our way to saying something about it when I sat beside Faye at that wedding.

Faye said I'd do her too. But it was different. She'd actually said it, like no one else could – the crease at the left side of her mouth, the half shut left eye. Faye wanted me. When I was inside her, I knew it was me she wanted inside her. It was me on top of her. It was me she was pulling to her. It was never her face, her shape, an ankle, a hand. It was Faye.

—Nice to meet you, Mister Walsh, she said.

All she was wearing was my jumper.

147

Cathy had offered to put on the kettle. They'd spoken about their counties – she was from south Wexford, my father was from Waterford – and the people, the families, the farms, they might both have known. He'd said more to Cathy than he ever said to me. He'd chatted to her, with her. I'd watched him respond to the presence, and the attention, of a woman. I was getting to know him. I was making him happy.

—Was Cathy a lesbian? he asked me, a few years ago.

—Cathy?

—The girl you went out with that time, he said. —I've often wondered.

—No, I said. —Not as far as I know.

—I wondered, he said.

—Back then?

—No, he said. —No, no. The thought wouldn't have occurred to me back then.

—Same here, I said.

—Did you ever think it, yourself?

—No, I said. —No. I didn't.

—Would you think it now? he asked.

—Why would I?

—Well, he said. —With what we know now. And the same-sex marriage referendum and all that. And she was a *Bean* Garda too, remember. So, there's that as well.

—I don't think she was gay, I said.

—Right.

—I don't think wearing a uniform indicates you're gay – if you're a woman.

—Back then, though.

—I don't think so.

—Well, I liked her, anyway.

—So did I.

—Do you ever hear from her?

—No.

—I liked her.

—Yeah.

He sat up when he met Faye. That was the big thing. He sat up.

No – he stood up. My father stood when Faye stood in front of him in my blue jumper, at the opposite side of the kitchen table. He walked around to shake her hand.

—It's very nice to meet you too, he said. —I've heard all about you.

He turned, walked back around the table, and sat. He looked at Faye, the nineteen-year-old girl standing in his kitchen – my mother's kitchen. I thought his face was melting. It was shifting, sliding – something was happening to it. I thought he was going to do what I'd just told Faye I'd never seen him do: cry.

But that stopped.

He sat up. My father was a man and there was a woman in the room. He sat up – and I knew my father like I hadn't known him before. I could imagine him now with my mother – holding her, being with her, kissing the back of her neck. I saw what he'd lost and I loved him.

Then something happened. The man fell from his face – the admiration, the longing. He looked at me. He stared, then looked away. He pretended to read the paper. He waited for us to leave.

—You're crap at this, Joe, I told him.

He was back from the toilet, back beside me.

—Crap at wha'?

—Explainin' yourself.

—I'm not, he said. —Fuck off. Seriously, though –. Davy –.

He looked at his pint.

—I don't want this, he said.

I picked up mine. I drank, took an inch off it.

—I haven't been fair to Trish, he said.

—You left her.

—That's not the point, he said. —Fuck off. Although it is.

—Wha'?

He picked up his pint.

—Despite her anger, he said. —Whatever. I was the one tha' made the move. Left, you know. She didn't tell me to. But anyway –.

—Wha'?

—It's the salacious thing again, he said. —I've been makin' a bit of a joke of her, haven't I?

—I don't know, I said. —I don't think so.

—I have, he said. —Yeah, I have. It's not good. I love Trish.

—Okay.

—I do, he said. —Tha' doesn't stop. I tried to tell her.

—Did she listen?

He didn't answer. He didn't need to. He knocked back more of his pint than I thought he would.

—But when I met up with Jessica, he said.

—The first time?

—First, second, all the times. I knew this was my life. I felt at home.

—So you said.

—Literally, he said. —At home.

—Where were you?

—I told you, he said. —It doesn't matter. It was bein' with her. I was at home. Finally, Davy.

—Finally, Joe?

—Finally. Yeah – finally. I'm tellin' you how I felt. I know it sounds feeble – I can't do anythin' about tha'.

—What about your other home?

—Look, he said. —I'm just tellin' you what it felt like. It's not – I don't know – it's not a chessboard. Or Monopoly. Houses an' property. An' it's not logical, I know – believe me, I know. Or maybe even sane. But it's how I felt.

—What's home? I asked him.

—Wha'?

—What d'you mean by it? I asked. —Me – it's the house. Faye and the kids. The house and the people in it. And the years we've been in it. The whole history. My father's house – it's not home. Not now, any more. I hate bein' there.

That was true. I hated sleeping in that house. I hated waking up in it, knowing where I was. It was always a shock.

—It's a big word – home, I said.

—Yeah.

—So, wha' d'you mean by it?

—Well, it's hard, he said. —If we'd been here a year ago –

—Exactly a year ago.

—That's right, yeah. A year. If it was a year an' a day ago, then. I'd be agreein' with you. Every word. Trish an' the kids, in the house. Tha' was home.

—Not now?

He didn't answer. He took his phone from his pocket, looked at it, put it back in his pocket.

—No, he said. —I wish –. But I don't know.

I took my own phone out and looked at it.

Nothing.

—I don't know, he said now. —I used to think tha' was good.

—What was?

—Sayin' I don't know, he said. —I used to think it was a sign o' somethin'. Maturity. An' equality. Trish said it once. After one o' the kids asked me somethin' an' I said it. I don't know, I mean. She said, A man admits he doesn't know. We laughed. I thought it was great. Liberatin' or somethin'. An' it was. In work as well. Because I've been there so long. It doesn't really matter what I say, I'll do the job anyway. I said it at a meetin' once. Lads, never be afraid to admit you don't know. Their faces – Jesus.

—I can imagine.

—Trish said I was overdoin' it, he said. —Like I was claimin' it as a philosophy or somethin'. Some lifestyle bullshit. An' I was – in a way. But she said the kids were startin' to think I was just thick. An' a proper dad should be a cranky know-all. But, anyway. Now, it kills me.

—Does it?

—No, he said.

He rolled down one of his shirt sleeves.

—If I'm being honest, he said. —No.

—Drink talkin'.

—No.

He buttoned the sleeve.

—It's what I'd wish for, he said. —I think. Between ourselves – I wish I could feel tha', that it kills me, not feelin' tha' the house – Trish an' tha' – is home. But it doesn't kill me. So –.

He pulled down the other sleeve.

—So, there yeh go.

—Okay.

—It's not, though. Okay. Is it?

—No.

—No, it's not. Somehow. I don't know, Davy. Tha' part of it.

—Wha' d'you mean?

—The family, he said. —They just –. Look –. They don't seem there now.

—Joe.

—Wha'?

—Have you any idea how many men I know who've left their wives for other women? Men our age. An' you know them too – men who've done wha' you've done. We could spend the night countin' them.

He hadn't buttoned the second sleeve. It almost slapped him as he lifted his pint. He put the glass down and buttoned the sleeve.

—Younger women, he said. —For younger women.

—No, I said. —Not always.

—Jessica's older than Trish.

—So wha'?

—You're not listenin' to me, Davy. You haven't been listenin'.

—An' you're bein' a pain in the arse, Joe.

—You're soundin' like Trish now.

—Fuck off, I said. —I've been listenin' to every fuckin' word. You walked out on your wife an' kids an' you're calling it a philosophy.

The barman was looking at us. He stayed where he was but he stared at us. I didn't stare back.

—Are we bein' loud? Joe asked.

—Don't know, I said. —I didn't think we were.

—Fuckin' prick, said Joe. —The head on him. Wha' time is it?

—Half-eight, I said.

It was good, saying that – 'half-eight'. It always made more sense than 'eight-thirty'.

—What're we doin'? he said.

—Don't know.

—I don't know why I'm doin' up my fuckin' sleeves, he said. —Habit. Are we havin' another one?

—I suppose so.

—Or a short, maybe – instead.

—No.

—No, you're right. Madness. Whose round is it?

—Don't know. I don't –. Actually, I don't want a drink. I've had enough.

—One more, he said. —It's my twist. An' I need to finish this.

—Finish wha'?

—You were there at the beginnin', he said.

—I wasn't, I said.

—You were, he said. —In George's. Back then.

—No, I said. —I wasn't. You're makin' this up. You're on your own.

—What d'you mean I'm makin' it up?

—Just that, I said. —You are.

—What d'you mean, though? he said.

—Well, look, I said. —Wha' you say you remember an' what I know I remember don't tally.

I felt like I'd slammed a door on my own hand.

—You know you remember?

—Yep.

—You fuckin' *know* you remember? Are we havin' tha' pint?

—Go on – yeah.

—I'll pour the fuckin' thing over you, he said.

—Excuse me?

I was in his way. He lifted himself off the stool and leaned over the counter, so the barman would get a clear view of him.

—Two pints, please.

I watched the barman nod.

—Thank you.

Joe sat back down.

—Fuckin' Noddy, he said. —Did you see him?

I knew what he was doing. He'd become Joe again – the man I used to know – so he could have another go at me. The new version was lurking there behind him.

—Right, he said. —What d'you remember?

—It's what I don't remember, I said.

—What's tha'?

—I don't remember you gettin' off with her.

He closed his eyes, and opened them.

—Okay, he said. —I did.

—Okay.

He looked at me. My eyes slid.

—Okay, he said. —Look. Let's agree on somethin'. I've a suggestion. Davy?

—Yeah, I said. —Go on.

—Okay. I'll accept you don't remember an' you can accept you don't remember, an' tha' way we'll both accept that it happened –

—What happened?

—For fuck sake, he said. —I remember her better than you do. That's reasonable, isn't it?

—Okay.

—It's human, isn't it? he said. —We remember things differently. I've siblings –.

155

—Yeah.

—An' we never agree on anythin' tha' happened more than thirty years ago – or even last month. An' we grew up in the same house. It's only a matter o' time, we'll be arguing about who our parents were. We won't be able to agree on even tha'. So –.

The barman delivered the pints.

—Two good ones, he said.

—Good man, I said.

I took money from my pocket and found him a tenner.

—Thanks very much.

He went and left us alone. I saw him put the change into a poor box at the taps.

—So, said Joe.

—Was it even my round? I asked.

—I'm not sure, said Joe. —It might be.

—I don't even want it.

—Same here, he said. —But it has to be done. Are we not men?

—We are Devo.

—Fuckin' sure, he said. —So, anyway. I remember what I remember an' you don't remember what I remember. Because you weren't fuckin' there. On tha' particular occasion. But wha' I'm suggestin' is, we bypass that an' continue.

—Okay, I said. —Right.

I'd listen and leave. I knew the man I was listening to and in a minute I wouldn't. It didn't matter. I'd have to be going.

—I'll keep on track, he said. —No distractions. She spoke to me –

—When're we talkin' about?

—Wha'?

—When did she speak to you? I said. —Recently or –?

—Recently, he said. —Yeah, no – I mean last year. When I started meetin' her again.

—Okay, I said. —Sorry – go on.

—I felt it immediately. Like I said. That I'd known her all the time.

—Okay.

—That the first time was actually the five hundredth or whatever the number would be. Before tha' – this is true, I'll admit this. It was the gap in the years an' the fact that I hadn't thought about her – although that's not strictly true either. I often thought about her. But it was the sudden arrival of – I don't know – the possibility. The novelty. I'm not sure if it was sex, Davy. The reality o' tha'. I don't know if I'd have gone tha' far. It was more the fantasy. The thinkin' about it, the anticipation. An' there must be a scent. A fuckin' vibe – energy or somethin'. Because Trish an' meself –. We won't go there again.

—No.

—Grand. So. I go an' I meet her. You know already. An' I feel it. We're already together.

Again, I wanted to hit him. Again, I wanted to go. But I wanted the story; I wanted to hear much more.

—Was it deflatin'? I asked him.

—How d'you mean? he said.

—Well, I said. —You were half hopin' for some sort o' sexual liaison. Sorry – that's crap. But you know what I mean. You said novelty there. An' you said well-preserved earlier.

—Was tha' not you?

—No. You.

—Okay.

—Maybe both of us.

—Right – go on.

—Tha' was wha' was on your mind, I said. —A fling with a woman tha' used to be the girl of your dreams. But then you sit down with her an' it's like the two o' you are in your slippers an' dressin' gowns an' there's nothin' goin' on at all.

—It wasn't like tha'.

—Was it deflatin'?

—No.

—No?

—It was different.

—Okay. And unexpected?

—Very.

—An' deflatin'.

—Fuck off.

—It must've been, I said. —For fuck sake. Or maybe it was a relief, was it?

—Well, there you go, he said. —Tha' might be nearer the truth.

—Is it?

—Jesus, Davy, when did you join the fuckin' FBI?

—Was it a relief? Go on.

—It might've been.

—You could still go home an' ride Trish.

—What's your fuckin' problem? he said. —Hang on, but, I know what it is. I forgot there for a bit. You fancied her as well.

—Trish?

—Stop bein' such a spa, Davy, he said. —Jessica.

—Whose name I didn't know until a few hours ago. It's a long time since anyone called me a spa.

—Well, you are a fuckin' spa.

—You can't say that any more.

—I know.

158

—It was a relief – you said.

—*You* did.

—You agreed with me.

—Okay, he said. —It was. A bit. I'm not sure. Because it stopped bein' abou' tha'. Abou' me meetin' up with a woman I hardly knew. The effort involved.

He surprised me now.

—Did anythin' like this ever happen to you?

—No.

—Really?

—No. You asked already.

—Did I?

—I think so, yeah.

—Okay, he said. —Seriously, though, Davy – there was never another woman?

—Not really, no.

—Not even a deflatin' one?

I didn't answer. It wasn't really a question. Joe lifted his pint. He knocked back a good bit, two swallows, three. He put the glass back down on the beermat.

—But anyway, he said. —Somethin' happened to me.

There was a Saturday, one of the last Saturdays, maybe the last. She was there, with her friends and the cello case. She was sitting under the window when we came in. I walked straight into Joe's back. He'd seen her first. But I'd recovered in time to see her look our way and smile.

And smile.

—Hi, guys, she said.

Guy wasn't the word it is now. Every waitress and lounge girl will address a group of two or more men as guys, no matter their age, the lounge girl and the men. But not back then. We weren't guys; there were no guys. We were young lads, boys, men. But only men in American films were guys.

But we were guys now too, apparently. Although speechless guys – we were in a silent film.

I eventually managed a word.

—Hi.

It was me who said it, not Joe. I was the first guy to speak to her. I know that. I knew it then, and I thought I knew its significance. I was the first to respond, so she must have been talking to me.

We kept on going. I followed Joe, down to our end of the bar.

I was the one who had spoken. Mine was the only voice. I knew it then, at that exact time, and it thrilled me.

It seems pathetic. But it's not – not as I understand the word. We were children when we were together. I was a functioning adult most of the time – all week. But something happened when we were together; joy rushed in and drowned us. Before I met Faye, I experienced happiness only when I was with Joe. I think that's true. Happiness that could be trusted. Happiness that, somehow, I could measure, feel; it was a thing in my chest. When I was with Joe.

I liked being a boy. I loved being a boy. The rush of it, the rib-breaking ache of it. I'm not sure that I'd ever been one before. I couldn't be happy at home. I can't feel it now; I can't construct it. Because it wasn't there. I remember once, when I was twelve or thirteen, watching *Coronation Street* and one of the characters – I can't remember which; a woman – she said to another woman, 'You'll have to fend for yourself.' I knew exactly what she meant.

160

I said Hi to the girl I know was called Jessica. And I knew: it might be the end of happiness. And it might be the start of something new. A different kind of happiness. An adventure. A night. A life.

And I ran.

I took a look at her. She wasn't looking our way. She was listening to one of her friends. She was devoting herself to whatever her friend – another woman; I've no other memory of her – was saying. I could hear words but I couldn't catch meaning; I didn't try to. She wasn't waiting for us. I was disappointed, and relieved. I was safe.

I was shy but I wasn't crippled. I'd stepped up to women and slept with them hours later. I'd met looks and I'd managed to hold them when I'd wanted to, when I'd thought I had to. When I'd trusted my judgement, when I knew – when I thought I knew – I was reading the look correctly. I was surprised if a woman smiled at me, but never shocked. I was shy, but not of women.

I don't know about Joe. I don't know why he didn't say anything to Jessica that time, why I was allowed to be our spokesman. We'd had a few pints on our journey across town to George's. We'd been running, pretending to rush, to get out of the rain. He'd hit the door first. I'd had to negotiate a puddle, hop over the thing – I don't remember. He got there first and was inside before me. He saw her first. But I spoke.

Why devote the space to this? It was the only time I spoke to her. And I was the one who spoke.

—So tell us, said Faye once, after we were married. —What do you find desirable in a woman?

—Words, I said.

I didn't hesitate. I didn't think. I felt I'd had the answer ready, just waiting for the question.

Faye pretended to unblock an ear with one of her little fingers.

—Excuse me? she said. —What?

—Words, I said.

She was pregnant, six or seven months. We were sitting in our new house. I was just in, from my new job. There was no food. The smell of fresh paint would always be the smell of our happiness.

Faye thumped my arm.

—You'd prefer to ride a dictionary than a woman, she said. —Is that what you're telling me now, David?

—I'd prefer to ride a woman who could say I'd prefer to ride a dictionary, I said.

—A big mouth?

—A clever dick.

—She'd have to be a dickess, so she would.

—A clever dickess, then.

—Am I one?

—Yeah.

—Well, I'm lost for fuckin' words, she said.

We were in England. Away from Gorey and her house. Away from Dublin. Away from the ghost of her dead mother and from the ghost of my living father. We were fresh paint. There'd been nothing here – no one here – before us.

—I'm not sure that I approve, said my father.

He'd never said anything like that to me before. It was a few weeks after he'd met Faye. I'd just told him we were getting married.

I was ready for the fight. I knew – I know it now:
I'd been expecting it. It was just the two of us in the
kitchen – his kitchen. It wasn't my home. It wasn't my
country. I wanted to be pushed out. And so did Faye.
We both wanted the shove.

—Approve of what? I said.

He hadn't been looking at me.

He looked now.

—I'm sure she's a nice girl, he said.

—She is, I said.

—I don't doubt you, he said.

—You do doubt me.

He picked up the kettle. I wanted to dash across and
grab it from him. I wanted to open the back door and
fuck the thing out into the garden.

—I haven't been a very good father, he said.

He'd raised his voice, almost to a shout, so he'd be
heard over the roar of the water rushing into the
kettle.

—I wouldn't say that, I told him.

He'd turned off the tap.

—I would, he said.

He was putting a match to the gas. He was an old
man at the cooker. His thin hair was standing, lit by
the sun coming through the window beside him. I
couldn't see his face but, the way he stood, he was
reminding himself, trying to remember why he was
standing there. I wanted to hold him.

I heard the gas. I watched him waiting, not trusting
the flame. He didn't want to turn, to face me. He was
looking for something else he needed to do. All this
was seconds, not minutes.

He turned.

163

—I mightn't have the right, he said. —But I'll say it anyway. I think you should be careful.

—Careful?

—Yes.

—Fuckin' careful?

—David.

—Sorry. Careful, though? What d'you mean?

—She's very young.

—So?

He shrugged. He smiled.

—Right, he said. —Before you say it. Yes, your mother was younger than me.

—Six years.

—Yes.

He wasn't smiling now.

—She's wild, he said. —Your lassie.

—Faye.

—She was half naked.

—We'd been upstairs.

—I don't want to interfere, he said. —I can see why you –. She was attractive.

—She still is.

—You were introducing her to me and she wore – what was it? – one of your jumpers. I could see her *hair*. For God's sake, David. I'm your father and she was displaying herself. Here! And you, son – you let her. In case you hadn't noticed, David, we're not the bloody Borgias.

The kettle was starting to hiss.

—And it's not that, he said. —If you want to bring a girl upstairs – even though you don't actually live here, let me remind you. But I have no problem with that. I bloody envy you. One-night stands – whatever you call them. They're none of my business and good

164

luck to you. She's a lovely-looking lassie. But I can see, you're serious.

He looked at the kettle, and the steam that was taking over the room.

—Aren't you? he said.

He grabbed a tea towel and lifted the kettle off the hob.

—Is she pregnant? he said.

He'd always been a gentle man. Too gentle, I often thought – gentleness as a type of absence. But he'd never been brutal, or crude.

Faye *was* pregnant.

—No, I said. —She isn't.

If I could relive that evening, I'd do several things differently and I'd say different things.

I'd tell him she was pregnant.

I'd say nothing and walk out of the house.

I'd go home to the flat I'd started sharing with Faye but I wouldn't tell her what my father had said.

I'd go home and tell Faye *all* that he'd said.

I'd stay with my father and ask him why he'd asked if Faye was pregnant, instead of saying Good man or I'm delighted. I'd try to know him. I'd ask him why, so long after my mother had died, he'd finally lashed out. I'd ask him why he was pushing me away.

Faye laughed when I told her.

—Why did you tell him at all? she said.

—I don't know. I just wanted to.

—Without me there?

—I thought he'd be happy.

—That fella? she said. —He doesn't want to be happy. And come here.

She put her arms around me. Faye's a tall woman, as tall as I am, and she looked straight into my eyes.

Faye did that: she was able to hold a gaze – she always won the staring matches.

—Your daddy's misery is none of your business, she said. —And you'll be getting plenty of misery from me. Does it give you the horn?

—Yes, it does.

My father looked at me.

—I wouldn't mind if she was, he said. —Pregnant.

—She isn't, I said.

—Grand, he said. —It must be love, so, is it?

He turned, and took two mugs from the shelf beside the cooker.

—Your mother would be very happy, he said.

—Would she?

—She'd have loved Faye.

I don't know why I didn't tell Faye that my mother would have loved her. I didn't feel it, I didn't know it. But he'd said it to be kind and I never told Faye. I left it out, deleted it, told her half of what had happened. She'd have loved Faye. Maybe that was why he didn't – couldn't – love her. She was too like my mother. But I don't know that either.

We make up our own stories.

—We'll have the baby in England, said Faye that night. —Will we?

—Yeah.

We'd been going, anyway. Faye talked about distance – from Gorey, from family, from expectations and inspections. I'd never thought about leaving. Until Faye said she wanted to wake up some day in air that wasn't Irish. Then I'd wanted to pack.

—Sure, fuck him, she said. —He'll have to come over to see his grandson or his granddaughter, so he will.

166

She was holding me.

—He'll have to spend a few shillings and vomit on the boat, she said.

—He's never been mean, I said.

—Not with the money, maybe, she said. —But he's tight with the kindness.

She kissed my shoulder.

—So, he can fuck off with himself, she said. —We both deserve better.

I've often wondered if we'd have gone, if I'd told Faye the full story. We'd have left but perhaps not as quickly. We had Faye's money, from the sales of the shop and the house; we didn't have to charge. And she'd made it clear.

—I don't want to be settling in Dublin.

—Okay.

—I don't like Dublin. Does that shock you, David?

—No.

—You're a liar.

—I'm not.

—D'you know what Dublin's problem is?

—What?

—It's only the capital of Ireland, she said. —And that's fuckin' nothing to be stuck up about.

We were going. The real question is, why I never told Faye all that my father had said, why I'd lied to her, why I'd worked myself up to believing what I'd told and hadn't told her. I wanted to be like her, I sometimes think. I wanted to feel isolated, and homeless; I wanted to match her.

We were riding for children, from the start. That feeling was there: we were changing our lives, making something new. We were always going to leave. But I still don't know why I hurt my father, hurt Faye, hurt my children. None of the answers answer the question. There'll never be an answer.

Five years ago – about five years ago – we were sitting beside each other, half watching something on the television. The ads came on and there was one in particular, warning the viewer of the perils of unprotected sex. Immediately, I felt it – I was in our flat in Dublin, with Faye, in bed. Doing something dangerous and wonderful, together. Making up our lives – our life.

I turned to look at Faye, and she'd already turned to me. We said nothing and we kissed, and adjusted our older selves on the couch to face each other.

—Unprotected sex, Faye.

I held her face.

—It was the making of us, so it was.

She held mine.

—So, yeah, said Joe. —Somethin' happened.

—Okay, I said. —Wha'?

—Well, he said. —I still don't know how to say it.

—Did she cast a spell on you or somethin'?

He pushed himself back from the counter. He exhaled loudly – he almost whistled.

—No.

—You hesitated.

—No, he said. —No, she didn't. That'd be fuckin' daft.

—But you hesitated.

—Fuck off, he said. —Look –. There's a film, a kids' thing Holly used to love. I can't remember the name of it. But there's a wall an' when the characters go over it, they're enterin' into a different world – different rules, different everythin'. *Stardust* – that's wha' it was called. D'you know it?

—No, I said. —Don't think so. I mean, I might've seen it – I don't know.

—It's not the film, he said. —It's good, by the way. Holly loved it. But it's not the plot that I mean. The main chap has to cross the wall, into the realm o' the fairies or somethin', I think it's called – I can't remember. Carrie from *Homeland*'s in it, now that I think of it. She's a kid in it – it's goin' back a good bit. D'you watch *Homeland*?

—It's brilliant.

—Yeah, he said. —Although I haven't seen the last couple o' series.

—The new one's great, I said. —Bang up to date. The Russians interferin' with the elections and everythin'. Claire Danes.

—Yeah, he said. —But look, there was no wall or anythin' dramatic like tha'. But I did feel like I'd stepped into another world. Just a bit. I don't want to exaggerate it.

—Sorry, I said. —Is this magic we're talkin' about, or wha'? Hypnosis?

—No, he said. —No. It's psychological, maybe. I don't know. But somethin', anyway. Somethin' definitely happened. In my head – so to speak. D'you know anything abou' tha' stuff?

—Psychology?

—Yeah, he said. —How the brain works an' tha'.

—No, I said.

I didn't want to let us stray. I didn't want to talk about myself.

—I had to have a brain scan, he said.

—Did you?

169

—Yeah, yeah. An MRI.

—Because o' this?

—Wha'?

—Because you met your woman?

—No. No – fuck off. Two years ago, or so. Before me an' Jessica. Yeah, two years ago.

—Why?

—Did I never tell you?

—No, I said. —You didn't.

—Did I not? You sure?

—Yeah, I said.

But I wasn't. I wasn't sure at all. I'd had an MRI of my own, a year before. Mine was more recent than his. I hadn't told Joe. And I didn't want to hear him telling me about his. I could already feel him leaking into me.

—What's wrong? said Faye. —David?

Her voice was different, distant. I was standing at the kitchen door. I was looking out at the sky. I'd decided to stand up. I'd felt like I was waking, suddenly conscious, when I'd moved, stood. And I'd felt that way – waking up, waking repeatedly – as I'd moved to the back door.

Faye must have seen me. She must have been watching me.

—What's wrong? Dave?

I turned to her – I woke.

—Hi.

—Are you okay?

—I've been asleep – have I?

—No.

—No?

170

I walked past her to the chair I'd been sitting in. The chair I always sat in. My chair – when there was no one else in it. I sat – the chair was under me.

—What's wrong with your back?

—Nothing.

I looked at her. She sat beside me – she pulled a chair from under the table. She was staring at me.

—What's going on?

—I keep waking up, I said.

I was looking around me, up, around.

—Are you stoned or something? she asked.

—No.

It wasn't a ridiculous question. Nothing was ridiculous.

I looked at her, straight at her – woke up. She looked worried.

—What did you eat?

It was Saturday, early afternoon.

—Breakfast, I said. —I think.

—What?

—Toast.

—Did you go anywhere?

—No.

I stood – woke up. There was a rush – I had to sit down. I held the arms of the chair. I sat, woke up.

—I keep waking, I told her.

—You look stoned, she said. —You look doped.

—It's really slow, I said.

—What is?

—It. Every –.

I stood.

I'd forgotten words.

—Jesus, David –.

—Air, I said. —Fresh air.

—D'you want to go for a walk?

I woke up.

—Yeah.

We brought the dog. I bent to put the lead on him – I woke. Faye's hand was there, on mine. I was on my hands and knees. She took the lead from me. She grabbed the dog's collar.

—Dave?

I stood, straightened – woke.

—For fuck sake, David, stop messing.

I smiled. I turned. I smiled at her.

—I'm fine.

—You're not, she said. —Are you having a stroke or something? David?

I walked down the hall. I found my jacket at the end of the stairs. I put it on. Woke. The dog was under me, at my feet. I opened the front door. Faye was beside me. We were out – I closed the door. Woke. I walked between the cars. Faye's car. And mine. The trees were there. And other cars. I looked at Faye. I looked at my feet. At the path. Woke.

—David?

I stopped. I turned – turned – turned.

—Yes, Faye?

—We need a bag. Harry's shit. Did you bring some?

My hand was already in my pocket. I took out my hand. It was holding three or four orange nappy bags.

—Yes.

I opened a bag. Licked a finger, to separate the plastic sides. Put my hand into the bag. Woke. Opened my fingers. Looked at the ground. Saw the shit. Bent down – got down. Woke. I picked up the shit. Three half hard, dark brown lumps. I closed my hand around them. Heat through the orange plastic. Stood up. Woke up.

Looked at the bag. I turned it inside-out. Shit in. Fingers out. I tied the bag.

I saw Faye.

We walked. Under the trees. I heard – I could hear something. Wind. In a tight space. Wind screaming. In the distance – and near. Faye held the dog's lead. That was the noise – the wind noise. The retractable lead. Nylon screamed, in – out, in – rubbing against the plastic handle. A car passed. I heard no noise, no engine.

I stopped. I woke.

—This is taking for ever, I said.

—What is?

I woke up.

—We've been walking for hours.

—Come on, she said. —Come on. I'm getting you to the hospital.

I looked. At the next-door neighbour's gate. I looked at Faye.

—Okay.

—You're worried too, she said.

I wasn't.

I walked.

—Stay here, said Faye.

—Where?

—Here, she said.

She took one of my hands. She put it on the roof of her car.

—Here, she said. —I'll just get the key and bring Harry in. I wish the fuckin' kids were still here.

—Do you?

—For once, I do. Stay there.

I stood beside her car. My hand was on the roof when she got back. I watched her double-lock the front door. I woke. I watched her looking into her bag. I watched her shake it. I watched her take out her phone and drop it back into the bag. The car door – my door, the passenger door – was open. I felt Faye's hand on top of my head.

—In.

She pushed slightly – she made me bend. I watched as I lifted my feet into the car. I looked at them. She closed the door. She didn't slam it. Her door was open. I could see her waist. She leaned in. She held out her bag.

—Hold this for me.

I looked at the bag.

—Jesus Christ, David.

She leaned in further. She dropped the bag on my lap. I held it. She was beside me.

—Can you see properly?

—Yes.

—The tree there – the branches. They're clear, are they?

—Yes.

She started the car.

—Is there any point asking you to phone ahead?

I looked at the bag.

—No, she said. —I didn't think so.

The car moved.

—Put your belt on, she said.

I looked – I felt the belt. I'd already done it.

—Are we going to the hospital?

—That's right, we're going to the hospital.

I woke.

My phone was in my hand. I looked at it. I was supposed to do something.

—You're scaring me, Dave.

174

—Sorry.

—Are you, though?

—Head injury, said Joe.

—What happened?

—I stood up in the attic.

—You're jokin'.

—I fuckin' amn't, he said. —I nearly broke a cross-beam with me head. I was lucky, though, as well because I landed righ' beside the hatch, you know. If I'd fallen through that –. Cos I was unconscious, ou' for the fuckin' count.

He loved this story.

—I was only startin' to stand up, he said. —An' a mouse ran across me hand. I thought it was a rat. I just shot up – bang. Ou' – gone. Nothin'. Trish heard the thump an' she was ou' the back, sunnin' herself. She was callin' me for ages. But I hadn't a clue. I was knocked ou'. Were you ever unconscious, Davy?

—Not like tha', no, I said. —Literally knocked out. No.

—It's amazin', really, how it can happen.

—Must be.

—When you think about it, he said. —We're so fuckin' frail. I only woke up properly in the Mater. But, apparently, I was conscious when they got me down from the attic.

—Who did that?

—The ambulance lads. I don't remember them – nothin' ever came back. One o' them was a woman. So Holly said. She found me – Holly. That's the legend. She came out of her room when she heard Trish shoutin'. She saw the ladder on the landing an' she climbed up an' saw me. Saved me life.

—Was it tha' bad?

—I'd a fractured skull, Davy – for fuck sake.

—Lads –.

It was the barman. He was looking at us – staring at us.

—Sorry, I said.

—Were we loud? Joe asked me.

—You were, I said. —You must've been.

—Fuck'm, he said, quietly. —There's no way we were tha' loud. It's a fuckin' pub, for fuck sake.

—Did you need a plate or anythin'? I asked him.

—No, he said. —No. Luckily. So, but –. Good ol' Holly.

—It must've been a bit shatterin' for her as well, I said.

I was thinking of Róisín. I was missing her. We skyped, but neither of us liked it. It's like we're in a shit film, she'd said once, months before. You don't look like you. You look, like, stupid.

—She clung to me for months after it, said Joe. —It was –. I don't know, Davy. I *do* know. It was great.

—I can imagine.

—She was terrified I'd die, he said. —Afraid I was goin' to drop dead. I was out o' work for a month, you know.

—Jesus.

—Yeah. An' I never told you?

—No.

—Weird, he said. —Cos I'll tell you now, I told everyone else. But, there – anyway. I had my daughter back, my little girl. You know what I mean, I'd say.

—I know exactly what you mean.

—She stopped bein' a teenager an' became human again. Yeah. So. Tha' was it for a while. An' then I went an' fuckin' blew it.

He sighed again, almost whistled.

—Did I? he said.

I told the neurologist.

—I keep waking up.

—Do you like a drink?

I didn't understand. He looked too young to be asking the question.

—He's not an alcoholic, said Faye.

—Was he drinking?

—Today?

—Yes.

—No, he wasn't.

—Is that true? he asked me.

I looked at him.

—I was reading a book, I said.

—And last night? he said. —A party? Drinks after work?

—Are you Irish? I asked him.

—Yes, I am, he said.

—Me too.

—Yes.

I woke.

—It happened there, I told him.

—You felt you woke up again?

—Yes.

—And last night? he said.

—He was at home, said Faye. —With me. But you're Irish, so you'll know we're more than likely lying when it comes to the drinking.

—Were you?

—A bottle between us, she said. —And it wasn't empty when we turned off the television.

I was standing beside the bed.

—Put one foot in front of the other, said the neurologist. —Toe to heel.

I looked at my feet.

—Take a step now, please. Back foot to the front.

—The drink-driving test, said Faye.

—Similar.

I looked at the foot at the front.

—Take a step.

—I can't.

—Try.

He grabbed me as I fell. He helped me sit on the
bed. I looked at his hands. I woke.

—Again.

—Thank you, he said. —That's helpful.

—It's like a dotted line, I said. —Instead of a straight
line. Dot to dot.

—Yes.

There was paper in front of me, below my eyes – a
writing pad. And a pen – a biro.

—Draw a clock, please.

I held the biro. I looked at the paper.

—It doesn't have to be perfect.

I heard Faye.

—Go on, David.

The doctor – the neurologist – was young, much
younger than a specialist should have been.

I drew a circle. It wasn't good.

—Can I draw it again?

—It's fine.

—It's not like a clock.

I woke up.

—I'm interested in the numbers, said the doctor.
—The hours.

—He knows his hours, don't you, David? He's very advanced.

I looked at Faye – I looked for Faye. She was behind me, against the window. I couldn't see her – I couldn't turn. I looked at the paper, at the circle that wasn't a circle. I put the pen at the top of the circle. I didn't know what to do.

I woke.

—Again, I said.

—Fine, he said. —The hours – do you know them?

—I think so, I told him.

I brought the biro down a bit, to the right, and wrote a 1. I had it now; I knew what to do. 2, 3, 4, 5, 6, 7, 8, 9, 10, 11.

It took hours – it seemed to be taking hours. I looked at my hand holding the biro.

I stopped. I was back at the top of the circle. I didn't know what came next.

—David?

I woke.

I didn't know the number.

He took the writing pad.

—Thank you, he said. —Stand up.

—Me?

—Yes.

I couldn't. I couldn't make myself do it. I kept waking up. He helped me stand. He didn't have to pull. I stood. I couldn't see the floor – I couldn't look at it. I watched him wrap the black rubber around my arm. I saw the rubber expand, I felt it tighten.

—I'm going to take your blood pressure, he said. —Both standing and sitting.

I felt the rubber loosen.

—It's very low, he said.

—Okay.

—Very low. Sit now, please.

—Sorry?

—Sit down. On the bed.

I felt his hand on my arm.

—Yes, he said as I lowered myself onto the bed.

—I don't care, I told him.

—I'm sorry?

—I don't care.

I felt the rubber tighten, and loosen. I didn't look at it.

—Low again, he said.

—How low? Faye asked.

—Very.

He was looking into one of my eyes. I didn't blink.

—Who's the President of Ireland?

—We're in Britain, I said.

I could see him smile.

—Good man, Dave, said Faye. —Put him back in his box.

—Nevertheless, he said. —Who is he?

—I keep waking up, I said.

—And who is the President of Ireland?

I knew. I knew but I didn't know. I knew I'd known. But nothing would come. It was like the clock – the number at the top. I didn't know what I knew.

I waited for Faye to fill the silence. To rescue me.

She didn't.

I didn't care.

I woke up.

—Michael D. Higgins.

—She'll come round, I told Joe.

—D'you think?

180

—Ah, she will.

—When, though?

—I don't know, I said. —But she will.

—Just have to be patient, I suppose, he said.

—Yeah, that's it.

—It's hard, though.

—Yeah.

—Fuckin' hard.

—Must be.

—Where were we?

—Wha'?

—I was tellin' you, he said.

—You were climbin' over the magic wall, I said. —Go on.

—It wasn't a fuckin' wall.

—You used the analogy.

—Yeah, I did. But it wasn't a wall.

—I know –. Just –. Does the knock on your head have anythin' to do with this?

—Wha'?

—It's a genuine question, I said.

—Okay, he said. —But it wasn't a knock on my head. I fractured me fuckin' skull.

—Okay.

—Fuckin' fractured, Davy.

—Lads.

It was the barman again.

—Sorry, said Joe.

He looked at me, and smiled.

—We might get ourselves barred here, he said.

—I'd kind o' like that, I said.

—It'd do us good. Gettin' barred.

—Probably, yeah, I said. —Definitely.

We'd never been barred from a pub. We were reliving something else that hadn't happened.

—But the wall, he said.

—Yeah?

—I thought I could cross an' recross it, he said. — Although I only thought o' the wall – tha' film – a few minutes ago. But d'you know what I mean?

—Wha'? I said. —Like, keep two households on the go?

—No –

—A gap in the hedge?

—Would you ever fuck off, Davy.

—Why're you sayin' tha'?

—Right, lads – finish up. Come on.

The barman had come out from behind the counter. He was quickly standing between us, against us. He held the stools, as if he might pull them from under us.

—Are you barrin' us? said Joe.

—If that's what yis want to call it, said the barman. —I don't know yis, so just finish up and hop it – come on.

—Thanks very much, said Joe.

He looked at me.

—There you go, Davy. We're barred.

I listened.

—This one will last five minutes, said the voice. —Do you understand?

—Yes.

I was in the sausage, the scanner. I was lying down, tight against the walls of the bed – or whatever it was. The base, the shelf. My head was trapped. I couldn't move.

I didn't care.

I woke.

—I will be counting down from three, said the voice.
—Do you hear me?

—Yes.

They were scanning my brain. Looking for clots.

—Three –, two –.

I knew: the noise was distressing – it should have been distressing, it could have been distressing.

I woke.

This might be the last time. I thought that, exactly that. Every time I woke. This might be the last time. I didn't care if I died. If I didn't. I didn't care.

—Can I go to the toilet first? said Joe.

The barman didn't answer. He was a sheepdog and he'd herded the two of us through both sets of narrow doors, and out. He didn't touch us, he didn't say another word. He went straight back into the pub. I tried to feel amused but I couldn't quite catch it.

—Should've thought o' tha', said Joe. —Men our age. Always go to the jacks before you get yourself thrown out of a pub.

—It's a bit of a let-down, I said. —I expected more.

—We could smash a window, said Joe. —Do a legger.

I was going home – not home – to my father's house. I'd have a shower, sleep, go back to the hospice. I was done. Joe's story was inside, still at the bar. It hadn't come out with us. I was going to shake myself away, make the decision. I didn't care. I wanted to sleep. I didn't want to be struggling or stupid in the morning. I wanted to sit with my father.

Joe was looking across the road, at the trees and the promenade.

—We'll have a piss over there, he said. —Behind the pumpin' station.

He walked across the parking spaces outside the pub, onto the road. There was no traffic – I couldn't see or hear anything. I followed him.

—I'm goin' now, Joe, I told him.

—We'll go into town, he said.

—No.

—Fuckin' yeah, Davy. Don't desert me now.

He crossed and I followed him. We went in behind the strange structure.

—What is this?

—A pumpin' station, said Joe. —It's won awards.

He pissed against its side.

—Shite or water? I asked.

—Don't know, to be honest, he said.

He groaned – he made himself groan.

—If you can piss like this – a steady stream, like. At our age. You're grand. Your prostate's fine.

—Did Jessica tell you tha'?

—Fuck off, he said. —Have a piss there an' we'll grab a taxi.

—I'm goin' home.

—No, you're not.

—I am.

—No, he said. —Davy. I have to tell you.

—You've spent all night havin' to tell me, I said. —I still haven't a clue wha' happened. Except you fell over a wall.

—Come on an' stop bein' a cunt.

I unbuttoned my fly. The wind in the trees – the branches were alive, creaking.

—Remember we used to come down here?

—No, I said.

—We did.

—We didn't.

—Well, I did.

—Grand.

—Hurry up, for fuck sake. Four or five taxis have gone past while you've been unravellin' your langer.

I knew as I stood there, feet apart, staring at the pumping-station wall: I'd go with him. We were going to go to George's. I wasn't tired and I wasn't being dragged. It was my decision. I wanted it.

We stood at the side of the road, opposite the pub.

—No fuckin' taxis, he said.

I didn't let myself apologise.

—It's not too hot now.

—No, he said. —It's grand. The way it should be. Here's one now, look it.

A car – a taxi – was coming towards us. Joe lifted his arm.

—Here we go.

It slowed. I could see the driver, an African, looking at us. He stopped.

—Grand, said Joe. —We're elected.

He opened the back door and got in. He kept moving across the seat, and I followed him into the car. I waited for him to say something over-friendly, faintly sardonic to the driver. But he didn't. He told him we wanted to go to South William Street or as near as he could get us, and he thanked him. He put on his seat belt and sat back, head back, as far as he could make it go. His eyes were shut for a second, two.

—There was nothin' tellin' me I couldn't – I don't know. Balance it.

185

He spoke softly, just to me.

—I could be fair to both, he said. —Jess and Trish. Jess.

That was new. It caught me on the hop. I didn't know who he was referring to at first. She'd been Jessica all night. There was no radio on in the car. I looked out the side window. We were passing the old Clontarf Baths. The building seemed to have been converted into a restaurant; there were lights on, and two lines of parked cars outside. I said nothing about it.

—I sound like a slug, he said.

I took my eyes from the window, to look at him. He was looking at me.

—Don't I?

—I don't know, I told him. —I don't know wha' to say.

—I know, he said. —Yeah. But I think it's true. I wasn't actin' the maggot, though, Davy. Or just actin' the maggot. At all. I wasn't. She needed me.

—Which?

—Jess.

—What d'you mean she needed you?

—I knew it. When I met her. She –. I just – I don't know. She needed me.

—You haven't told me about it.

—No, you're right, he said. —I haven't.

We were through Fairview, passing the fire station, where we'd been chased when we were walking home from the Ramones film. I didn't remind him.

—Look, I said. —You've suggested it – you said it. You might have a son.

—Okay –

—And you've told me you're livin' with Jessica an' that you're –. Estranged?

—It'll do.

—You're estranged from your family.

—Yeah.

—But you've told me nothin' else – not really.

—I know.

—So –

—I love her, Davy.

—Jessica?

—Yes.

—What about Trish?

—It's different.

—For fuck sake.

—It is.

—I said it earlier, Joe. You sound like every middle-aged man who's ever fallen for a younger woman. Except in your case the younger woman isn't any younger. She might even be older than us, is she?

—A year.

—You're infatuated.

—Ah, fuck off.

—Listen, I said. —I talk to one of you, some man just like you, every time I go for a few drinks after work. Which is a big reason why I never go.

—What about you?

—Wha'?

—Have you ever been fuckin' infatuated?

—We're not talkin' about me.

—Go on.

—Listen, I said.

We were still speaking softly, but hissing. I could see the driver's face in the rear-view. He was keeping an eye on us. We were drunk men. We were probably trying not to be, pulling ourselves back. But I was drunk and so was Joe. We were drunk men and we were right behind the driver.

187

—No offence, I said to Joe. —Honestly – no offence. But middle-aged men an' the rediscovery of their spunk eyes.

I saw Joe smile.

—It's boring, I said. —It's really fuckin' borin'.

—I know, he said. —I agree with you.

—I'm here, I said. —I wanted to go home, back to my da's. I've had enough. But I'm here. Because you said you wanted to tell me about it.

—Okay.

—Because I was there when you met her.

—We're buddies.

—I don't know you, I said.

We were over Matt Talbot Bridge, turning right on to the quays.

—I can't believe they named a bridge after Matt Talbot, I said.

—Wha'?

—He was a fuckin' nut, I said. —With his penance an' chains an' feedin' his dinner to his fuckin' cat.

—Now you're startin' to do it.

—Wha'?

—Avoidin' the subject, said Joe. —Evadin', avoidin'. Whatever the fuck. Like tax.

—It's just, I said. —When we were young, when we were goin' to George's, they were namin' the bridges after religious fanatics. And now –. The new one back there, with the Luas tracks on it.

—The Rosie Hackett.

—Who was she?

—A union leader, he said. —I think.

—She was a member of the Irish Citizen Army, said the driver.

—Was she? Thank you.

—She was a very great lady.

—She must've been.

—So, there, I said. —It's a different place.

—Not really, said Joe. —You don't live here.

—Well, it must be, I said. —In some respects. Because you thought you could live with two different women at the same time.

—Okay –

—You thought tha' was possible.

—That's the thing, though, he said. —I didn't think. Think – as in think. It wasn't logical.

—Is he your son? I asked.

—It doesn't matter, he said. —What I'm tryin' to tell you. It doesn't matter.

—It's a shite story then, I said.

—It kind of is.

He took out his phone and looked at the clock.

—We'll have one in the Palace.

It was exhaustion. I hadn't had a stroke; there were no blood clots. Everything was fine.

I was exhausted.

—How? I asked him, the neurologist.

I don't know if I ever knew his name.

—Only you can answer that one, he said.

I woke.

—It's still the same, I told him.

—The dots.

—Instead of a straight line.

—It's a good image, he said. —I might use it with my students.

—You have students?

—Yes.

—Jesus, we're getting old, Dave, said Faye.

She was behind me. Her hand had been on my back, my shoulder, but not now. The neurologist smiled.

—I'm sorry.

—So you should be, she said.

I woke.

—So, said the neurologist. —I go back to my original question.

He was looking at me – down at me. I was sitting in a wheelchair. Just back from the third scan. I thought I could walk now. But they wouldn't let me.

—Are you a drinking man?

—No, he isn't, said Faye.

—Are you? he said.

—No, I said. —Not really.

—Listen, said Faye. —If you asked me, I'd say yes. If this was an Irish conversation we were having. But David – no. He likes his bottle of IPA but he looks at it as much as he drinks it. One or two a week, just. And the odd glass of wine. He used to drink a bit but not now.

—Alright, said the neurologist.

—You think I'm lying.

—No.

—Exaggerating.

—No.

—You do so, said Faye. —Look at him, Dave, he's blushing.

He smiled – he grinned. He grinned over me, at Faye. He grinned at me.

—We'll keep you for a few days, he said. —If that's okay. Is that okay?

—Yes.

—We need to build up the fluids, he said. —You're very dehydrated. Dangerously so. We'll get you into the bed, so we can get you hooked up.

He took his phone from a jacket pocket. He looked at it. He lifted his other hand and tapped.

—I want you to look at this, he said.

His phone was a mirror.

—Is that an app?

—Yes. Look, please.

He was showing me my eyes. My eyes – the irises – are brown. Everything else was red. A consistent, even red. As if I'd coloured in the whites with a marker. I blinked. The red eyes in front of me blinked. I believed what I saw. And I didn't care.

I woke.

I saw him put his phone in his pocket. I saw him adjust his jacket. The weight of the phone had made it slide off one shoulder.

—It's not my business, he said. —But it is. You need to think about why you're here. Why you might be exhausted. *Are* exhausted. Do you understand?

—Yes.

—Perhaps you could talk about that, he said.

He was at the door.

—I'll see you again tomorrow, he said. —No, sorry. On Monday. I'll see you on Monday.

—What day is today?

—Saturday, he said. —My day off.

—Did you come in for me?

—It's the job, he said.

He was gone. I was alone.

—He's such a little fella, said Faye.

I wasn't alone. I couldn't see Faye. She was behind me.

191

—A little fella playing doctors, she said. —So fuckin' young – Jesus. I'd say the nurses love him.

I woke. I was alone.

—They can pick him up and put him on their knees.

Faye was in the room. The ward. I heard her feet, her heels.

—They can give him a bath and wash his botty.

She put her hands on my face and pulled it – me – to her.

—It's nice to hear you laughing, she said.

I wasn't aware that I'd been laughing. I hadn't felt it. I didn't feel it.

She let go of me.

—I like your clicks, Faye, I said.

—Jesus, David.

She walked up and down, in front of me, in the space between the wheelchair and the door.

—Here's some more clicks for you, so.

She says it to me. When she looks at me, when she makes me look at her. You like my clicks, so you do. You like my clicks, apparently. When we look at each other. When she makes me laugh.

The driver took us up D'Olier Street, around past the Bank of Ireland and down the piece of Westmoreland Street, to the corner of Fleet Street. I paid him and looked at the change before I identified a two-euro coin and gave it back to him, my hand between the two front seats.

—There you go.

—Thank you, sir.

—Goodnight.

—God bless you, sir. And your friend. You are good people.

—Thanks.

—I hope you are happy.

—Seeyeh.

Joe was looking down Fleet Street.

—Fuckin' Temple Bar, he said.

—We're not goin' down there, I said.

—I know.

—We're too old.

—We've too much taste.

—We're snobs.

There was a crowd outside the Palace, smoking, chatting, laughing. But it wasn't too bad, too packed, inside. There was a free stool not too far from the door. The driver's words had pleased me. He'd seen something in us that I hadn't felt. Something in me, something about us, our past, our present. It wasn't just drink. It wasn't just anger.

Joe took the stool.

—Whose round is it?

—I haven't a clue.

—Okay.

He ordered two pints from a passing barman. He looked around, and at me.

—Good pub, he said.

—Yeah.

—Remember the jacks, back in the day?

—No.

—Ah, you do. Down the stairs, into the Black Hole of Calcutta. The light never worked, you just hoped you were pissin' in the right direction.

—They were all like tha'.

—That's true, he said. —We've come a long way. So, yeah –.

I thought he was going to say something. I thought he'd get going on what he'd wanted to say in the taxi, what he claimed he'd been trying to say all night. But he didn't. He took out some coins and made a neat pile of two-euros, six of them, on the counter.

—They're heavy fuckin' things to be luggin' around, he said. —If you've too many o' them.

I didn't respond. It was up to him.

—It's only a matter o' time before there'll be no cash at all, he said. —It'll all be cards. Would you miss it?

—Cash?

—Yeah.

—I like a bit o' cash in me pocket.

—Same here, he said.

The barman had arrived with the pints.

—Good man; thank you.

He picked up the coins and put them into the barman's hand.

—There you go.

I watched the pints settle as if it was the first time I'd seen it happen, the tan darkening to black and the arrival of the collar. I couldn't help myself.

—It's a fuckin' miracle, really, isn't it?

He knew what I was talking about.

—It is, he agreed.

It wasn't the first time he'd heard it. It had been one of our lines, since we'd heard some oul' lad say it, probably where I was standing now.

Joe picked up his pint and placed it a few inches closer to him. I did the same – I leaned across him and put my glass on top of a wet bar mat.

—I don't think I want this one, I said.

I meant it.

—I'm fuckin' full o' drink, I said – another phrase we'd got from an old man when we were young men, an old man who had probably been younger than we were now.

—We'll take it slowly, he said.

It was up to him. He could use the time we'd left or we could fill it with drivel; we'd hug and never see each other again.

He took the top off his pint.

He put it back down. I really didn't want my one. I held it but I didn't pick it up.

—It's a strange one, Davy, he said.

—Is it?

—I'm a different man, he said.

—Are you?

—You're bein' aggressive.

—Am I?

—You fuckin' are, yeah. An' there's no need.

—I'm not.

—I don't really blame you, he said. —It's all fuckin' weird, I suppose.

—I'm not bein' aggressive.

—Okay.

—You said you're a different man.

—That's right, he said. —Well, we all are. You are.

—Ah, fuck off.

—No, we are, he said. —We're older, we change. We do. But, like, now. I feel like I used to – I think I do. Because I'm with you.

He smiled.

—It's good.

He picked up his drink.

—Come here – cheers.

I picked up mine. We tapped our glasses.

—It's good, he said again.

He wanted me to agree.

—An' tha' makes me think how strange it's been, he said. —How strange it must seem.

—I don't know, I said. —You still haven't really told me anythin'. But yeah, it's a bit fuckin' weird.

—I understand.

—So, educate me, I said. —The only thing you've really mentioned is the wall.

—The wall.

—The wall in the film.

—I know which wall, he said. —Maybe the wall wasn't a good one. A metaphor or whatever. But it probably was. But anyway, that's it.

—What's it?

—Well, I don't know, Davy, he said. —I keep tryin' to think o' the words. Words to do it justice. On paper, like – I'm guilty. I can see tha'. I left me wife an' family for another woman.

—Spunk eyes, I said.

He smiled, he shrugged.

The smile was gone.

—We haven't had sex, he said.

—So you said.

—Did I?

—I think you did.

—Okay.

—Have you not, though?

—No.

—With Jessica?

—Yeah – no. With Jessica. Who else?

—It was just for clarity, I said. —The question.

—Okay, he said. —But yeah. Jess. Just so you know.

—It's none o' my business, I told him.

—Just so you know, he said again. —So, in fact. It's not a case o' me walkin' out on my family – for the gee.

I laughed – it burst from me. I hadn't heard the word in years. It wasn't one of Faye's words.

—Sorry, I said. —I know it's serious. But the gee –

—Drink talkin', he said. —But I hope that's clear, Davy. I didn't do what I've done for – like, a cliché. Okay?

—Right, I said. —Okay. Understood.

—We haven't had sex, he said.

The pub was full but there was no one looking at him.

—I don't care, I told him.

—An' I don't either, he said. —That's my point. It hasn't happened. An' I don't care. An' you mightn't care either but I bet you think it's weird.

—The whole thing's weird.

—The sex, I mean.

—No, then, I said. —Not really.

—Unusual then – a bit.

—Probably, I said. —Yeah. Definitely.

—Interestin'?

—Yeah. I think – yeah.

—Good.

—Why is that important? I asked him. —Why would you care if it's interestin'?

—Well, it has to be somethin', he said. —Jesus, man – I mean.

—What?

—I've – wha'? – erased more than half me life. In a way. An' not even for the sex.

—You haven't erased anythin', I said. —Are you tellin' me you've murdered Trish an' your children?

197

—No, he said. —No. No.

He looked away, at the window and doors, the snug in the corner, the bottles on the shelves in front of us, and back.

—No, he said. —But I've murdered somethin'. Not literally, but I've done somethin' fuckin' dramatic an' maybe wrong. I love my kids, Davy.

—I don't doubt it.

—No, I know you don't. I'm talkin' to myself, really. But it's as if they didn't exist.

—Didn't?

—Don't exist, he said. —No –. Didn't. They exist. But –.

He looked at me. His eyes were wet.

—They didn't matter, he said.

—An' she isn't even a femme fatale.

—No, he said. —No, that's right. Anyway, that's all bollix, the femme fatale business. Blamin' the woman.

—Spunk eyes.

—There you go, he said. —Exactly. My spunk, my eyes. I'll take full responsibility for them.

—You're bein' very noble, Joe.

—Fuck off, he said. —It's true. Those fellas you were mentionin'. The ones tha' go after the younger women. They're responsible for their own decisions. They're not bein' led down a fuckin' path by their mickeys.

—Joe, I said. —This is really borin'.

—Talkin' about women is fuckin' borin'?

—Don't start now, I said. —Be honest. You're not talkin' about women.

—Fuck off, Davy.

—You're still tryin' to avoid talkin' about the one particular woman.

198

—That's not true, he said. —I did start. I'm startin'
– I am.

—Stop it, I said. —I'll tell you what it is – I'll tell
you. You sound like you've been caught sayin' the wrong
thing by – say, Trish or Jessica. An' now you're tryin'
to talk your way out of it, or you're tryin' to make them
forget wha' you're afraid they might've heard.

—That's a load o' bollix.

—No, it isn't, I said. —An' come here.

I felt so happy saying that – an' come here – so
exultant and free, I almost cried. I could feel it too;
and I understood him – just a bit. I was slipping back,
to a different man. A man I might have been once – I
wasn't sure.

—I'm not interested, I said.

—Not interested?

—No.

—You've been fuckin' plaguin' me all night –

—No, I said. —I fuckin' have not. You've been wantin'
the opportunity to tell me about your adventures an'
I've been willin' to listen.

This wasn't how we'd been. Joe had always been the
one who drove us. I could see him thinking, trying to
catch up and trip me.

—I'm still willin' to listen, I said. —But spare me
the fuckin' all men bad, all women good shite.

I picked up my pint. I could feel my arm shake
slightly, my wrist ached, but the weight of the glass and
its contents steadied me.

—Okay, he said.

I put the glass to my lips. The cold on the bottom
lip felt good; it felt right. I filled my mouth. It was
okay; I'd be able for it. I put the glass back on the
counter; I leaned across him to do it.

—You're right, he said. —There are some slappers out there. Lurin' poor lads onto the rocks.

I didn't respond.

—But, he said. —Anyway. This time –. It wasn't about sex.

—You said it was.

—When?

—At the start, you did.

—Ah, Jesus, Davy, just fuck off, would yeh. Stop bein' so fuckin' pedantic. I love tha' word, by the way.

—Same here.

—A brainy oul' lad's word. Anyway. Yes, when I saw her –

—Jessica.

—Yes, Jessica. For fuck sake. When I saw her –

—In the school.

—Yeah. There was a part o' me thinkin', I definitely would.

—That's reassurin'.

—Oh, good. Great. I'm glad. So, yeah, I admit. We were outside the maths room but I was thinkin' honours biology.

—That's still reassurin'.

—Part o' me was, anyway, he said.

—Part of you?

—Don't be fuckin' crude. I thought she looked great. She *did* look great. Really – fuckin' lovely now. But when I actually met her, all tha' stopped.

—Literally?

—Literally.

—But you went home an' you shagged Trish.

—That's true as well, he said. —But you're a bit of a cunt for bringin' it up.

He looked around again, and back at me.

200

—I'm makin' it up as I go along, Davy, he said.

—I know.

—I don't mean I'm lyin'.

—I know.

—I'm tryin' to make sense of it.

—So, keep tryin', I said.

—I am, he said. —I fuckin' am. The drink is funny, though, isn't it? You see things clearly but then you can't get at the words to express them properly.

—Or somethin'.

—Or somethin', yeah. But anyway. Here goes – again. I met Jess an' I was hopin' – half hopin' – there'd be a thing. That I'd finally, after nearly a fuckin' lifetime, get to go to bed with the woman of my dreams. Our dreams.

—Your dreams.

—Yours as well – fuck off now. Admit it.

—It's your story, I said.

—Yeah, but –.

—Go on.

—You fancied her too, he said. —But okay. So – yeah. It was there – yeah. The excitement. But more than, way more than excitement. To finally, Jesus –.

He quickly looked around again at the other men and women close to us.

—To ride her. Just be with her. She's lovely, Davy. To feel her under my hands. An' her hands on me.

—Honours biology.

—At least a B+.

—But –

—No, stop, he said. —We're bein' salacious again. I don't like it. We'll leave it at tha'.

—But.

—Wha'?

201

—I wasn't going to say anythin' salacious, I said.

—Wha'?

—This would've been your first time. With Jessica.

—Yeah.

—But come here, I said. —You said –. Earlier, you said it. Tha' you think you might be the father of her son.

—I did, yeah.

He didn't look cornered, or caught.

—An' you said it didn't matter.

—Yeah.

—Well, I said. —Fuckin' hell, Joe. How does tha' work, for fuck sake?

—Davy, he said. —Give me a fuckin' chance.

—Are you his father or aren't you?

He stood up off his stool, although he didn't quite stand. He lifted both shoulders and extended his arms. Like a half hearted Jesus on a cross built for a smaller man. He sat down again.

—What does tha' mean, Joe? I asked him.

—It means –.

He lifted his shoulders again.

—It means I know an' – I suppose – I don't, he said. —It means there might not be an answer. Or a satisfactory answer.

—Jesus –

—I know, he said. —An' it's the problem with drinkin' like we are. The stories should be gettin' dirtier or whatever. But this one isn't, an' it isn't going to.

—That's not the point.

—I know, he said. —But it kind of is.

—I'm lost, I said.

—Well, he said. —I'm tempted to say the same thing, Davy, an' I nearly would. But I won't.

—Even though you say – what is it? – you might or you might not be the father of a middle-aged man?

—Yep.

He didn't hesitate, or grimace, or smile. Or shrug.

—I think I might go now, Joe, I said.

—Ah, no.

—I'm too drunk to listen.

—Ah, go on to fuck, Davy. It's the only way to listen.

—Bollocks.

—Spoken like a true Englishman.

—Fuck off.

—Look, he said. —Look it. You can't go. Be a pal. Give me a chance.

—What chance? I said. —Wha' fuckin' chance? Wha' d'you even want, for fuck sake?

He'd spoken as if it had been his turn to unburden himself and I was being selfish. He'd endured my late-midlife, early-elderly confessions and now it was his go.

And maybe I was selfish. I hadn't told him about my spell in hospital, the scare that hadn't scared me until months later when I started crying. I'd never mentioned it, yet I resented his lack of curiosity. I needed him to be a bad man, somehow. I had to be the good man. There couldn't be two of us.

—The thing is, he said. —I don't think it matters.

—Wha' doesn't?

—Whether I'm his father or not. His biological father.

—You've never fuckin' met him.

—Doesn't matter.

—You never had sex with her.

—Well, he said. —There now.

—Ah, Jesus, I said. —Wha'?

He gave me the shrug again.

203

—Did I say never, Davy – actually?

—Did you?

—Does it matter?

—I'm definitely goin', I said.

But I picked up my pint and drank from it. The stout went down without a protest. I felt stupidly pleased; I was holding my drink.

—I love her, Davy, he said.

—So wha'?

—It goes a long way.

—Wha' the fuck does tha' mean?

—I want her to be happy, he said. —It's all I want.

—So fuckin' wha'?

—Literally, he said. —Literally. It's all I want. It's not an easy one when you're a bit pissed, is it?

—Wha'?

—Literally. Sayin' literally.

—You keep sayin' somethin' serious, I said. —Or it seems to be serious. An' then you say somethin' frivolous like tha'. To distract us.

—Yeah.

—Why?

—Because I hear meself, he said. —An' I can't fuckin' believe it.

—Because I have to say, Joe, it's very fuckin' irritatin'.

I wanted to go but I was leaning in, almost resting against his shoulder.

—When I met her, he said.

—Jessica.

—Yeah. When I met her. When I met her. I don't know. I felt happy.

—Fuckin' happy?

—Not delighted. Or giddy. Or aroused, or any o'
tha'. Just happy. I'll tell you – I'll tell you what it was
like. You're pushin' me off the stool, Davy.

—Sorry.

—D'you want it – d'you want to sit down?

—No, I said. —No. I'm grand.

—Okay.

—You were sayin'.

—Was I?

—What it felt like when you met Jessica.

—Yes, yeah – brilliant. Yeah. So. We were cleanin'
out the house, me an' the sisters, when me ma died.

—How long ago is that?

—Does it matter?

—No.

—Four years. Five. Five years ago. We were puttin'
the house on the market. Strange fuckin' experience,
by the way. Emptyin' a house like tha'. Because they'd
lived in it all their lives together, my ma an' me da.

—Same as mine.

—Yeah, of course.

—Well, my father did – does.

—Yeah, yeah, he said. —So anyway, I thought it was
horrible, just a horrible fuckin' experience. Throwin'
all their stuff ou'. It made me feel really shite – guilty,
I think. Their lives, you know – into a skip. Or down
to the Vincent de Paul. An' my sisters felt the same
way. The cryin' – Jesus. Everythin' we picked up. An'
the laughing. We can't throw this ou', there's no way
we can throw that ou'. But it had to be done. But the
things we found tha' we didn't even know were in the
house.

—Wha'?

—Nothin' dodgy. Calm down. We didn't find an Armalite or a vibrator –

—Ah, Jesus.

We were laughing.

—Nothin' like tha'. At all. But stuff tha' should've been thrown out years before. Things we'd had when we were kids tha' we'd have forgotten even existed.

—Toys?

—No.

—We've kept the kids' first shoes.

—No. Same here – but no. Trish put them somewhere. But not tha'. Or teeth. Did you keep your kids' baby teeth?

—Some.

—Same here, he said. —After the tooth fairy came down the chimney. No – that's fuckin' Santy. But anyway. Like, we made the decision to save the shoes an' the teeth. Me an' Trish. But this was different. Or, half different. Maybe she decided – I'm guessin' it was my mother. I can't see me da givin' much of a shite. But she decided she'd keep the school reports. But she only kept one.

—Whose?

—Not mine. But we found one letter from the Gaeltacht. One. An' we'd all have gone there at some time – all of us. But she only kept one o' the letters. An' I'm nearly certain I'd have written letters to her when I was there.

—So it wasn't yours.

—No. But then. It was Orla found it. My Holy Communion prayer book.

—Jesus.

—Well, yeah. Exactly. It was in this little – this small suitcase. At the back o' the wardrobe. Like a suitcase a teenager would've had when my ma was a teenager. With a clasp, you know – the lock.

—Yeah.

—It wasn't cardboard like those old suitcases, the ones people emigrated with. It was – I suppose – plastic. Vinyl or somethin'. Lacquer – I don't know. Cream coloured. An' I think Orla was worried openin' it. She was afraid there'd be clothes in it – that our ma might've planned on runnin' away at some time, or somethin'.

—An' what was in it?

—The prayer book – I told you.

—Besides tha'.

—Letters, he said. —Sent to her when she was a kid. Most o' them were from a cousin or somethin' in New York. An' two from a boy called Colm. An' a few photographs. A couple o' bits of ribbon. An ol' record – a 78, believe it or not. Called 'The Old Refrain'. It was stuff she brought with her into the house – into the marriage. Her life before she got married.

—But your prayer book too.

—There you go, he said. —It was slipped into a little side pocket.

—Only yours?

—Only mine. It was the only thing in the case tha' came from after she married my father. An' tha' got the girls' backs up a bit. They were callin' me the white-headed boy. But then Sheila admitted she couldn't remember if she'd had a prayer book. She said she'd almost definitely have had one but she couldn't actually remember it. An' the others were the same. They couldn't remember their own prayer books. But there's the thing.

—Neither could you.

—Exactly. I'd no recollection of it. Even when I was holdin' it in me hands. It's a lovely little thing, by the way. The print is nearly faded off the cover but you can still make it out. Souvenir of First Holy Communion. An' a cross, of course. An' inside it has – on the first page. It has my name an' address, an' the date.

—What was it?

—The 29th of June. 1965.

—Christ.

—Yeah.

—That's brilliant.

—Yeah.

—An' the best thing – come here. The thing tha' really fuckin' floored me. It's my father's handwriting.

—Brilliant.

—Ah, man.

—That must've been incredible.

—Well –.

He took off his glasses and gave his eyes a quick rub.

—Look at me, he said. —Fuckin' eejit.

He put the glasses back on.

—But yeah, he said. —You can imagine, Davy. An' you know me an' religion. I hate the fuckin' Church, everythin' about it. But this thing – the little book. Jesus –. This is true now. It was the first thing I packed when I was leavin'.

—Leavin' wha'?

—Trish an' tha'.

—Yeah – sorry. Gotcha.

—The first thing, he said. —It's mad, I know. Given wha' was goin' on, like.

—I can kind of understand it.

—But it made me – I don't know. Happy. So, like – so full of happiness. Even though I'd never missed it or even knew about it. She probably put it away the same day, the day of the Communion. We'll never know why she put it into the little suitcase – why in there. But, anyway. There you go. I just felt so happy. So complete. Complete – yeah.

—Yeah.

—An' that's exactly how I felt when I met Jess. When I was with her again.

He looked happy now too. He'd got there; he'd explained it all to me. He thought he had.

—A complete surprise, he said. —Out o' nowhere. But it still made sense.

I was officially exhausted. And I didn't know why. Nothing had clicked, no one good cause had made itself known. Work, money, sex, kids, grief, marriage – a line of not-reallys. I was a fraud. I believed that.

I'd woken up the morning after I'd been admitted. I knew exactly where I was and why I was there. I was exhausted; I'd been told that the day before. Time had been broken into unjoined moments. But not now. I sat up in the bed; I did it carefully. I knew I had to, because my blood pressure was low – interestingly low, the neurologist, whose name I never knew, had said. I wasn't linked to the drip-stand beside the bed. I would be again, later; the IV valve was taped to my wrist. There was a heart monitor sitting on my chest. It looked like an old-fashioned smartphone, some early prototype, wrapped in thick plastic. It hung around my neck; I had to bring it with me. I sat on the side of the bed. I waited some time. Then I stood.

209

Wake, know, sit, stand – it was a line, linked moments and knowledge. I stood slowly, one hand still resting on the bed. I stood straight. My head didn't spin. I looked at my feet; I looked down. There were slippers beside my feet. They weren't mine. I didn't own slippers. But they made sense. Faye had bought them in a shop, downstairs. The yellow pyjamas I was wearing now, the slippers, the bottle of Lucozade, *The Girl on the Train* – she'd brought them back up to me before she'd gone home. I was interested in my feet. If I could use them. If I could walk. I lifted the right foot and placed it in front of the left; I'd be stepping away from the bed. I'd be stepping out of something – and I wasn't sure I wanted to. I liked exhaustion. I liked not knowing, caring, not living the measured life.

I took the step. I took the other. I walked to the window. Around the bed. I opened the curtain. I looked out for the first time. At a wall. I smiled – I felt myself do it. A wall – no windows. And a patch of sky the same colour as the wall, just as badly painted. I liked it – I'd tell Faye.

I'd tell Faye.

I was able to eat breakfast; I was hungry. I was told to stay on the bed. I was dehydrated. But I was fine. Fine, but I didn't care. It was what I wanted: I wanted not to care. I looked at the window, at the wall to the side of the window. I waited for, I pressed for the differences – the colours, glass, sky – to stop. I tried to go back to broken time. I wanted it back. I didn't know what I didn't want to face. I didn't know and it didn't matter. I tried to gaze my way back, hypnotise myself. Escape. Unhappiness. Redundancy. They'd been gone. I tried to get back there.

Faye was in the room. But I saw her come in – she wasn't just there. I heard her open the door, I saw her. I saw her look at me – smile.

—How are we this morning?

I saw her look at the clear bag suspended from the drip-stand; I was being fed again. I saw her frown – I saw her decide to.

—Is it doing the trick, is it?

She held the collar of the pajamas.

—Yellow's your colour, David.

She had a shopping bag with her. I wanted to see what was in it. I wanted to watch her empty it, comment on each item, place each on the table in front of me. I wanted to look at her do things. I saw: I understood. She wanted this too. She wanted me to watch her. She wanted me to follow her. She wanted to feel my eyes. She wanted to lift me out of death.

—I'm feeling better, I told her.

Regret immediately drenched me; I'd been fooled, found out. I wanted to go back. This might be the last time. I wanted to go back behind there.

But I wanted Faye. I wanted to be with Faye. To look at Faye. I wanted to feel her. She placed an Innocent smoothie, mango and passion fruit, on the table in front of me.

—That'll put hairs where you want them, she said.
—And not the grey lads, either.

She stepped past the table and leaned down, right to my face, my eyes. She kissed my lips.

—I want you better, she said.

She examined both of my eyes.

—They're not as red. Only pink. Pink's your colour, Dave.

211

—Yellow and pink, I said. —My colours.

—Oh, God, I'm getting the lady horn.

I laughed – it burst out of me.

—That's music to my ears, she said. —Are you back?

—I am.

—Great.

—I think so.

—No thinks, she said. —No fuckin' thinks. You're back or you're not back.

—I'm back.

I said it, but I hated saying it. I hated believing it. Exhaustion was safe and I wanted it back. I shut my eyes but I couldn't keep them shut.

We made it to a party one night. We hung on, we followed. We got into the back of a car. A Mini, I think. We'd no idea where we were going. The two other lads in the car booed as we passed a set of big gates, then clapped, and laughed.

—What's that about? I asked the girl beside me, the Emmylou girl. She was on a lap, to my left.

—Blackrock College, she said.

—Did they not like it?

—They fucking loved it, she said. —They never fucking left it.

—I can't remember the name o' the school I went to, I told her.

—My kind of guy.

The car stopped. I got out, followed others, made sure I was with Joe, went through a gap in a wall. A path under trees. A lantern. But no door.

—How do we get in?

212

There was an open window. There were people inside. There was music. There was a door around a corner. And the mother.

—Oh, fuck.

A formidable mother. A mother like nothing we'd encountered before. There were steps up to her – this must have been the front of the house. We were never going to get past her. She was gorgeous. Too full of sex to be a mother but definitely the mother, the owner of the huge house right behind her.

Joe got up on the first step.

—Two more 'Rock boys for you, he said.

—Oh, dear God, she said, and raised her colossal eyes to the porch above her stiff hair, and smiled, and moved aside just enough for us to pass and smell her, and rub against her, as we went.

—Fuckin' hell.

—This is a bit fuckin' different.

A house from American television. A flow of people up the stairs, and down. The people coming down held bottles of Heineken. We went up, joined the queue, to a bath full of ice and bottles, and a child with a bottle opener sitting on a shower seat beside the bath. Joe pulled up a sleeve and took two bottles from the bath. The Heineken labels were floating on the water. One of them stuck to the hair on his arm. He pulled it off and threw it back in the bath.

—What's the occasion? he asked the child.

A boy.

The boy stared up at us.

—Why don't you know? he asked.

—I'm testing you, said Joe. —And I asked first.

—Jess is engaged to Gavin.

—Correct, said Joe.

We left the child and went back downstairs. We stood in a full room and shifted to let the traffic pass, and looked at the people who had always known one another – the couples, the friends, the gorgeous tribe.

—Where is she? said Joe.

She was why we were here. Somehow. Our girl – our woman. *Hi*. She'd dragged us here. I looked around. I looked at every chair, along the walls, through both doorways. Where was she? She'd left George's with the rest of them, with us. She'd been outside. We'd seen her get into one of the cars; she'd dragged her cello in with her. We'd heard her laugh. Not *your* lap?! Be good now! The Mini we'd pushed ourselves into was just a bit further down, near the corner of Fade Street. We were all going to the party. She was here, somewhere.

I didn't care. I feel it now, I felt it then. The impossible dream – but I wasn't dreaming. Joe, though – I don't know. I'd been infatuated before; I knew what it was like. The spunk eyes, and the wish to protect the girl from spunk eyes, my own eyes. To be engulfed, protected, changed. To disappear into a woman. To be killed, born. To feel the woman right against you. I don't know about Joe. He was in love with a woman he didn't know. But I don't know. I was looking half heartedly for the Emmylou girl. I wanted to smile at her. See what happened.

—We'll try the kitchen, said Joe. —This is shite.

We battled our way out to the hall – the house kept filling – and found the kitchen, a home in itself. There was a fireplace, a huge black metal oven, a silver fridge. The place was packed. And she was there. She was sitting on a chair, the only person in the room sitting. It took a while to realise that the thing she seemed to

214

be leaning on was the cello. Had she played, was she about to play? She moved to the side, bent down – she disappeared. And reappeared – she'd been getting her bow from the case on the floor. She was going to play. I looked at Joe, at the side of his face. I saw his sneer. Not there for long. He killed it, wiped it from his face. It was how we always reacted to things we didn't know – art, food, the world: we sneered. And that was what Joe did when he saw that she was about to play the cello. At first.

She threw her head back, and brought her hair with her. But it almost immediately fell back in front of her face as she sawed at the strings and, gradually, her movement produced notes and a sound that began to flow and rise. It was probably Bach – I don't know.

I saw the Emmylou girl. She was at the door, looking – like everyone else – at the cello. I left Joe and went across to her. She was by herself. I stood beside her.

—Hi.

She looked.

—Oh. Hi.

We both looked at the woman playing the cello.

—She's not very good, said Emmylou.

—No, I agreed.

I looked across at Joe, to make sure he hadn't heard me. He was gazing – I think that is an accurate word – gazing at her, at her bow hand, at her, hidden behind her hair. It was the look of a man who fancied the woman he was looking at. That was it. He was waiting to see her face again.

I'm making this up. I saw Joe's face that night, almost forty years ago. But I'm lying. I don't know what his expression was like. I didn't care. The woman beside me was holding my hand. I'd made my hand touch hers and she'd taken two, three of my fingers and held them, then opened her full hand to mine. I think her name was Alice – I'm not sure. I slept in her bedroom that night and met her mother the following morning. I remember that but not the girl, the woman, herself – not really.

I didn't stay. Alice started to turn, away from the music. She pressed my hand and I went with her.

We didn't know the cellist's name was Jess. When we watched her play, when I was watching Joe. We didn't know she was engaged, and that she was playing Bach at her own engagement party.

I look again – I try to remember – to see if I can spot Gavin, the fiancé. I have no idea who Gavin was. I can't see him standing beside her, over her. I can't see him leaning against the fridge, staring around, making sure that no one interrupts the performance. I can't see him in George's, with his arm around her shoulder. I don't think I ever did see him. I'm not certain that the child with the bottle opener said Jess and Gavin. I slept with a girl that night and I think her name was Alice, but I'm not sure.

The woman we'd been staring at and thinking of for months was called Jess – I know that now. We were in her house. And I remember, Alice didn't like her. I remember, it had helped me to like Alice, to reach for her hand. I'd done that when I'd heard – she'd let me hear – her irritated sigh. I liked her then, I'd liked her before then. But not enough to remember her name. I'm calling her Alice because it seems fairer – nicer – than calling her the Emmylou girl.

I know that the woman was called Jess. She was the boy in the bathroom's sister and she was engaged. But – before we went into the house and upstairs to the beer – we didn't know her name. We hadn't heard it, we hadn't asked it. That – what we didn't know – is true. Downstairs, in the kitchen, we didn't know we were looking at the fiancée. That must be true. We didn't know she was Jess.

I look again at Joe before I leave with Alice.

I can see it: he's smitten. I decide this.

Joe had gone downstairs, to the Black Hole of Calcutta. I'd been down already. It was well lit, almost beautiful, probably protected; it was like descending into the nineteenth century. I sat on the stool while he was gone. The place was filling and it was the easiest way to protect it. And I was tired. Wired and tired – and drunk. I checked my phone. I was dreading the call and wanting the call.

He'd had another go at explaining to me – and to himself, I thought – how he had felt. Finding Jess, finding what she meant to him, had been like finding something that he'd lost and would have given up on if – in this case – the growing sense of despair, and terror, hadn't made that impossible.

—This is somethin' that happened, I said. —What you're talkin' about now. This is somethin' that happened?

—Yeah.

—It did?

—Yeah, he said. —Yeah.

—Wha'?

—My weddin' ring.

—You lost your weddin' ring?

—Yeah.

—What happened?

217

—Another fuckin' cliché, said Joe. —The Christmas party.

—You took your weddin' ring off.

—Don't ask me why.

—Why?

—Well, there you go, he said. —It makes no sense. The woman knew I was married. So it was – ah, it was stupid. An' nothin' happened, like. Nothin' was ever goin' to happen. But I took it off anyway. In the jacks. Put it in me jacket pocket.

—Where were you?

—Some fuckin' place I'd never heard of. The younger ones always lead the way. So anyway, I'm chattin' to her. I think I might even have been talkin' about the kids, for fuck sake. But somethin' – the drink. Or the fact tha' she *is* a very good-lookin' woman, an' dead-on. I take the fuckin' ring off when I go out to the jacks. Like I'm announcin' somethin' to myself. Givin' myself permission. Connin' meself, I suppose. Totally illogical. Totally fuckin' stupid. An' like I said, I wasn't particularly frisky or anythin'.

—You didn't say that.

—Well, I'm fuckin' sayin' it now. But anyway, I come back from the toilet an' there's someone else sittin' where I'd been, an' I'm glad. I really am. A few more drinks. Mad things – cocktails, you know. Buckets o' fuckin' gin an' vegetables. An' I slide out, I've had enough. Into a taxi an' home.

He remembered the ring in the morning. He was lying in bed. He'd moved to the side that Trish had just vacated, into her warmth, when he remembered. His jacket was downstairs, draped carefully over a chair in the kitchen. He was nearly sure that that was where he'd left it. He was always very tidy and methodical

218

when he was drunk. The jacket was down in the kitchen and the ring was in the pocket and Trish would go through the pockets and find the ring, and she'd know exactly why it wasn't on the third finger of his left hand. She'd know immediately, without having to think it through. There was nothing to think through. He'd taken off the ring because he'd wanted to unmarry himself for the half hour it would have taken him to get into some young one's knickers, and he'd forgotten to remarry himself on the way home because he'd been so drunk – the smell off his breath, off his skin, was proof enough of that.

He sat up in the bed, too scared for a hangover. He was hoping he'd see the jacket on the floor, although he knew he wouldn't. His suit trousers were draped over the back of the chair beside the window, with his shirt and the tie. His shoes were side by side, parked under the chair. His underpants were on him.

—Me heart, Davy, he said. —I'm not jokin' yeh. The poundin' tha' should've been in me head – it had emigrated to my fuckin' heart.

Had he had sex with the woman the night before? He knew he hadn't – he was positive he hadn't. But he was sniffing himself and checking his crotch. Even though he knew nothing had happened. And he hated himself because nothing had happened and he was thanking Christ that nothing had happened. He couldn't think of anything to tell Trish, to explain the ring. She was down there now – he was sure of it – holding the jacket up in one hand, slipping the other hand into the first of its pockets.

Joe had forgotten about Jess or he was trying to make sure that I forgot about Jess. But it didn't matter. It was him at his best, his own hero and villain, genius

219

and eejit, bringing himself to big life in a story. The boy and the man I think I'd wanted to be.

—D'you have form? I asked him.

—Wha'?

—Well, why would Trish have been goin' through your pockets?

—Oh, he said. —That's just Trish. She's a pain in the arse – no. No, sorry – that's not fair. But you know the way I'm tellin' you a story? Now, like. Here.

—Yeah.

—Well, she'd've been tellin' hers, he said. —If tha' makes sense. In her head – livin' the story as she went around the kitchen. Searchin' the pockets – that's what they're there for, kind o' thing.

—A pair of fuckin' drama queens.

—Fuck off, but yeah.

He wanted to go downstairs to the kitchen but he was afraid to. There was a chance she hadn't searched the pockets, and wasn't going to. But she might have been waiting at the foot of the stairs with the ring sitting on the palm of her hand. Or in the kitchen, waiting, pretending there wasn't a fight and a separation on the way. He couldn't think of anything to tell her if she'd found the ring. But he got out of bed and put on his dressing gown. He lifted the shirt and trousers off the chair, to make sure that what he knew was true: the jacket was downstairs. He checked the trouser pockets – and no ring. He thought of a story on the landing. He'd tell her he'd got the ring caught in a towel, one of those small white towels that they stack beside the sinks in hotel toilets. The Clarence – he'd say they'd been in the Clarence; they'd all gone there after the food. They'd been to the Clarence before, him and Trish, so she'd know exactly what he was talking about.

He'd had to take the ring off to free it from the towel because it had become snagged, somehow – he didn't know how; he'd been drunk. And he'd forgotten to put it back on. He must have slipped it into the pocket so he could wash his hands.

Trish was there, in the kitchen. She was making a list, opening and shutting the fridge and the presses. It was a couple of days before Christmas. He'd forgotten all about Christmas. It was why he'd been out with the office gang.

—The dead arose, she said.

Her back was to him. She was looking in the freezer above the fridge. The jacket was where he knew he'd left it. He lifted it off the chair, exactly as he'd pictured Trish doing. He put his free hand into the pocket he'd slipped the ring into the night before. Trish was still rooting through the freezer. The pocket was empty; the ring wasn't in there.

—No fuckin' ring, Davy, he said. —An' I knew I'd put it in there. I fuckin' knew.

Trish had turned.

—What are you lookin' for? she asked.

—Nothin', he said.

—You're not smokin' again, are you? she said.

I'd forgotten: Joe used to smoke. In fact, it was un-usual that he hadn't mentioned it tonight because he often had a smoke – just the one, or two – when we were out together.

—No, he told Trish. —My wallet.

He was delighted – relieved. She hadn't been search-ing the pockets. She'd have known there wasn't a packet of Silk Cut and matches or a lighter in the pockets if she'd already been through them. But Trish loved her drama. She might have been leading him to the trap.

221

He still had to be careful, and the hangover was kicking in. He was dying. He checked the other pocket as Trish pointed to the black wallet – an anniversary present, from Trish – on the kitchen table.

—There it is, look.

The ring wasn't there. It wasn't in the only other pocket it could have been in. There was just one inside pocket and he would never have put the ring into that one. He was reliving the moment, the night before, soaping the finger, sliding it off, putting it in the pocket – the outside pocket, right side. Trish was looking at him. She'd shown him the wallet on the table and he was now putting his hand into the inside pocket, searching for something he no longer needed to search for.

—Joe, she said.

—What?

—Your wallet's on the table.

—Yeah.

The inside pocket was empty. He was hoping his face was too. But he thought he was going to vomit.

—There's Coke in the fridge, said Trish. —D'you want some? You look like you need the bubbles.

He put the jacket back on the chair. He lifted the shoulders, to make sure it sat well. And saw the wedding ring. On his finger.

—Ah, Jesus, I said.

—I swear to God. On my fuckin' finger.

—That's brilliant.

I laughed. I leaned against him. I put my forehead to the side of his head, for a second. I lifted my head.

—Jesus, Joe, I said. —You're a terrible fuckin' messer.

I knew we'd be having another pint.

—My fuckin' heart, Davy, he said. —An' she asks if I want a fuckin' Coke. An' there was me thinkin' she was goin' to murder me – stab me – or wallop me with somethin' out o' the fuckin' freezer. A leg of lamb or somethin'. The fuckin' turkey.

He kept looking at the ring; he couldn't help it. He kept expecting it to be gone. He couldn't believe that nothing was going to happen. He was almost disappointed.

—I loved fightin' Trish, he said. —I have to say tha'.

—Joe, I said.

—Wha'?

—Why're you tellin' me this?

—Wha' d'you mean?

—You told me this – the story, like. It's brilliant, by the way. But you said it would – I don't know – illustrate how you felt when you met Jess again. And now you're tellin' me you liked the fights with Trish.

—Well, it's true.

—What is?

—The fights.

He looked around; he'd just heard himself. He looked back at me.

—Rows, I meant. Arguments.

—I know wha' you mean.

—Trish, he said. —She's like an opera singer when she's arguing. She's fuckin' amazin'.

—Yeah, I said.

I'd met Trish only a couple of times but I remembered her tearing the face off me once and I'd felt tiny, torn apart and lucky to have been the focus of such attention. She'd held my arm when she'd finished with me. She'd run her hand up and down it, elbow to shoulder, shoulder to elbow. She'd patted it. We were all drunk in a back garden. Any friend of Joe's is a friend

223

of mine, she'd said. I have your back, remember that. I came away feeling lucky and lonely.

—You still haven't told me, I said.

—I miss Trish, he said. —There's a part o' me tha' misses Trish. I have to say.

—You still haven't told me.

—Fuck off, Davy, for fuck sake. I'm gettin' there – I've lost track. It made sense when I started. Yeah, that's it – it was tha' feelin' of elation when I saw the ring. I thought I was fucked, then there it was. But that's goin' off track again. But it was the feelin'. Like a miracle but, actually, it was easily explained. I must've remembered the ring was in me pocket, probably in the taxi on the way home, an' I'd put it back on. Simple as. So, yeah. I found Jess.

—An' it felt miraculous.

—It kind of did, he said. —But a slower burn, if you're with me. Gradual. Like, I can't quite believe this but it's happenin'. At the school an' then when she texted me, I was thinkin' – I suppose – here we go. But then the first couple o' meetin's. An' it settled into this other feelin' – tha' there'd been no reunion, it'd been like this all along.

Joe was back from the toilet. I stood, and he got past me and sat. He brought his pint closer to him with his right hand. I looked at the left.

—You still have your ring on, I said.

—Wha'?

He caught up with what I'd said and he held up the hand.

—Yeah, he said. —An' you spotted it as well. You're a bit of an oul' one, aren't you, Davy?

—Fuck off.

224

—Well, Jesus, he said. —I can't think o' one other man
– not one – who'd've noticed or given a shite. No offence.

—Only because you were talkin' about it, I said.

—You're grand, he said. —I'm only slaggin' yeh. But,
yeah. I still have it. Trish flung hers at me.

—Did it hurt?

—She missed.

He grinned.

—It broke the glass on a photograph of her mother.
Knocked the fuckin' thing off the wall.

—Brilliant.

—Well, it was. An' she started laughin' before I did.
She's great, Trish.

He tapped the ring with a fingernail.

—Anyway, we're not divorced, he said.

—Hedgin' your bets.

—No, he said. —Fuck off. No. What's done's done.
I've no regrets.

—Is that true?

—It is, I think, yeah. It's true enough. But tha' sayin'
– no regrets, like. It's a bit callous. Is it?

—It could be, I said. —An' it's definitely unrealistic.

—Exactly, he said. —How could you not have regrets?
Some, at least. Everyone has a few regrets.

—Yeah.

—So, then, yeah, he said. —I do have regrets. Fuckin'
big ones. The whole family thing. I miss them – fuck
me. I don't even have to admit tha' – you'd be the
same, I know.

—Yup.

—It'll iron itself out in time, he said. —Whatever
tha' fuckin' means. So I'm bein' told. Every time I open
me fuckin' mouth. But it's true. It has to be. You don't

go from bein' a good dad to an evil one, just like tha'. Or a husband. They'll calm down.

—Probably, yeah, I said.

—Eventually.

—Yeah.

—Fuck it, he said.

—What about you?

—What about me?

—Will you calm down?

—I am fuckin' calm, he said.

—Grand.

—Calm as – whatever.

He watched me – he was looking at my hand as I took my pint off the counter. He bent slightly and grabbed my other one, the left. I let him do it, so we both looked at the palm and fingers.

—Come here, you, he said. —Where's your own fuckin' ring?

He let go of the hand.

—I don't have one, I told him.

—No?

—I've never had one.

—How come?

—Well, I said. —It wasn't unusual back then, remember. For the groom not to have one. I'd've been happy enough but Faye wasn't havin' it.

—How come?

—She used to find weddin' rings on the table at home, when she was a kid. After her father died.

—Jesus, he said.

—Yep.

—But did men have weddin' rings back then?

—I know what you mean, I said. —But some must've. Cos Faye found them.

—An' her ma was a bike?

—A tandem, I said.

I felt disloyal, and cruel. But there was no real point in trying to explain Faye's mother to Joe. It was too complicated; the drink was drowning the words.

—But it doesn't make sense, he said.

—What doesn't?

—These lads takin' their weddin' rings off. Before they went up with her mother.

—Faye used to hide them.

—The rings?

—Yeah.

—Brilliant.

—Her mother paid her to do it, I told him. —After she did it the first few times.

—That's mad, said Joe. —Kind o' not funny, really. Did Faye think it was funny?

—No.

—She took the money, but.

—She saved it.

Faye was all set to go, before her mother died. She just had to pull herself away from the conviction that she was needed; and the fear that she wasn't. She'd made it to Dublin once, when she was sixteen. Her mother guessed she'd be at her aunt's flat, her father's sister, Mary; and she phoned. Come home, pet. I'm dying.

—The whole ring thing, though, said Joe. —Two women, Davy. Tha' was me for a bit. I sound like a fucker.

—A bit, yeah.

—I know. But I'd like to think I'm not. The fuckin' Mormons an' their polygamy, there's no way it'd work out fairly. For the women – sure it wouldn't?

227

—No.

—Now there was a religion designed by a man.

—They all were.

—Wha'?

—Religions.

—True, he said. —It's all bollix. I'm feelin' these pints now.

—Behind the head.

—Exactly, he said. —I'm out o' practice. Still, though. Great to see you, man.

He held out his glass. He wanted me to tap mine against his.

—Good to see you too, I said.

We tapped.

I wanted to go now. I wanted to get back before the call. I wanted to sit with my father. Just sit. I wanted to tell him I loved him. I wanted to say it out loud.

—But men have managed it, said Joe. —The two households thing.

—Jesus, Joe –

—I know, he said. —But look it. Tha' was me – in a way, it was me, how I was livin'. For months.

—It must be fuckin' exhaustin'.

—No, he said.

—It must be, I said. —It has to be.

—No, I swear, he said. —I see why you'd think it. But it wasn't.

—It wasn't two households, was it, though – really? Two houses, the works.

—No, he said. —An' – I don't know. Dividin' the time – a night in one place, a night in the other place. Tha' must be a killer. Never mind the economics. Keepin' track o' the lies – fuckin' hell. But look, I wasn't

228

messin'. D'you know what I mean, Davy? I wasn't actin' the prick.

—Well, you must've been.

—No.

—To an extent, I said. —You must've been. Did you tell Trish wha' you were up to?

—No.

—There, I said. —So, you withheld the information –

—Are you fuckin' jokin' me? Trish?

—What I'm suggestin' is, just because you didn't think you were messin' around, that doesn't mean you weren't.

—Lower the voice a bit.

—Was I shoutin'?

—A bit.

I looked to the sides – I saw no one looking away. The barmen were busy. We were okay.

—Did you stay away from home? I asked him.

—The house?

—Yeah.

—Yeah, he said. —A couple o' times. Before –

—Trish found out.

—I told Trish – but yeah.

—How many?

—Wha'?

—Nights.

—Four. For a night, just. You know – a single night. Each time.

Now I lowered my voice; I wasn't sure why.

—But you said you didn't have sex with Jess, I said.

—No, he said. —But –

—Wha'?

—You'll have to get past tha' – the sex. If you're goin' to understand wha' I've been tryin' to say.

—Give me a fuckin' break, Joe.

—Fuck off now, Davy – you give *me* a fuckin' break. I'm not a slug an' I'm not fuckin' stupid either. I knew it couldn't last an' that I'd have to tell Trish. An' I knew what would happen. An' it did. Boy, did it – fuckin' hell. Although even tha' got complicated. But there was a spell – that's what I'm sayin'. There was a spell when it felt perfectly, nearly perfectly fuckin' normal to be livin' the way I was.

He grabbed his pint. I thought for a second that he'd pour it over my head, or his own. But all he did was drink from it.

—What's this? Faye said.

—What's what?

It was two years or so after we'd moved to England. We were still a bit lost and Faye was pregnant again. She was holding a piece of paper, a receipt.

—What the fuck is this supposed to be, David? she said.

She slapped my nose with the paper and stepped back before I could grab it.

—Stop it, Faye, I said.

—Stop what? Stop what, exactly?

—It's not funny, I said. —Stop it.

She looked at the receipt. She brought it up to her eyes, although it was another twenty-five years before she'd start wearing reading glasses.

—Bombay Indian Restaurant, she read.

She stepped up to me again, and slapped me with the receipt. Harder this time; her knuckles brushed the side of my nose.

—Lay off, Faye – please.

—Who is it? she said. —Do I know her?

She was looking at the receipt again.

—Two starters, two mains.

—I hope you're enjoying yourself, I said.

—I am.

—It's boring, Faye.

—What's boring, David? Indian food or adultery?

I laughed.

—What's so funny?

—You are, Faye, I told her. —You're brilliant.

She looked at the receipt. She'd been upstairs, putting Cathal, our eldest, to bed.

—It was in your pocket, so it was.

—No, it wasn't.

—Maybe it's mine, so.

—Maybe it is, I said.

—Who did I meet, I wonder? she said. —Are you interested?

—No.

—Don't worry, though, Dave, she said. —I'd never let any man's tongue near my fanny after he's had a vindaloo.

—Wise move, I said. —It was us, by the way.

—What was?

—You were the woman, I told her. —We ate in that place a couple of weeks ago. We had Cathal with us.

—A likely story.

—You said it yourself, I said. —You'd be the only pregnant woman in England who liked spicy food.

There were times when I knew she was messing and times when she frightened me, when I thought I was sharing the house with a woman I didn't know or like. Her unpredictability became a threat. I thought sometimes that she didn't trust herself, she didn't trust what

231

we were; she was testing herself, rehearsing her mother's madness. It was nasty, brief, sporadic and strategic. She never performed in front of the kids. She let them grow up and when they left, she let them stay gone. They never got the phone calls, Come home, pet, I'm dying.

—Guess what, Dave? she said the day we came home after driving Róisín to college in London.

—What?

—We can do what we want, she said.

—That's true.

—The first time in fuckin' for ever, she said. —We can starve the dog if we like.

—Do we want to do that?

—It can go onto the agenda, she said. —Is what I'm saying. We can do anything we want. Does that appeal to you, David?

It didn't.

I'd no children; I'd nothing. I'd nothing to do and nothing I wanted to do, other than lie down and wait – I didn't know for what. A revelation or a disease – both made equal sense.

She put her arms around me and she cried; she drenched my shoulder.

—They're ungrateful little cunts, she said.

—Are you talking about our children, Faye?

—I am.

—We could watch telly, I said.

—My God, she said. —There's a thought. Telly.

I kissed the top of her head. I knew what she was going to say.

—Never fuckin' kiss me there, David.

I was finally getting to know her.

★ ★ ★

I watched Joe. He'd stopped talking. He'd stopped needing to talk. He was looking around again, as if we'd just arrived.

—This place hasn't changed, he said.

He pointed at a line of old photographs.

—The dead writers are still dead, he said.

—That's reassurin'.

—It kind of is, he said. —I go with it.

—Sorry?

—I go with it, he said. —I'm tryin' to think of a way to describe it.

—Describe wha'?

—I don't know, he said. —That's part o' the problem. The whole thing. What's happened – since I met Jess.

—You go with it?

—Yeah – I think so.

—With the flow, d'you mean? I asked him. —You go with the flow?

—No, he said. —No. Definitely not tha'. Tha' sounds like I'm bein' led by the flute or somethin'. An' I'm not. At all – fuckin' at all.

—Okay.

—I'll tell you what it is, he said.

But he didn't – not immediately. He was looking at the bottles on the high shelves, and at the pictures. He didn't look drunk now. The wetness had gone from around his eyes. He looked older – older than he'd looked a few minutes before. And turning – when he was turning his head – he seemed stiffer; his body had to go with him. The back of his head, down around the neck, looked fleshy.

I waited.

I wanted to leave again. Suddenly. I didn't like my position here, the listener, the tape recorder. I wanted to call Faye. I wanted to see my father.

233

He put his hand on his glass again.

—It's a thing abou' gettin' older, he said. —At least, I suppose it is. So many memories, you know. It becomes harder to separate wha' happened from wha' might've happened an' wha' didn't happen but kind o' seemed to.

He was looking at me.

—Is it? he asked.

—Is memory reliable? I said. —Is that wha' you mean?

—I think so, yeah.

—Jesus, Joe.

—I know.

—For fuck sake.

—I know, he said. —I remember once. Listen –.

He lifted his glass. He drank. He took the glass from his mouth and held it to his chest.

—Not tha' long ago, he said. —Only – Jesus – only a bit more than a year ago. We'd a do in our house. Aaron's graduation, it would've been.

The name, Aaron, meant nothing but I knew he was one of Joe's kids.

—College graduation? I asked.

—No, no, he said. —He's not the eldest. That's Sam. No, just school. End o' sixth year, you know. A big deal these days – fuckin' hell. Anyway, my sisters were there, an' Trish's sister, Grace. An' the husbands. You know, yourself. The gang. We were ou' the back, in the garden. We've a pond out there now, an' a deck. A barbecue as well, one o' the big lads. Like a fuckin' helicopter under the cover, if you're lookin' ou' the window at it durin' the winter.

—We've one o' them too, I said.

234

—There you go, he said. —Half the gardens in fuckin'
Ireland have them.

—Does Jess?

—No, he said. —No. D'you know wha', though? I'm
not sure. I haven't been ou' in her back garden.

—Really?

He seemed to be thinking about it, going back over
the months.

—Yeah, he said.

—You live there.

—I know, he said. —It's – wha'? – a bit odd, I suppose. But I don't know. I just haven't gone ou' there.
The wheelies are all out in the front, so –

—You've looked out the kitchen window, surely.

—I have, he said. —Yeah. An' I haven't seen a barbecue. But anyway, where was I?

—Your back garden.

—That's righ', he said. —Thanks. We were all ou'
there, sittin' around in a big circle, like, an' Trish starts
tellin' a story, somethin' tha' happened when the kids
were smaller, a few years before – another couple o'
years back. There's a school at the end of our road,
d'you remember?

—No, I said.

I'd never been to his house.

—Ah, you do.

—I don't.

—Well, there is, he said. —On the corner. A girls'
school – the national, you know. An' if you're tryin' to
get out, off the road, when all the parents are droppin'
their kids off in the mornin' just before nine, you haven't
a hope. It's jammed. It's a pain in the arse. So, anyway,
Trish was tellin' everyone abou' this one time. The car

– our car, like – was stuck behind a jeep. The woman drivin' the jeep had parked it nearly in the middle o' the road an' she was out of it, gettin' her kids ou' from the back. An' Trish was tellin' them all how I rolled down the window an' called out to her, Excuse me? Exactly like I did do it – I'll never forget it. So, the woman – a big girl, by the way, with a baseball cap. She takes her head out o' the back of the jeep an' turns. The way Trish was tellin' it, it was fuckin' brilliant. An' we were all in stitches – all ages, you know. Kids an' oldies, all laughin'. So anyway, I ask her – your woman with the baseball cap. I say, Would you mind movin' your car, we're just tryin' to get out? An' your woman just says, Fuck off.

—No.

—Yeah, said Joe. —That's all. Fuck off. Straight at me. An' Trish's face, Davy, when she was sayin' it. It was the funniest fuckin' thing. Trish wasn't wearin' a cap when she was tellin' it but, the way she was holdin' her head, you'd've sworn she was. It was fuckin' hilarious. But.

—But what?

—She wasn't there.

—What d'you mean?

—She wasn't in the car – Trish wasn't. I was drivin' an' Holly was beside me. Just me an' Holly. I was droppin' her off to a football summer camp before I went on to work. She's a great footballer, Holly. All sports, really. But it was June, like, so Holly was done with school but the girls' school, the primary, was still open till the end o' the month. That's why she was with me. But the point is, Trish wasn't there. She didn't witness the woman's performance. I told her later.

236

—Okay.

—You don't think it matters?

—I don't know, I said. —But not really – I don't think so. We all do it, don't we? Embellish stories, add to them. Especially in this country.

—No, I know wha' you mean, he said. —As far as tha' goes, yeah, I'm with you. She hears it from me, she hears me tellin' it fuck knows how many times. So, she makes it her own.

—Yeah.

—Yeah, he said. —It's understandable. It's natural. An' she's a brilliant storyteller – a raconteur. Brilliant. You should see men lookin' at Trish when she's in full flow. Jesus – d'you remember?

—Yeah, I said.

I was lying: I didn't remember watching Trish telling a story. But I'd seen Faye, and men watching her as she spoke, loving her, resenting her, leaning in to take over, sitting back open-mouthed.

—So, I'm happy to hand it over, said Joe. —She's the entertainer. I just happen to be the one who endured the wrath – the fuckin' contempt of Missis Baseball Cap. It doesn't matter. We're joint owners o' the house – still are, by the way. An' we'd a joint account, so we might as well share the stories. I don't know – our fuckin' autobiographies. An' she's better at it.

—Same with me, I said. —Me an' Faye.

—There you go, he said. —An' it's a good thing. We don't feel threatened or undermined.

—No.

—An' they glow, he said.

—Yeah.

—Don't they?

—Yeah.

—So, he said. —It's grand. It's more than grand. But.

—The fact remains.

—The fact fuckin' remains. She wasn't in the fuckin' car.

—But, I said. —So wha'?

—So wha'? he said. —Nothin' – nothin', really. But this is my point, I think. If Trish an' myself hadn't – if we were still together, we wouldn't be havin' this particular conversation, you an' me. Because I'd've let her into the car. I'd've remembered her bein' there beside me, with Holly in the back – eventually. That's wha' would've happened.

—That's possible.

—That's definite, he said. —That's wha' would've happened. I've no doubt about it at all. It's wha' was already happenin', the more I heard her tell the story. I wanted her to be in the car. An' I'd've eventually remembered it tha' way. I'd've seen her beside me in the passenger seat, maybe even me in the passenger seat an' her drivin'. I'd've genuinely remembered it. But then we split up.

—An' she's not in the car any more.

—She's not in the fuckin' car. Are we having another?

—Go on, I said.

I was trying to recall a case of my own, some event that Faye had made her own. But I couldn't remember the last time we'd been in company, when I'd have heard and watched her tell a story. For years now, I've been her only audience. And I'd been hiding from her.

It's my fault.

—Two more, please, Joe said to a barman, the same one, I thought, who'd served us the last time.

The barman raised a hand.

—Two, he said, and kept going to the taps.

Joe took out his phone and looked at the clock.

—Loads o' time, he said.

He put the phone back into his pocket. I checked my own, took it out. I held it beside my leg and looked down. I slipped it back into the pocket.

—I asked Holly, he said.

—Wha'?

—I asked her – Holly. I asked her wha' she thought o' Trish sayin' tha' she was in the car with us.

—When was this?

—Well, when she was still talkin' to me, anyway, he said. —It would've been before meself an' Trish split up. Before she threw me ou'.

—Is tha' what happened?

—Not really, no, he said. —It wasn't really like tha'. I threw myself out. Truth be told – whatever tha' fuckin' means. No, we were arguin' alright, but I was still at home. But Holly would've heard us, I suppose. Definitely. Shite –. But anyway, Holly said she'd been in the car.

—Trish.

—Yeah. She said Trish was there with us. An' I'll tell you. I found tha' very hurtful.

—Why? I asked.

—Well, these things, he said. —Memories. They're precious, aren't they? I used to think tha', anyway. Special. There was me an' there was Holly beside me, an' your woman with the cap tellin' me to fuck off an' we were laughin', the two of us, once we were off the road an' your woman couldn't see us. Just me an' Holly.

—You didn't have it out with her, no?

—Who?

—The woman.

—Are you jokin' me? he said. —Never – Davy. Seriously. Never disagree with a woman who's wearin' a baseball cap. If you remember nothin' else tonight, remember tha', for fuck sake. But Holly. It was like she was erasin' me. From her memory. It hurt.

—Did she say you weren't there?

—No, he said. —No, she didn't. It's just, she inserted her mother. She was takin' sides.

—Jesus, Joe, I said. —Do you really think tha'?

—I do, yeah – I think I do. An' look, I don't blame her. She's heard Trish tell the story as often as I have. An' then there's me – she's furious with me. That's what I mean about her erasin' me. I'm bein' punished. Here's the pints. Whose twist is it?

—It might be me.

—It might be me as well, said Joe. —It was never a question back in the day, was it? We'd've known. Part o' the muscle memory or somethin'.

He was searching his pocket for notes. So was I, and I got there before him. I pulled another twenty from my wallet and held it out, across Joe, to the barman. He took it and turned to the till.

—I'll get the next two rounds, said Joe.

He watched the barman put the change on the counter.

—If I fuckin' remember, he said.

He watched me gather the change, the fiver and coins, and slide it into my pocket.

—So, yeah, he said. —Memory.

—Okay, I said. —What about it?

—Did you ever tell a lie so often you ended up believin' it?

—Probably, I said.

—Probably me hole. You did.

—Okay.

—So often it becomes a memory, he said. —Some porky you told to get you out of a corner becomes an event tha' you can remember. You cross a line or somethin'. D'you think that's feasible? I'm not so sure.

—No, I said. —Same here – I think.

I was getting drunk for the second or third time that night. I was feeling young. I was feeling thin and tall. I was feeling less than careful.

—But how would you know? I asked.

—Wha'?

—Well, if a lie becomes somethin' you remember, you have to forget it's a lie. Surely. Don't you?

—Good point.

—I mean, I said. —I remember lyin' so convincingly, I almost believed it. But I still knew it was a fuckin' lie. I didn't really believe –. I was impressed, tha' was it.

—When was this?

—Are you askin' me if I've only told a lie once in me life?

—No, he said. —No. Just a – for example. I seem to be doin' all the talkin'. Am I?

—Yeah.

—Fuck off, he said. —Go on.

—Well, I said.

I couldn't think of anything.

—Why are we talkin' abou' this? I asked. —Memories an' stuff – wha' started it?

—Good question, said Joe. —I was – I think I was, anyway. I was tryin' to explain –

I remembered something.

—I've got one, I said.

—Good man, he said.

—I told Faye I had a stalker.

241

—Fuck off.

He laughed, and so did I.

—Brilliant, he said. —That's fuckin' mad. What happened?

—Well, I said. —It's ages ago. Before the word stalker was even a thing.

—Before you went to England?

—No, I said. —No. Not tha' long ago. I've been livin' in England longer than I haven't been, remember. If tha' makes sense.

—It does.

—Does it?

—Yeah, he said. —You're in England more than thirty years.

—Yeah, I said. —Exactly.

—Fuckin' hell.

—Yeah, I said. —It's hard to believe sometimes. Especially tonight. Somehow. It feels like I've never been away.

He picked up his old glass.

—Good to see you, man, he said.

I picked up my glass and we tapped them again.

—Fuckin' great, isn't it?

—Yeah.

—Fuckin' great, he said. —Move back, Davy – you have to.

—No.

—Go on, he said. —Come home.

—Can't.

—Why not? What's stoppin' you?

—Faye wouldn't have it.

—Fuck her.

* * *

242

Faye was watching a film. She'd heard the key in the door. She thought she'd heard a car – the taxi moving away from the front of the house. All the sounds were expected – the car, the key, the front door being carefully opened. Then the unexpected. A rhythm that wasn't mine. Strange feet in the hall.

—David?

I remember my hand on the wall. Beside the light switch.

—Dave?

She found me looking at my feet.

—What's wrong?

I lifted my foot, the one that I'd just realised lacked a shoe. I felt the sock – the sole. It wasn't wet. Was it raining outside, was it wet out there? I didn't know.

—What's wrong with your foot?

I let go of the foot. I let go of the wall. I looked again. The shoe still wasn't there. I looked at Faye.

—God, the state of you, she said. —Come on – come in. Where's your bloody shoe gone? Shut the door there, for God's sake. The dog will fuckin' escape again.

I couldn't speak. I couldn't remember getting home. I couldn't remember being in a taxi; I couldn't remember paying for a taxi. I couldn't remember opening the door. I couldn't turn to close it. Faye did that; she went past me. I heard the rush – the door across the mat, the slight thump and the click. Faye was gentle. She was smiling as she put her arm around me, under my own arm, and escorted me to the couch and let me drop. I lay there, facing the television. There was sound, a gunfight, music, then no sound. The dog was looking at me. Whatever dog it was back then. Front paws up on the couch, right in front of my face.

Faye sat on the floor.

—Are you going to be sick, are you?

I tried to shake my head. I lifted it, I got up on my elbow. I moved my head, right, left.

—Saying no would've been easier, Dave, said Faye.

—No, I said. —No, Faye.

—You remember my name – lovely.

I closed my eyes. But it wasn't nice there. I opened them again.

—Where's your shoe?

—Somewhere.

—Grand.

Something about the way she spoke, about the way I heard it. She thought I was a child. I was lying on my side, my hands were under my cheek. I'd lost one of my shoes. I was a child. My mother was beside me, looking after me.

I didn't like it. I didn't want a mother.

—There's a woman in work, I told her.

—Is there?

I sat up. I felt like I'd slept. I was ready.

—What about her? said Faye.

—What?

—This woman you're dying to tell me about.

—She won't leave me alone, Faye.

—Did she take your shoe?

—No, I said. —I don't think so. I don't know. She's gorgeous, Faye.

—I'm sure she is.

I wanted Faye to slap me. I wanted her to rage. To stand over me and beat me. I wanted to feel her over me, on me.

She was sitting on the couch now. She was holding one of my feet.

—And she's taken your shoe hostage, has she?

I was lying down again.

—You're Cinderella, David, she said.

—What?

—That's who you are, said Faye. —You left the shoe behind when you ran away at midnight. And – sure, look. It isn't even midnight. It's hardly even dark. She'll be going from door to door now, getting all the men to try on your shoe.

—She's gorgeous.

—I bet she is. And she'll be ringing the bell any minute, will she?

I was crying.

—I'd never do it, Faye.

—More fool, you, *Daithí.*

—I'd never do it.

—I know, she said. —I know you wouldn't.

Her face was close to mine. I opened my eyes. She was still there, further away. I closed my eyes. I opened them. She was gone.

—Faye?

—Go to sleep, David.

There was something on me. Faye had put a duvet over me. The television was off, the light was off.

—Faye?

—Go to sleep, for fuck sake.

—Where are you?

—Near, she said.

—Where?

—Go to sleep.

—I don't want to.

—You do.

—I don't.

—Please yourself, so.

—I don't want to.

245

—You're a pest, so you are. Go to sleep. Don't get up and fuckin' wander. Let the kids stay asleep.

—She was gorgeous, Faye.

—Sure, I know, she said.

She was beside me again. Looking down.

—Make sure you stay on your side, she said. —The basin's beside you there. In case you want it.

She was gone.

—I want to hold you, Faye.

I couldn't get up. I wanted to, but I couldn't. I had to sleep – I had to roll away from this. I needed to shut my eyes. I needed this to end. I needed to start. Start again. Find her. Look at her. Hold her.

—Why did you say tha'? I asked him.

—Wha'?

—Fuck her, I said.

—I didn't mean it like tha', said Joe. —Fuck her. I didn't say tha'.

He smiled.

—More fuck'r, he said. —That's what I said. An' not aggressively. Or dismissively – none o' tha'.

It was like he was ready; he'd planned his response.

—Wha' makes you think you can fuckin' say tha'? I asked.

—Okay, he said. —Look, I shouldn't've said it but – fuck it – I didn't say wha' you're sayin' I said. But I do apologise.

—It's always the fuckin' same.

—Jesus, he said. —Here we go.

—Fuck you, Joe.

—Drink up, Davy, he said. —Before we get fucked ou'.

This was more like it. This was what I hadn't been remembering.

—Just fuck you, I said. —You can't fuckin' say tha'.

—I'm sorry.

—It's like – for fuck sake. It's like you expect me to make a decision – not a decision either. Just fuckin' obey you, just like tha'.

—Where's this comin' from?

—From deep down an' far away.

—What's tha' fuckin' mean?

—Fuck you.

I was going to do what I wanted to do. I was going to go. I'd had enough.

—Seeyeh, Joe.

—I'm sorry, he said. —I didn't mean anythin'. I was bein' flippant – stupid. Sorry.

I was going.

—I don't even want you to come home to Dublin, he said. —Not really. I was just enjoyin' meself an' I thought you were too. So – yeah. Sorry.

—You can't fuckin' say tha'.

—I didn't mean anythin'.

—You can't fuckin' say tha', I said again. —I'm still married, you know. I understand the fuckin' rules.

—Ah, now, he said. —For fuck sake.

He laughed and I still didn't want to hit him. But I wasn't going yet – the need had gone from my legs. I wanted to want to hit him. I wanted to feel myself deciding not to. To forgive him because he needed me to.

—You're a desperate fuckin' bitch, Davy, he said. —I understand the rules. For fuck sake.

—It's always been the same, I said. —But it's not. Not now.

—What're you on abou'?

—I always had to drop everythin', I said.

—That's just bollix.

—It isn't, I said. —An' you fuckin' know it isn't.

—An' I'll ask you again, he said. —Where's this comin' from?

—Fuckin' always.

—Wha'?

—But I'll fuckin' tell you, it's different now.

—I'm sure it is, he said. —What is?

—I don't even live in this poxy country.

—Thank fuck.

—You don't even know Faye.

—I know I don't an' I'm sorry for tha', he said. —I am. I didn't mean to – to – hurt your feelin's. Or insult you. Or her – Faye. I really am sorry.

—You even insisted that I fancied Jessica, I said. —Before we even knew who she was. Which we never fuckin' did, by the way, I don't care what you're sayin'.

—Fuckin' hell.

—Just because you fell for her, I had to as well. I broke it off with tha' one – Mags.

—Mags?

—Yeah.

—Mags? he said. —Are we inventin' people now? Fuckin' Mags?

—Yeah – Mags.

—Who's Mags?

—I think her name was Mags.

—You think?

—Yeah.

—Who was she?

—I went with her, I said.

—The love o' your life an' you can't remember her.

—I didn't say she was the love o' me life, I said.
—An' I do remember her. Quite well. I'm just not sure of her name. It was years ago.

—I'd hope so, he said. —Because, let's face it, you're married an' you understand the rules.

—Ah, fuck off.

—I'm only quotin' you, he said. —Who's Mags?

—Back, just after I left college, I said. —She had a flat on Leeson Street.

—You broke it off with a bird with a flat?

He was winning again. He was taking my anger and clarity from me. And I was letting him do it. Just as I'd done years before. I was trotting along behind him. Letting myself be his sidekick.

I drank from my pint. It was warm – it protested; it didn't want to be drunk. I swallowed.

—I'm goin' to the jacks, I said.

—Good man.

I hadn't been sitting but I felt like I'd just stood up. I was dizzy. I didn't stagger – I don't think I did. The spots stayed away from in front of my eyes. But I could feel myself deciding to take the steps I needed to take to get to the door down to the toilet. I was remembering the hospital, trying to put one foot forward, failing.

I watched the steps down, I held the rail. It was good to be away. Away from him, away from warm drink. I wanted to go now, to piss – urgently. I unzipped my fly while I was still on the stairs. I let go of the rail. I was fine.

I pissed. It was fine. It was normal – strong. I hated this getting old, the surprises. The quick indignities. It was supposed to be a slowing down, but it wasn't; it was a series of shocks. I'd been told that my hearing wasn't great in one ear. I'd been told that I had low

249

blood pressure, high cholesterol. I'd been told that I had a blocked artery, coronary artery disease. I'd been told that I had a cataract on my left eye – a small one, a growing one. All in less than two years. From man to old man. Dying man. Careful man. Self-pitying, pathetic man. I'd been told not to drink and I was getting hammered – I was already hammered. I was my young self, drunk, sober, drunk, sober several times in a day. I was drunk. I was drunk and angry, drunk and happy. Drunk and lost. Drunk and just drunk. I was missing something.

I checked my phone. I'd missed nothing.

I washed my hands. It was cold here – it was nice. I was still alone. I went to the wall opposite the sink. I kept my eyes on the door upstairs and I put my face, my left cheek, against the wall, the white tiles. I felt the cold go through me. Down me. I was steadier, sturdier. I went back to the stairs. I remembered what he'd said, I remembered what I'd said. I wanted to keep going. To keep going at him. I had to keep the anger. He had to know and I had to get it right.

I was steadier, lighter. I was ready to beat him.

I checked my phone again; I took it out. I'd done it already – I remembered that.

—You said you had a stalker, he said when I got back.

—No, I didn't.

—You did.

—I told Faye I had a stalker, I said. —That's what I said. But you weren't listenin'.

—Ah, Davy.

—No, no – sorry, I said. —But I need to get this straight. You'd no right to say wha' you said abou' Faye there. It was just crude an' you were tryin' to make me

250

go against her, even though you might not be conscious o' that. An' her name was definitely Mags.

He looked at me. That was it – he looked at me. He didn't try to interrupt or contradict. He didn't smile this time, he didn't shake his head. He let me talk.

—There was a gig, I said. —In the Magnet. I'm nearly certain it was the Magnet. The Atrix – the band. I was goin' to bring Mags an' you said I couldn't. You said it was disloyal, I could meet her on Saturday night or any other night o' the week, but not Friday. Disloyal to fuckin' you, by the way. Friday night was our night. An' I remember thinkin' tha' that was a load of bollix, but I didn't say it. An' I didn't go an' meet her like I'd said I would, an' I only had her work phone number an' it was too late to phone her. I was supposed to be meetin' her outside Trinity, I think it was – at the gates. An' I didn't go. An' I really liked her.

—No, you didn't, he said now.

—I did, I said. —But I didn't know that until after.

—Jesus, Davy.

—It was always the same, I said. —I'm not blamin' you. I was always the sap.

I ignored the remains of my old pint and went for the new one. It smelt fine, it smelt good. The glass was cold in my hand. I drank. I put the glass to my cheek.

—We always did wha' you wanted, I said.

—Not true.

—True, I said. —I trailed along behind you. Until.

—Are we havin' another?

—Go on.

The barman didn't hesitate. We hadn't crossed a line. I wanted to stay there for ever. I wanted to go back down to the toilet and stay down there. I wanted to stay with Joe. I wanted to kill Joe.

251

—An' I didn't fancy Jessica, I told him.

—You did.

—Only the same way I'd fancy any woman, I said. —I fancied her, was infatuated or whatever, because you insisted on it. If you fell for her, the world had to fuckin' stop. But – me? Sorry, she was nothin' special. Tha' sounds wrong – sorry. But I wasn't fussed.

—Tha' was the fuckin' problem, Davy, he said. —You were never fussed.

—Wha'?

—The stalker, he said. —Go on.

—Wha' d'you mean, I'm not fuckin' fussed?

—Tell me abou' your stalker, he said. —And then I'll tell you if I'm right.

—I told you already, I said. —There wasn't a fuckin' stalker.

—But you told Faye there was.

—Yeah.

—Why?

—The buzz, I suppose.

He laughed.

—I'm changin' me mind, he said.

—Thanks very much, I said. —Tha' word, but. The phrase – the buzz. I feel so fuckin' old sayin' it. It just seems wrong. Like – there's nothin' worse than a fifty-year-old woman pretendin' she's twenty. An' I'm assumin' it works for men as well – that any self-respectin' woman would gag if she heard me sayin' the buzz.

—Does Faye try to be twenty, by the way?

—Leave Faye alone, I said. —An', no, she doesn't. But I'm bettin' Trish fuckin' does.

—More, thirty, he said. —No – forty. No, Trish is great. An' forty, like – I don't even know what it means. An' who said it was okay to have a go at Trish?

—Sorry.

—Fuck you.

—We're quits.

—Jesus.

—We're quits.

—Okay.

—I've no idea wha' bein' forty used to involve, I said.

—Same here, said Joe. —But a kid, bein' a kid – I remember tha', no bother. An' the twenties.

—Yep, I said. —Like yesterday.

—And now – the way we are now.

—Yeah.

—I could talk all fuckin' night abou' tha', he said. —But the years in between?

—We might as well never've fuckin' lived them, I said.

—It does feel tha' way sometimes, he said. —Maybe we were just too busy. The stalker – go on.

He didn't care about the stalker. He was trying to get me back. He was letting me talk. He was asking me to forgive him. I already had.

—It was just a work thing, I told him. —Like the one you were talkin' about. A Friday.

—Dress As You Like Day.

—I'd say it was before all tha', I said. —The whole dress as you like thing. How long has tha' shite been on the go?

—Oh, fuck. Ten years? Twenty? I don't know. I'd know if it'd started when we were in our twenties. I'd remember the fuckin' day.

—Exactly, I said. —But anyway, the kids were still small – I remember tha' much. It was just down to the pub after work. The English are funny – more formal tha' way. But now an' again someone would just say

253

let's go for a pint an' it would happen. I'd have phoned Faye, to tell her.

—An' no problem?

—No – no, I said. —None. Never. But, anyway, it was just one o' those ones. That's why I was so hammered by the time I got home. I don't think I even had a packet o' crisps all nigh'. I don't do it any more.

—Eat crisps?

—No, I said. —Fuck crisps. I don't do the drinks thing after work any more.

—Same here.

I could tell, my time with the mic was running out.

—I'm the oldest person in the place, I said. —By a distance. An' I feel it if I'm with them.

—I know wha' you mean.

—An' it's not the drink, I said. —This – tonight, like. I haven't drunk like this in – Jesus. Years. But it's the company, the others. I haven't a clue wha' they're talkin' about.

—Same here, he said.

—The words, I said. —The language. I end up wonderin' is it English. An' I'm living in fuckin' England, by the way. But anyway, this was years ago. Down to the boozer with a gang.

—English pubs are shite.

—Not all o' them. But, yeah. This one was okay.

—Wha' d'you drink over there?

—I drink bitter.

—Ah, Jesus. Fuckin' bitter?

—It's an acquired taste, I said. —An' I've acquired it. When in Rome.

—Drink piss.

—I like it, I said. —Anyway –.

I hung there for a while – over a bowl of words and sentences. I could pick one up – woman – and see where, how far I could carry it. I could make up a life to match his. Have an affair. Launch one here, see what I could do with it.

—It was one o' those days, I said. —When you're so tired, so – I don't know – wired as well, you can feel the first pint nibblin' away at you immediately, you know. I was drunk before I was drunk, if tha' makes sense.

—Been there.

—Half an hour later my head was hangin' over the table – I was bollixed. I remember gettin' into a taxi an' it was still daylight – it was the summer, like. An' I got back out of it before it started movin'. I just thought the kids would still be up when I got home an' I wasn't havin' tha', the state I was in. I didn't want them seein' me. So I was staggerin' around the town. Tryin' to walk straight, you know. An' failing fuckin' miserably.

—Where is it again?

—Wantage, I said. —It's in Oxfordshire.

—Strange name.

—Yeah, at first – a bit. A lot o' the place names sound strange, when you're away from the towns tha' have football teams.

—Scunthorpe.

—Macclesfield.

—Hartlepool.

—Halifax, I said. —So, yeah, it's all a bit confusin', even though it's only over the water. But you get used to the names. East Challow, East Lockinge, Stanford in the Vale. It's just English an' that's where we are, so fair enough. An' they haven't a fuckin' clue abou' the place names over here.

—The ones that'd bother comin' over.

—Ah, lay off, I said. —But, anyway, I couldn't remember wha' pub I'd come out of.

—Did yis always go to the same one?

—Yeah, we did, I said. —The Lord Alfred's Head. But I couldn't remember it. I was so drunk, it was like I'd taken tha' date rape drug – what's it called?

—Rohypnol – is it?

—Sounds right, I said. —I was wiped.

—Come here, though, said Joe. —Did someone slip somethin' into your drink?

—I never thought o' tha', I said. —Christ –. There's a fuckin' thought, though. After all these years. But no. I don't think so. An' I found the pub – I figured out where I was. An' I went back in. But I didn't go over to the gang again. I didn't sit down. I went back out an' got into another taxi. But all I remember then is being in the hall, at home, an' one of me shoes was missin'.

—Rohypnol – I'm telling you.

—No. No – but maybe you're right. Why would someone from work do tha'?

—Your stalker.

—But there wasn't a stalker.

—Maybe there was, he said. —Tryin' to get into your boxers.

—She wouldn't've needed to drug me.

—Maybe she did, though, said Joe. —The happily married man. She'd've had to drug your smugness.

—Fuck off, I said. —But, anyway, I had nothin' to tell Faye, so I told her about the stalker, the woman who wouldn't leave me alone.

256

—Out o' nowhere, said Joe.

—Not quite, I said.

—Oh, oh.

—But basically, yeah, I said. —I made her up.

—How did she take it – Faye?

—She was all set to get me into the car an' back to the pub, to point her out an' confront her.

—Brilliant, he said.

—She was hoppin', I said. —Fuckin' furious.

—Fuckin' sure she was. An' there actually was a woman, was there?

—Not really.

—Go on, yeh fucker.

—It was nothin'.

The feeling, the rush of happiness, of achievement, surprised me. I was worth listening to.

—But you see, said Joe. —There's the thing. Faye would've known there was somethin'. She'd've sensed it. She'd've felt threatened.

—There was no need for her to feel threatened, I said.

—You're missin' the point, Davy. You're missin' the fuckin' point. She'd've been feelin' elated, up to the fuckin' challenge. Like Trish.

—You split up with Trish.

—Yeah – but.

—Wha'? Trish can't've been all tha' fuckin' elated, Joe. She threw you out.

—Oh, she was, he said. —She really was. A fight on her hands – she was fuckin' delighted.

—A fight for you?

—For herself.

—Jesus, Joe.

—Wha'?

257

—You sound – you sound like such a cunt sayin' tha'.

—Wha'?

—Tha' you were doin' Trish a favour by havin' it off with Jessica. Sorry – I don't mean to be crude there. But for fuck sake.

—I'm not sayin' tha'.

—You kind of are.

—Maybe I am, he said. —But it's not as simple as tha'.

I could think of nothing I wanted to say. I didn't want to make up the woman now, or Faye's reaction to her. I didn't trust myself. I didn't trust Joe. He'd examine every word; he'd catch me out. I didn't want to hear his male-infidelity-was-good-for-women theory, and he didn't either. He'd gone silent too. He was looking at his pint. He picked it up. He drank. He put it down. I put my hand around my glass. It still felt cold; I'd be able for it. I picked it up.

—Where were we? said Joe.

—Don't know.

—Tha' stuff there, he said. —Abou' Trish comin' alive an' tha'. I wish I hadn't said it.

—Okay.

—I didn't really mean it, he said.

—Grand.

—Was there a woman?

—No, I said. —There was – no. It's not worth mentionin'.

—Did she get in the car?

—Faye?

—Yeah.

—No, I said. —No, she didn't. I fell asleep.

—You didn't even get a ride out of it.

—Joe.
—Sorry.
—Okay.
—Drink talkin'.
—Yeah.

The air outside was good. The day's heat was gone. I examined my walk, my feet – I was fine. I was surprised, pleased. Joe was beside me at first but the numbers coming at us on the path around to College Green made walking together tricky. There was no talking. I led the way. That surprised me too.

He was beside me again.

—Dublin is unbelievable, he said. —The fuckin' crowds.

—Yeah.

—It's never quiet, he said. —We could drink all night if we'd a mind to.

—There's a fuckin' thought.

We walked side by side, and separately when there wasn't room, beside the new tram tracks, to the bottom of Grafton Street. I wondered if I was fitter than him, if that was why I was in the lead; I could walk faster than Joe. I didn't think so. He wasn't overweight; his breathing wasn't laboured. I half expected him to trip me.

We were on Grafton Street now.

—I need to get cash, he said.

—I've cash, I told him.

—I want some of me own, bud, he said.

We were at the AIB, beside Weir's jewellers. My father had bought me a watch in there, when I started secondary school. I remembered him giving it to me the night before the big day. It was in a box, not wrapped.

—I quite liked school, he'd said.

—Thanks.

—The Brothers weren't the worst.

—Okay.

—Your mother would be proud, he said.

—Thanks.

—Very proud.

Joe had joined one of the queues at the cash dispensers. There were two homeless men – young lads, wrapped up for a much colder night – sitting against the wall, on the ground beside the machines. There was a couple – man and woman – putting down a flattened cardboard box in a shop porch across the street. They were young, my children's age. I'd noticed it before, the last time I'd been in Dublin. But I'd forgotten. Every shopfront seemed to have a lone man or couple.

I looked at Joe. He was at one of the machines, his face close to the screen. He was holding his glasses over his head with one hand as he tapped in his PIN with the other. He looked at the homeless lad beside him; he'd put his glasses back on. I saw him put a hand in his pocket. He bent down slightly and dropped a coin into the lad's paper cup, then straightened and took his cash and card. The lad sitting on the ground said something, and Joe laughed and said something back. The money and card went into the breast pocket of his shirt, before he turned and saw me. He was buttoning the pocket as he came up to me.

—All set, he said.

—Wha' did your man say to you?

—He offered to mind my card for me.

—Brilliant.

—Off we go.

And, again, I was leading. My shoulders, my muscles, seemed to protest; they were pulling me back. But I pushed through the stiffness. I didn't turn, in case I'd see he'd gone and left me alone. I expected to hear him laughing.

We were at the corner of Wicklow Street.

—We could go this way, he said.

I kept going straight.

—Fine, he said.

He'd increased his pace and he came up beside me again.

—I'll go with the flow, he said.

—You said that earlier.

—I was remindin' meself, he said.

—Abou' Jessica, I said. —Yourself an' Jessica.

—Yeah, he said. —A pint in the International would've been nice.

—We're goin' to George's.

—True, he said. —But en route. Wha' was it we used to call them?

—Pit stops.

—That's right, he said. —The pubs between the pubs.

—It's more piss stops these days, I said.

—That's clever.

—Jesus though, Joe, the homeless people.

—I know.

—It's desperate.

I'd been looking at another couple in a doorway. They were both lying down, under an open sleeping bag and a damp-looking blanket. The man – the boy – was leaning on an elbow. She looked even younger; she was lying back, her head on a backpack. He was holding a thick paperback and they were both reading

261

it. Further up the street there was a trestle table, flasks, Tupperware full of sandwiches. Like the remains of a street party – until we got up to it, and passed. There was laughter, there was friendship, I thought. But the faces – caved in, haunted, frightened, and – somehow, some of them – childlike.

—It's desperate, I said again, quieter.

I loved the sound of the word, and the feel of the word, coming from me. I was still a Dubliner and I liked being a Dubliner, despite the homeless men and women – because of the homeless men and women, the wit of the kid back at the bank. It made no sense – it made drunken sense. I felt hopelessly angry, stupidly proud, close to crying. I felt at home. But I wouldn't be coming home. Dublin wasn't my home.

We were on Chatham Street now. I saw the bronze arms holding up the lights on either side of the door.

—Neary's, I said.

—Pit stop.

—Piss stop.

—George's is only a minute away.

—My bladder doesn't do minutes.

We were going where I decided we were going.

Pubs, the world of men. There were women too. But the world – the pub – was made by men, put there for men. There were no women serving, no lounge girls, very few women sitting on the stools along the counters. Dark wood, old mirrors, smoke-drenched walls and ceilings. And photographs of men. Jockeys, footballers, men drinking, writers – all men – rebels, boxers. The women were guests. The men were at home. There was a day, I parked myself on a stool and, although I'd never sat on it before, I knew it was mine. All of the stools were mine. That particular stool was in George's but it was the stool we found in every pub in Dublin. I'd discovered my life. The shy man's heaven. A string of pubs, connected by streets and lanes, the streets in plain sight but secret. Poolbeg Street, Sackville Place, Fleet Street, Essex Street, Dame Lane, Wicklow Street, Exchequer Street, South William Street, Chatham Street, Chatham Row, Duke Street, South Anne Street, Duke Lane, George's Street, Fade Street, Drury Street, Stephen's Street, Coppinger Row, Johnson's Court, South King Street. The streets were sometimes crowded, sometimes deserted, but only we knew why they were there, their real, hidden purpose. They got us to Mulligan's, Bowe's, the Sackville Lounge, the International, the Stag's Head, the Dame Tavern, the Long Hall, the Dawson Lounge, Neary's, Rice's, Sheehan's, the Hogan Stand, Grogan's, Kehoe's, the Duke, the Palace, George's. The one big pub, the Dublin pub, the light, the smoke, the other men. We were men, with other men. The voices. The man at the bar of Sheehan's telling other men – and telling us – how he'd escaped from John of Gods, where he'd been sent by his sons to dry out. His eyes watered, his hand shook as he reached for his glass, but his voice told us what lay ahead and what we already had. So this chap stands up and he says, My name's Jim and I am an alcoholic, and another chap gets up and he says, My name's Fergus and I'm an alcoholic as well, and then the chap sitting beside me, he gets up and he says, My name's Paddy and I'm an alcoholic, so then it seems to be my turn, they're all looking at me, so I stand up and I say, My name's Tommy and I'm going over the fuckin' wall the minute it gets dark enough. The laughter, the love, defiance. Nothing about him scared us. The voice in Mulligan's, the deep voice that shook the glasses on the nearer tables, although it was never loud. Today's Cunt was what we called him. He'd see us come in; he was always there. Today's cunt is Charlie Haughey, or Today's cunt is Leonid Brezhnev. He never repeated a name. Haughey. Brezhnev. Reagan. Johnny Logan. Thatcher. Mr T. Garret FitzGerald. Garry Birtles. Pat Spillane. Today's cunts are Def Leppard. He worked in the *Evening Press*, one of the barmen told us, but he was there whenever we walked in. There was the man with the suit and ponytail who read the *New Statesman*. He sat for hours at the bar. He stood, he left. He ordered his gin and tonic without opening his mouth. He paid for it, he took his change. He never spoke a word. The world of men. Where they – where we – could be who we wanted to be, who and what we were going to be. Today's cunt is the Reverend Ian Paisley. The men stepped out of a world, into their real world. The secret one. The sacred one. The one that only men knew. Today's cunt is Billy Ocean. Everything outside was an act, an endurance. Inside the pub – that was where life was. Nothing mattered, and that was all that mattered. We entered it. I thought we'd stay there.

—You made it, said Joe.

—Just about, I said.

—Never pass a jacks, he said. —Advice for the agein' man. Never waste an erection, never trust a fart, never pass a jacks.

I started to laugh, and so did he.

—The fart one's great, I said.

—Isn't it? Ever do it?

—Shit meself?

—Yeah.

—No.

—Same here, he said. —A few close calls, but.

—Close calls don't count.

—That's probably true, he said. —We didn't come in here much, did we? Back in the day.

—Ah, we did.

—It was a pit stop, though, wasn't it?

—Yeah, I said. —I don't think we ever stayed here. For the night, I mean.

—No, he said. —Good pub, though.

—Yeah.

—They're all fuckin' good. There's still plenty o' good pubs in Dublin.

He'd ordered the pints while I was in the Gents. I'd checked my phone but I'd missed no calls or messages. And that was worrying me now; I wasn't sure why.

The place wasn't full. There were empty stools. But we stood. He picked up his pint and brought it to his face, his eyes. He looked at it over his glasses. Then he looked at me.

—Come here, he said. —It's really good to see you, man.

I picked up my pint. It felt good in my hand. We tapped our glasses. We were careful doing it.

—Good to see you too, I said.

—Really fuckin' good, he said. —I'm glad we came into town.

—Yeah.

I looked around.

—It hasn't changed much, I said. —Has it?

—Don't think so, he said. —It's much the same.

—That's good.

—It is.

—We're the oldest people here, I said.

—An' it isn't tha' long ago we'd've been the youngest.

—It feels tha' way, sometimes.

—It fuckin' does, he said. —Fuckin' *tempus fugit*. Look at your woman over there, though. Jesus, the legs. No – sorry. She's half our age – fuckin' less. Jesus, though – fuck it. She's amazin'.

I shrugged. I'd looked at her, the woman – the girl. She was lovely. They were all lovely.

—No harm, I said.

—No, he agreed. —An' I suppose –. I think, anyway. Here's my theory. If we didn't notice things like tha' – the girl there. If it didn't make us sit up, if it didn't give us tha' little bit o' joy. It'd be time to bow out, wouldn't it? Am I righ'?

—No, you're right.

—The one-way flight to Switzerland.

—Yep.

—One last wank an' then the electric chair, or whatever they use over there.

—I think it might be more humane than the chair.

—I read a book about electric chairs once.

—Did you?

—I did, yeah, he said. —I can't remember much about it. But I did – I read it. Very interestin', it was.

—Informative.

—Fuckin' very, he said. —An' great pictures.

—Ah, no.

—Yeah, he said. —Nothin' gory now. Just photographs of empty chairs, mostly. In the different prisons, like – the different states of America. They were like art. They *were* art.

—The chairs?

—The photographs. The chairs too, but. They're spectacular an' – the straps.

—I used to think wha' made them really frightenin' – and fascinatin' as well – was tha' they were nearly like ordinary chairs.

—That's righ' – you're right.

—Big armchairs tha' were designed by a chap who could only design kitchen chairs.

—That's it, he said. —Brilliant. Anyway, I don't think I'd mind goin' ou' tha' way. An electric chair made in Switzerland would be high-end, by the way. Well worth the fare.

—You don't have to go all the way to Switzerland to get yourself electrocuted.

—Tha' might be missin' the point, though.

—The trip is part o' the – the process, is it?

—I think so, yeah. The journey. A day shoppin' in Zurich, then the chair.

We were glowing – I was sure we were glowing. We were fresh again, young again, hilarious. In the world of men – even though there were more women in the place than men. And that, somehow, made it even more a world of men. We were the men at the bar.

He drank. He swallowed.

—Good pint.

—Good pint.

—Good pub.

—Very good pub.

—Good to be here.

—Yeah.

—I haven't forgotten.

267

—Wha'?

—I was tellin' you somethin'.

—About Jessica, I said.

—Abou' me an' Jess, that's righ'.

—You go with the flow.

—That's right, he said. —It sounds flippant, like I don't care – I couldn't give much of a shite. But that's not what I mean.

—That's not what I thought, I told him.

I was liking him. I was remembering him. I was happy here. I tasted my pint. It tasted good – it felt good.

—I love her, Davy, said Joe. —Simple as tha'.

—Okay, I said. —Good.

—Simple as.

—Okay.

—Trish says that a lot.

—Wha'?

—Simple as.

—Okay.

—A dam burst, he said.

—I don't get you.

—Just tha', he said. —I saw her –

—Trish?

—Jess, he said. —Fuck off. No –. No – shit –

—You're fine, I said. —I understand. You're not dismissin' Trish.

—No.

—Go on, I said. —You were sayin' abou' Jess. G'wan.

—I've forgotten wha' –

—The dam burst.

—I saw her, he said. —That's right. In the school. An' the dam burst. The thirty-five years or whatever. Thirty-seven. The missin' years.

—Missin'?

—Kind o', yeah, he said. —I'm not denyin' I'd a life – a good fuckin' life, by the way. I'm not sayin' tha' for a minute. My kids – fuck me, I'd die for them an' that's not the drink talkin' now.

—No, I know, I said.

I wanted to agree with him, I wanted to follow him. I wanted to get this finished.

—An' Trish, he said. —We had a good life. I love Trish – I really do. If she walked in here now, I think I'd start cryin'. I love her. So, like, I haven't been sleep-walkin' around the last four decades. Or – what's the other one? Livin' a lie. I haven't been livin' a lie. I'd never fuckin' claim tha'.

He was looking at me and listening to himself, to what he was saying. I was his mirror.

—I know tha', I said.

—If I could work it, he said. —If we could arrange it –. An' actually, I'm sure we eventually will. It'll be grand. I think it will. But I hate not seein' the kids. I hate, like – tha' they've turned against me. An' I don't blame Trish for that either, by the way.

—No.

—But –. Anyway.

—Goin' with the flow, I reminded him.

—Well, he said. —I wish I'd never said tha'. To be honest with you.

—I think it was me said it.

—Was it?

—I think so, yeah.

—Well, it sounds terrible, he said. —Not wha' I meant at all. What I feel.

—You said, the dam.

269

—The dam, he said. —That's right. The fuckin' dam. Good. This is what I mean. What I mean is – bear with me, Davy.

—I'm here.

—Good man. So. When I met Jess, it wasn't –. The dam didn't burst, exactly. It was more, the water level rose. Like a lock in a canal. A lock more than a dam. The lock gate opened an' the water level rose. Everythin' filled in, if tha' makes sense. The lock – like. It's the years between seein' Jess in George's back then an' seein' her again. It was empty –

—Empty?

—Not empty – fuck it. This isn't perfect, what I'm tryin' to say. Not empty. Why did you interrupt me?

—I didn't interrupt you.

—Ah, you fuckin' did.

—Lads.

It was a barman, a tall young lad with a white shirt and a dickie bow.

—Sorry, I said.

—Keep it down, he said.

—Yeah, sorry, said Joe. —We've had a few, you know.

—No problem.

—We're harmless, said Joe.

—I can see that.

We were twice his age and we probably reminded him of his father, or his grandfather. He moved away from us.

I waited a few seconds.

—Sorry, I said.

—Okay, said Joe.

—I didn't interrupt you, I said. —I didn't. I was just lookin' for clarification.

—Clarification?

270

—Yes, Joe. You know what it means. You said the lock was empty.

—Fuck the lock – fuck the fuckin' lock.

He was keeping his voice down. He was smiling.

—This is hopeless, he said.

He looked for his pint on the counter, then saw that it was in his hand.

—For fuck sake.

He laughed.

—Jesus, he said. —How did tha' happen?

—Wha'?

—How did I not know it was in me fuckin' hand? We're not tha' drunk. Are we?

—I'm grand.

I held up my pint.

—Mine's here, look it.

—Good man.

—The empty lock, I said.

—God, you're such a bitch, said Joe.

—Well, you dug the fuckin' thing, I said.

—I read a book about tha' once as well, he said. —Russian prisoners diggin' a canal. Political prisoners. Durin' Stalin's time, before the war. A huge fuckin' thing tha' turned ou' to be useless. Thousands o' men were buried under it. Fuckin' thousands o' them.

—The empty lock.

—It wasn't empty, he said. —It was just full o' the wrong liquid. No – fuck. Let's just abandon the canal. This isn't makin' me happy.

He wasn't joking. The glee, the messing, the drunk intelligence – they were gone. He looked tired. He even yawned.

—Sorry, he said. —Sorry.

271

He turned his pint on the counter, an inch, another inch.

—I've changed, he said. —But I keep forgettin'.

—We all change, I said.

—Well, I'm sure that's true. But I hate hearin' it.

—Why?

—It makes it harder to explain the thing, he said. —It's as if it's a thing that happens to every man. We were talkin' about it earlier, weren't we? A midlife thing. Or post-midlife. Or whatever it's called – if it has a fuckin' name. But, look it. I give up.

He looked at the counter. He looked at the floor. I looked at him looking at the counter and at the floor. He looked at the counter and he looked at me.

—She isn't happy, Davy, he said.

I said nothing. I wasn't going to interrupt. I looked at him. He was moving.

It was me. I was the one moving, swaying from foot to foot. Moving to a slowish song I wasn't hearing. I stopped. I put a hand on the counter. Anchored myself.

—No, he said. —I don't think she's ever been wha' you'd call happy. Isn't that terrible?

—Yeah.

—Sad.

—Yeah.

—Never, he said. —Fuckin' awful. It breaks my heart. Serious now – it does. Now –. Before I go on. I have to say this as well. She isn't fuckin' miserable. That's not wha' I mean.

—I know.

—A pain in the arse, I mean. She isn't. She isn't a whinger, Davy.

He was looking at the floor again. He looked back up at me.

—She's, he said. —She's lovely. An' one o' the reasons she's lovely is because she's so unhappy. Davy.

It was like he wanted me to say something. But I knew he didn't. He wanted me to look at him. Straight at him.

—I've never known an unhappy woman before, Davy.

—Trish?

I hadn't meant to say anything. But I loved saying the name. Trish. Its effect – what happened. It was like an electric shock, static electricity, a quick jolt up the arm.

—The happiest woman in Ireland, he said. —Happiest woman ever born – that's my Trish.

He smiled.

—She'd swallow the world, he said. —You know those yokes, Davy?

—Wha' yokes?

—On the water, he said. —The sea.

—I don't know what you mean.

—Ah, you do. The yokes. Noisy fuckin' things. But good crack.

—I don't know.

—You fuckin' do, he said. —You do. I can't think o' the fuckin' name. Jet ski – jet skis. I knew I knew it. D'you know what I'm talkin' abou'?

—Jet skis?

—Exactly.

—Wha' about them?

—Ah, for fuck sake. Wha' I'm saying – what I'm sayin' is. Fuckin' –. Trish is a fuckin' jet ski. That's what I mean. She's fuckin' brilliant.

—Wha'? I said. —You ride her in the water?

He laughed – he burst out laughing. He exploded.

—For fuck sake.

He wiped his eyes. I was laughing too. He put his hand on my shoulder. He staggered, a bit. He kept his hand there, then dropped it, and looked at the counter for his pint.

—Her energy, he said. —That's all I meant.

—Why didn't you just say energy then? I asked.

—Fair enough, he said. —Fair enough. Cunt.

He picked up his glass. It was half full. I was ahead of him.

—Forget jet skis, he said. —Dams, locks, fuckin' jet skis – forget all o' them. Here's one – here's –. Trish is a force o' nature. Is tha' clear enough for you?

—Yeah – grand.

—It passes muster.

—It does.

—Ah, good, he said. —If a force o' nature is a good thing – yeah?

—Yeah.

—Trish is a very good force o' nature, he said. —I'll tell you, man, I've been blessed.

—Okay.

I was wishing I knew Trish.

—Jess, he said. —Jess. Davy?

—Wha'?

—I'm talkin' abou' Jess now, okay?

—Yeah.

—Wha' sort of – wha' kind of a machine is Faye, by the way?

—Wha'?

—Trish is a jet ski, he said. —What's Faye?

—You said we'd forget about jet skis.

—Fuck jet skis. Come on. What machine is Faye? It is Faye – I'm right, yeah?

—Yeah.

It wasn't just the drink. He was being nasty again, when he could concentrate.

—I haven't thought about it, I told him.

—Go on, come on, he said. —She has to be somethin'. A toaster.

—No.

—A fuckin' –. I don't fuckin' know. A hairdryer.

—Forget it, Joe.

—A Dyson yoke.

—Fuckin' forget it, Joe.

He looked at me. He shrugged. He smiled.

—Grand, he said. —Point taken. No machinery.

He looked at his drink. He brought it to his mouth.

—Actin' the maggot, he said.

He drank.

—Sorry, he said. —It was wha' my mother always said. Anyway. You're actin' the maggot, Joseph.

He drank again. He put the glass back on the counter. He parked it. He brought it slightly forward, and back. It almost toppled.

—Yikes – shite. Leave well enough alone. Whatever tha' fuckin' means.

He picked the glass up again.

—The things we say. We don't even know wha' they mean. Jess isn't a force o' nature.

—So, I said. —Jess isn't a jet ski.

He didn't laugh. He shook his head.

—No, he said. —She isn't. You're right. I love her, Davy, d'you know tha'?

—You told me, yeah.

—Yeah, he said. —Yeah – well. I think that's why I love her. I think.

—She's different to Trish.

—Yeah. No – yeah. I don't know. I don't think so. It's not either or. Well, it is. Unfortunately.

—Is tha' wha' you want, Joe?

—Wha'?

—A *ménage à trois*?

—A wha'?

—You know what I mean, I said.

—No, he said.

He'd thought about it.

—No, he said. —No, I know wha' you mean. An' no. I don't want one o' them – a menage. An' come here. Not because it wouldn't work.

—It wouldn't.

—God, no. Fuck, no. Never. But it doesn't matter. It never really occurred to me – not the sex thing way, anyway.

He'd lowered his voice. He was looking at me now over his glasses. Then he lifted his head.

—I make her happy, he said.

I took a guess.

—Jess.

He didn't nod or shake his head.

—I don't have to do anythin', Davy, he said. —I don't really know how to explain it – sorry. It must be a pain in the arse.

—No.

—Listenin' to this shite. It must be.

—No.

—Go on to fuck.

—Okay, I said. —It is.

—Is it?

—No, I said. —I'm messin' with you. It isn't.

—I appreciate tha', he said. —Good to see you, man. Where's my fuckin' pint? Here – look it.

He put his hand around his glass, then – as if bracing himself – lifted it.

—I'm reluctant, he said.

He examined the word. He looked as it passed his eyes.

He was happy with it.

—I'm reluctant to say this, he said. —I'm nearly reluctant. But I'll say it an' we'll see where it gets us.

He looked at his pint. He drank from it.

—It's like livin' in a fairy tale, he said.

—Yeah, I said. —You mentioned the film – earlier.

—Did I?

—Tha' one –

—Wha' one? *Stardust*. It must've been *Stardust*.

—Yeah, I said. —You mentioned *Stardust*.

—No, he said. —No, I mean I did. But I don't mean I'm livin' in the story of tha' one. In the plot – I don't mean tha'.

—Okay.

—I mean, he said. —Like – I'm reluctant to say it. I said tha'. Cos it's mad. But there you go.

—I don't understand.

—Join the fuckin' club, Davy.

He finished his pint. He put the glass down, then picked it up and put it at the far edge of the counter, as far away as he could put it.

—The demon drink, he said. —That's a phrase I can understand. No problem understandin' tha' one. I don't drink much, by the way. That's why I'm hammered. Are we hammered, Davy?

—We are.

—Grand, he said. —I am, anyway. I have magical powers.

He looked at me.

—I do, he said. —Magical powers.

He held up his hands, wriggled his fingers.

—Not the spooky kind, he said. —I can't –. Fuckin' –. Bend spoons an' tha'. I can't bend spoons, Davy. I'm not Uri what's his name. Geller.

—That's a relief.

—There was a fuckin' chancer.

—Yeah.

—Spoons, me bollix.

He picked up his empty glass.

—What I mean, he said. —Wha' it is. The fairy-tale thing. It's like this. I can make her happy. An' by the way. I think I'm the first person to be able to do tha'. So – come here. Just let me concentrate for a bit. I'll sober up. Then I can explain it properly. Once an' for all. Once an' for fuckin' all. An' forget abou' magical powers by the way – that's not wha' I mean.

—Are you happy, David?

Faye had looked up from her plate. I didn't know what to say. It was a trap. It wasn't.

—Yes, I said.

—Good, she said. —So am I.

—Are you?

—Yes, she said. —I think I am. But.

—What?

—What does it mean? Happy.

—I don't know.

—I'm not giddy, like, she said. —I'm content. Are you?

—Yeah.

—Are you?

—Yes.

—Good, she said.

It was terrifying.

—That's all I want, she said.

—Same here, I said.

—What?

—I want you to be happy.

—Well, she said. —We seem to be quite efficient at it, so. Making one another happy. Aren't we great?

She smiled.

—How's the beef? I asked her.

—Oh, I'm very happy with it, thanks, David, she said. —Very happy. It's a lovely piece of beef. Fair play to you.

—It's not too pink?

—God, no. It could never be too pink. As the man said. You seem nervous.

—No.

—Tense.

—No.

—Are you happy enough, yourself? With the beef.

—I am, yes, I said. —I think I timed it well.

—I think you did too. It's all I want.

—Beef?

She smiled.

—You, she said. —You to be happy. Do you believe me?

—Yes.

—Do you?

—Yes.

—Good.

*　*　*

He was staring at his glass again. He looked up.

—All I have to do is listen, he said.

—To wha'?

—Jess, he said. —She –. Everythin' I say must sound mad. How long've we been drinkin'?

—Hours.

—Hours, he said. —We ate earlier, didn't we?

—Yeah.

—Tha' seems like days ago.

He was right. I couldn't remember what I'd eaten.

—So anyway, he said. —I've been tryin' to get to the point all night. Find the words that'll make sense. An' that's it – after all tha'. I listen.

He was changing again. His eyes had cleared. He'd said he was going to sober up, and that seemed to be happening. I looked at him and remembered what he'd said about having magical powers.

—So, he said. —Listen. I go home.

—New home?

—New home, he said. —Yeah. Yeah – I think I can call it tha'. It feels like home. I suppose.

—Where is it?

—Clontarf, he said. —Not far from where we were earlier.

—Right.

—Dollymount, more.

—Okay.

—So, yeah. I go home. An' it's like I've always been there. I said that earlier as well – or somethin' like it. An' it's not necessarily because I think I've always been there. But she does.

He seemed happy, relieved; he'd said what he'd wanted to say.

—I don't get you, I said. —Sorry.

—Wha' don't you get?

—She thinks you've been livin' with her for years?

—Not exactly, he said. —But yeah. That's it.

—Is that okay?

—Wha'?

—Are you alright with it?

—With wha'?

—Tha' she thinks you've been livin' with her since the early '80s.

—It's not fuckin' exact, he said. —I told you. Not literal. But she feels it. So – so do I.

—You're made for each other – somethin' like tha'?

—That'll do, he said. —Tha' covers it, I think. Like I said. I listen. An' I don't think I ever did tha' before. I don't think I had to. Trish didn't give a fuck if I was listenin' or not.

—Tha' sounds unfair.

—You're right, he said. —I regret sayin' it. Kind of. Not really, though. Fuck it, Davy, I'm in love. I run home, just to see her.

I remembered that. I remembered charging for the train, the bus, to get to Faye's house, our flat, wherever I was going to see her. She was often there ahead of me and I'd loved that too, watching her as she saw me arrive, the smile – the glee, the reined-back excitement – that it provoked. There was once, we'd just moved to England, and I charged in the door. She was watching *Neighbours*.

—I was lying back in the bed in my lingerie, she said. —But then I got up when you weren't coming home.

—What lingerie?

—Well, I'll tell you, David, I hid it. And it's going to stay hidden, so it is.

281

I could still imagine that charge, a man of my age, of Joe's age, racing to see a woman, to be seen by a woman. A sixty-year-old man's charge, but the excitement and the honesty could still be there. It didn't have to be a different woman; I wanted to run to Faye. I wanted to look at Faye and find her looking at me. Without the questions or the concern, or embarrassment.

I could feel it on my skin, in my legs; I wasn't drunk, again. We were stranded on some island of sobriety. We had a few minutes to talk. I had a few minutes to listen; the tide would be coming in again. Any minute.

—What's it like? I asked him.

—Like?

Aggression took over – I could see it – but he pulled it back.

—The house, d'you mean?

—Not really, I said. —But yeah.

—Well, it's nothin' like ours, he said. —Jesus, listen to me – ours. I mean –

—I know what you mean.

—It's in bits, he said. —I'm tellin' you. Trish would go fuckin' spare if she ever saw it. You left me for this? But it's cosy.

—Fuckin' cosy?

—Wrong word, he said.

He grinned.

—Comfortable, he said. —An' anyway, it's not the house tha' matters. The décor. I never gave a toss about tha' shite, anyway. It's her, Davy. I'm in a different world, man. I'm livin' in a life I never actually lived.

—Sounds mad, Joe.

—Fuck off, it's not. Well, it is. A bit, just. But I've been given a second chance.

—Joe –

282

—More to the point, he said. —Give me a minute here. More to the point. She's been given a second chance. That's what it is, Davy. I'll tell you a thing she said to me early on an' it nearly killed me. I shouldn't be tellin' you this but wha' harm, you're my buddy. An' you know her.

—I don't.

—You did. Back in the day. I hate tha' sayin' or whatever it is. Is it day or days?

—Day.

—Yeah, well. Only cunts say it.

He grinned.

—In our youth, he said. —You knew her in our youth. An' you fancied her as well.

—I didn't.

—You fuckin' did so.

—Wha' did she say?

—Will we have another pint here? he asked.

—Go on, yeah, I said. —We'll never get to George's.

—'Course we will.

He called the barman.

—Excuse me –. Yeah, two more, please. Thanks.

—Wha' did she say? I asked him again.

—Well, I could tell you. Word for word, like. But without the context, it'll sound dreadful. But come here, you're sound as a pound, I know tha'. But –

—Tell me an' then work backwards.

—Why're you so keen to know?

—I'm not, I lied. —But a minute ago you were all set to tell me.

—'I wish I hadn't lived.'

—She said tha'?

—Yeah.

—Jesus, Joe.

—Yeah.

—Jesus – on your second date?

—Fuck off now. But yeah. It was the saddest fuckin'
thing, Davy, I'm not jokin' you.

He looked at me. I looked at him. And we laughed. I
held his right arm, he held my left. And we laughed.

—It's not funny.

—I know.

—It wasn't funny.

—I know.

—It isn't.

We laughed. He took off his glasses and wiped his
eyes, and put them back on and took them off again.

—The fuckin' things are steamin', he said. —The
heat off me face.

—She said tha'? I said.

—Yeah.

—What age is she? Fifteen?

—It wasn't funny.

—Okay.

—It really wasn't funny. I swear to God. Don't look at
me, for fuck sake, I'll start laughin' again. I don't want to.

That got us going again.

—Laughin' like tha', I said. —It makes me want to
piss, sometimes it does. Is it the same with you?

—No, he said. —I don't laugh much, but.

—I'm not fuckin' surprised.

We laughed again.

—Enough, he said. —Enough.

We were wiping our eyes. Mine were sore, too big,
both dry and saturated.

—She's a bit of a clown, Joe, I said. —Is she? She
must be.

He was putting his glasses back on.

—Wha' did you fuckin' say?

—Come on, I said. —I didn't ask to be born.

—That's not wha' she said.

—Near enough.

—Fuck off, Davy. Fuck you.

—Wha'? I said. —We were laughin' a minute ago.

—It wasn't insultin' a minute ago.

—Only because she isn't here.

—Fuck off.

I didn't want this to happen.

—Explain it then, I said.

—Fuck off.

—I'm listenin'. Go on.

I could hear myself, and I didn't sound as I felt – how I wanted to feel. I sounded like my forehead was leaning into his; I was pushing him, goading him. I was rushing past myself, out of my own control.

—Sorry, I said.

It didn't matter. I didn't care about truth. I didn't want the fight.

—Fuck you, he said. —Listen.

—Wha'?

—Trish spoke to Faye once.

—When was this?

—Back in the fuckin' day, he said. —They had a good oul' chat, Trish said. So listen, pal, don't be callin' Jess a fuckin' clown.

—Ah, fuck off, Joe.

—A right fuckin' nut job, Trish said.

—Fuck off.

—You fuck off.

—Fuck off.

★   ★   ★

I looked at my eyes in the toilet mirror. They weren't too red. They fitted in the face; they weren't too bad. They belonged.

I'd say sorry again. I'd go back in and say sorry. I'd finish my pint and leave. He'd tell me to fuck off and I'd go. He'd tell me to fuck off and I'd let him have it; I'd rip his fantasy apart. I'd smash my glass across his head. I'd go back in and he'd be gone. I'd go in and he'd be waiting; he'd tell me something that would knock me to the floor, that would make me hit another man for the first time in my life, that would shut me down, destroy me.

I knew the man I was looking at in the mirror. I was okay, I'd be fine.

I'd apologise. And I'd go. We'd go on to George's, and then I'd go. We'd meet again, we'd keep in touch. He'd let me know he'd gone back to Trish. He'd let me know he'd never really left her. He'd send me a photo of Holly's graduation. I wouldn't apologise. I'd stand there with him and pick up my pint. It was up to him; we could move on, or we wouldn't. He could start a row, continue the row. I didn't care. He could fuck off – I didn't care.

I felt the phone in my pocket. I took it out and looked.

—I have to go, I told him.

—Wha'?

—I've to go, I said. —Sorry.

—What abou' the pints? he said. —We haven't touched them.

—Sorry – I've got to go.

—What's up? he asked.

He could tell I wasn't just deciding to leave; I hadn't come back from the toilet ready to storm out. He could see it was something else.

—Is somethin' wrong?

—My father, I said. —Yeah – my da.

—Is he okay, is he?

I wasn't sure if he heard my answer. I wasn't sure if I spoke the word.

—No.

—Wha'?

—No.

—Ah, Christ, he said. —I'm sorry, Davy. Let's go. Are you goin' home – to his place? I'll come with you.

—No, I said.

—Wha'?

—I'm not goin' home.

I watched Joe lift his fresh pint and take three or four fast gulps from it. The glass was half empty when he took it away from his mouth. I waited.

—Waste not, fuckin' want not, he said.

I wanted him with me.

And I didn't.

He put the glass back on the counter, then placed his hand on his stomach.

—Might regret tha', he said. —I might be climbin' into the bed beside your da. Come on.

I didn't want him to come – I don't think I did – but I got in behind him as he walked quickly to the door. He held it for me and we were out on to Chatham Street.

—Right – where's best for a taxi? he asked himself.

—Stephen's Green.

—South William Street, he said. —There's always a line of empty ones comin' up tha' way.

I followed him across to Chatham Row, to the corner of South William Street.

—Are you sure we don't have time for one in George's?

—No, I said.

—Only jokin', he said. —A pity, though. Here we go, look.

There was a taxi, its roof light lit, almost at us. Joe lifted his hand, and it stopped. He went to the nearest back door, and opened it. He stood back.

—In you go, bud, he said.

—Thanks.

—No bother.

I slid across the seat and he followed me in. He shut the door. And again, properly.

—Howyeh, he said to the driver. —Here, Davy, where're we goin'? Which hospital – Beaumont or the Mater?

—No, I said.

—Your da's house?

—The hospice.

—Jesus, he said. —Jesus, Davy. You never fuckin' said. The Raheny one?

—Yeah.

Joe leaned towards the driver's shoulder.

—Saint Francis Hospice in Raheny, he said. —D'you know it?

—I do, said the driver.

He was our age, maybe ten years younger.

—I do know it, he said. —Unfortunately.

We were moving.

—Brilliant place, though, said the driver.

—Yeah, said Joe. —So I'm told.

—Amazin' people, said the driver.

288

We were on Johnson Place.

—There's George's now, Davy, said Joe.

We both looked at the corner, and the doors, the porthole windows.

—Are you sure we don't have time for a fast one? said Joe.

I smiled.

—Sorry.

He spoke quietly now.

—Your father's in the fuckin' hospice?

—Yeah.

—How long?

—Two weeks, I said. —Sixteen days.

—Jesus.

The car had turned right; we were on Longford Street. The driver slowed, and stopped. The lights ahead were red.

—Have you been home for two weeks? he asked.

The words came from deep inside me. They were wet.

—Four months.

—Fuckin' hell, Davy.

I heard him breathe.

—In your da's house?

—Yeah.

The driver took us off Aungier Street, down on to South Great George's Street. We were passing another of the old pubs.

—We never made it to the Long Hall, said Joe.

—No.

—Next time, he said.

—Yeah.

—Great pub.

—Yeah.

—Smashin' pub, said the driver. —My da, God rest him, lived in there.

—Is tha' right?

—Oh, yeah, said the driver. —Lived in the place, he did. More than once my mother, God be good to her, sent me down to get him.

—Was he alright with tha'? Joe asked.

—Ah, he was. He just preferred the pub to the house. And he wasn't alone there.

—No.

—A lot o' men would've shared that preference.

—They would, said Joe. —An' still would.

Joe was looking at me.

—Is your belt on there, Davy?

—Yeah.

—Four months.

—Yeah.

—Why didn't you tell me? Even tonight, like – you didn't mention it.

—I didn't want to, I said. —I didn't think I could. To be honest.

—Okay.

—I've been –.

I looked out the window, at College Green and the crowds. I looked at the back of the driver's seat.

—I've been watchin' the man rot, I said. —For four months.

—Ah, Davy.

—Yeah.

—Alone?

I nodded.

—Davy –.

We were over O'Connell Bridge now, coming up to Beresford Place.

—Come here, said Joe. —I meant to tell you. Back there.

He indicated, with his thumb, the world outside the taxi.

—Wha'?

—The Sackville Lounge, he said.

—What about it?

—Gone.

—Shut?

—Yeah.

—Shut down, you mean?

—Yeah.

—For fuck sake, I said. —Tha' makes no sense.

—No.

—I often had a quick one in there, meself, said the driver.

—Sad, isn't it?

—Ah, it is.

—It's not sad, I said. —It's outrageous. It makes no fuckin' sense.

Joe spoke quietly.

—Where's Faye?

—At home.

—Okay, he said. —In England? Just –. Not in your da's house?

—No, I said. —Home, in Wantage.

—Okay.

I heard him adjusting himself, moving in the seat. I felt his hand on my shoulder. He patted it, held it, let go.

—You've been alone in the house.

—Yeah.

—With your father.

—Yeah.

—No help, no?

—No, I said. —There was –. There was a HSE nurse. Twice a week.

—Okay.

—Mondays and Thursdays. Two of them, actually. Job sharin'.

—Okay.

—They were good, I said. —Nice. Especially one o' them.

—Four months, Davy, he said. —Why didn't you fuckin' call me?

—I did.

—Today, he said. —Ten hours ago.

—I know.

We were past the Five Lamps, over the canal bridge, back the way we'd come earlier in the night, and all the nights decades before, walking home, swaying home, staggering, and running away from the hard men.

—I couldn't, I said.

—Okay, he said. —But I don't understand it.

—I don't either, I said. —I just –.

I had to do it alone. Devote myself to the man. Punish myself. Let him see me, make him see me. I'd had to endure it. Alone.

We were on Fairview Strand. We passed Gaffney's.

—Good pub.

—I remember it, yeah.

Joe was struggling to get something from his pocket.

—Here, he said. —Here.

I didn't know what he meant at first. Then I saw the chewing gum, Wrigley's Extra; he was opening the packet – he was trying to.

—I never come out without them, he said. —Or, I used to. I got them in the Spar on the way to the restaurant.

—What restaurant?

—We were in a restaurant.

—That's right.

—We met there.

—That's right, I said. —For fuck sake.

—Sorry, lads, said the driver. —Am I goin' straight up the Howth Road?

—The coast, I said.

—No, said Joe.

—I'll drop you off first, I told Joe. —It's on the way.

—You will in your hole, he said. —I'm comin' with you.

—No.

—Fuckin' yeah, Davy.

He put his open hand on my chest, and took it away.

—Howth Road, he told the driver.

—Grand.

—Wha' was the message, by the way? he said. —I meant to ask you.

—What message?

—From the hospice.

—Oh, I said. —I got a text from the nurse on duty tellin' me to phone her. She'd tried to phone me a couple o' times but I didn't notice.

—Jesus.

—I don't know why not, I said. —The phone was in my pocket all night. On mute, vibrate, like. I'd normally have felt it. But she phoned me when we were talkin'. In Neary's.

—Okay.

—Just before she texted me.

—Okay.

—So, yeah, I said. —I've been lookin' after him for four months and now I nearly miss his –.

293

I cried. Four months – sixty years – were behind my
eyes, pushing.

He patted my shoulder again.

—Have a chewin' gum, go on. You can't go in stinkin'
o' the gargle.

—Thanks.

—No bother. Why tonight?

—What?

—Why did you come ou' tonight?

—Oh.

I thought. I tried to think. The days were mush, my
life was mush. The hospice weeks were one long day.
The days at home were broken years. Broken sleep,
broken talk. Sliding thoughts and memories. My father
calling out to me at night, through the night, hauling
me awake – a voice I didn't know, I'd never heard
before.

—One o' the nurses, I said. —She said I should get
out for a while. She – well. She persuaded me.

—Nice one. How?

—Keep it clean, Joe.

—Okay – sorry.

—She said she didn't think there'd be anythin' dramatic happenin'. She's really sound – the best o' them.
They're all brilliant. Anyway, she said I needed a change
o' scenery. I needed to talk to someone who wasn't a
health professional or a priest.

—She sounds good.

—I nearly asked her out.

—Did you?

—No, I said. —Not really. But, anyway. I phoned
you.

—Well, I'm glad you did, Davy.

We passed Harry Byrne's.

—Not a bad pub, said Joe. —Unless there's fuckin' rugby on.

We passed the Beachcomber.

—Not a bad pub either.

—That would be my local, said the driver.

—Is tha' right?

—If I had a local, he said. —I don't be bothered much these days.

—How come?

—Lost the taste for it.

—How did that happen?

I watched the driver shrug. I saw one shoulder lift above the seat, and drop.

—Ah, sure, he said.

—I'm the same, said Joe. —Except for tonight. An' it wasn't planned. Sure it wasn't, Davy?

—No, I said.

—It just took off, said Joe. —We could stop for one in the Watermill, Davy. On the way.

—No.

—I'm only messin', he said.

He spoke quietly now – I thought he did. Sound was playing tricks – Joe was sitting to my left but I was hearing him from the right, from the window glass. I was hearing music that wasn't in the car. I could hear, and feel, something working its way up through me. Something growing, something liquid.

—Wha' did she say? he asked. —When you phoned the hospice. The nurse.

—She said –. She said there'd been a shift. I think she said a significant shift. In his condition.

—He's on the way out.

—Yeah, I said.

—I always liked him.

—Thanks.

—I did. I should've dropped in to him. Now an' again. I could've.

—Why would you have done that?

—To say hello – I don't know. See how he was. With you being over in England –. Sorry.

We were in Raheny village.

—He was always nice to me, said Joe.

The driver was slowing, to turn left on to Station Road.

—See they've renamed the Manhattan the Manhattan, said Joe.

I looked out.

—Ah, yeah – that's good.

—Isn't it?

—Why?

—Why did they do it – give it back the old name?

—Yeah.

—Don't know, he said. —D'you know? he asked the driver.

—I heard there was some sort of a referendum, he said.

—A referendum?

—In the area, yeah. So I heard.

—On the same day as the abortion referendum? said Joe.

We went over the bridge, over the railway.

—I don't know about tha', said the driver. —It wasn't a legal thing – I don't think. More, door to door. Or online – an opinion thing.

—Remind me, said Joe. —What did they call it before they changed it back? The Bull's Cock?

—The Cock an' Bull.

They laughed.

—I was close, said Joe.

—Not close enough, said the driver. —And it was the Station House before tha'.

—Why did they change it in the first place?

—No idea.

—New owners, I said.

—That's right, said Joe. —Tha' makes sense.

We were nearly there, and we were filling the car – pushing back the dread – with words. I'd have to get out. I'd have to go in. I could see the Hilltop Centre ahead, and the traffic lights. They were green and the road was empty. The driver took us right, on to Belmont – I knew the swerve and potholes by heart – and another quick right, up the hill, and over.

—This is it, said Joe. —Is it?

—Yeah.

The driver stopped at the front door.

—Here we go.

I didn't move.

—Davy?

—Okay.

I opened my door. The driver, in front of me, did the same; he opened his. He was out ahead of me – he hadn't been drinking all night. He put his hand out.

—I'm sorry for your trouble, he said.

He shook my hand. He held it.

—I've been there, he said. —It's dreadful. But I'll be prayin' for you.

—Thank you.

—No, he said. —The best o' luck now.

—What do I owe you? I asked him.

—You don't owe me anythin', he said. —I'm just glad to be able to help.

—Are you sure?

—I am.

—Thank you – thanks very much.

—I'm off, said the driver.

He got back into his car.

—Come on, Davy, said Joe.

The car moved slowly off, around, and back out on to the road.

—Your man didn't charge us, I told Joe.

—Saw tha', said Joe. —He was sound.

—That was a big fare, I said. —It must be – wha'? – twenty euro from town. More.

—There or thereabouts, said Joe. —Twenty-five, maybe. Come on.

—You sure about this, Joe?

—Wha'? he said. —Of course. You'll have to lead the way, though – come on.

There was a breeze. It was cool – it was reasonable – for the first time in weeks.

—Hang on, I said. —The heat in there, wait an' see. Just a sec.

He stood beside me.

I inhaled – exhaled, inhaled.

—Okay, I said.

I pulled open the door, felt myself do it, felt the effort, the decision, momentum. There was nothing holding me back. I nodded to Denis, the security man. He smiled back.

Joe was beside me.

Down the short corridor, through the land of the teddy bears – a couple of couches decked in large stuffed toys – and on to the longer corridor.

—Are there wards? Joe asked.

—They moved him to his own room, I said. —Three days ago – four. Here.

The blinds were down and closed. The 'Family Only' sign hung on the door.

I put one hand on the handle, the other on the door glass, and pushed as I also held it back. I realised, I recognised it: this was something I did – used to do – at home in Wantage, with the front door, to stop it from creaking, to stop myself from falling forward. I could hear Faye. You could always oil it. Or stop drinking. Whichever's handier.

The room was empty.

But it wasn't. My father was there. In the bed. *On* the bed, suspended just above it. He was hardly there. His size was a shock. It had been a shock for months, every time I left and came back.

Joe was behind me, beside me.

—Jesus, Davy, he's so small in the bed.

I nodded.

—Was he small? he asked. —Is he small? He wasn't, was he? I don't –

—No, I said. —The same size as me, about. I mean, everyone shrinks when they're getting older.

—He's tiny.

—Yeah.

—Jesus, Davy.

I could hear his breathing, my father's breathing. The rattle was sharper – both weaker and stronger. The death rattle. The name made sense in the room. It hadn't been like that when I'd left to meet Joe. The sister, the nurse – *my* nurse – Margaret, had told me that he'd days left.

—Short days, she'd said.

—How do you know?

—I've been doing this for years, she said. —Sometimes I feel like an Indian scout. In one of the old westerns. Looking into the sky or putting my ear to the tracks.

—What does short days mean?

—It means you can meet your friend for a meal and a few drinks.

—And he'll still be here.

—He'll be here – yes.

Joe had closed the door and now it opened again, behind us. We were standing at the foot of the bed.

I turned.

It was another sister, a different nurse. The different ranks wore different uniforms, different colours. She was one of the senior ones. They seemed to have more clout than the doctors, who I'd rarely seen. They were older, firmer; I believed what they told me.

—You're here, she said.

—Yes, I said. —I made it.

I hated what I'd just said. I hadn't felt drunk, I'd stopped being drunk. But now I was drunk again, just stupid. It was some sort of a game – touch the bed before your father dies.

—Good, she said. —You hear him.

—Yeah.

—He's nearly there.

She got past us.

—Sorry, said Joe. —I'm in your way.

—You're not.

She went to the top of the bed. She looked down at my father. She looked at the drip – the morphine. The room was dim, almost dark. The candle on the shelf above the radiator was electric. I'd show it to Joe when she left us alone. I'd turn it on and off.

—He's comfortable, she said.

—Thanks.

—He's very comfortable, she said. —We'll turn him again in half an hour.

—Thanks.

I couldn't remember her name. I couldn't read her name tag.

—I'm Joe, by the way, said Joe. —A friend of Davy – David's.

—You're very good to keep him company, she said. —I'm Maeve.

—I was just sayin', said Joe. —He's so small there.

She smiled.

—Like a child or somethin', said Joe.

—Did you have a good night, anyway, lads? she asked.

—Yes, thanks.

—Good, she said. —Good – I'll leave you alone for a little while.

—Will it be tonight, Maeve? I asked.

—Yes, she said. —I think so.

She was at the door.

—I'll just be across the way, she said. —You know where to find me.

—Yes.

She was out, gone. The door was shut.

—She's nice, said Joe.

—Yeah, I said. —They're all great.

—Nice room.

—Yeah, I said. —It is. It's very peaceful.

There was a little garden on the other side of the window.

—We can sit down, I said.

—Grand.

—You go that side, Joe, I said. —Go on.

I sat on the chair to the right, at the top of the bed, near my father's head – his face – on the pillow. Joe placed a chair opposite me.

—Is this okay? he asked.

—Bang on.

—He's –. He's right down to basics. Isn't he?

—Yeah, I said. —You're right. Did you see your father dyin', Joe?

—No, he said. —He just died, like. In the garden. I wasn't there. No one was.

—Was he there long?

—A couple of hours. My mother found him.

—That must've been awful for her.

—She was in the house the whole time, he said. — The doctor told her he'd died immediately – dropped dead. But –.

—The poor woman.

—Yeah.

We looked at my father. We listened to the rattle. His face was already stretched, at the mouth and cheeks, as if he'd already reached out for his last breath.

—You haven't seen anyone die before now, I said.

—No, he said. —Have you?

—No.

—We're both virgins, so.

—Yep, I said. —How long ago was that?

—My da?

—Yeah.

—Fifteen years. Yeah – fifteen.

—Jesus –. Time.

The window behind me was open.

—It's not too bad tonight, I said. —Not too hot.

—It's grand.

—There's a water fountain thing out there, I said.
—But they had to turn it off.
—'Cos o' the water restrictions?
—Yeah.
—Fair enough, I suppose.
—It was a nice sound, though, I said. —At this time o' night, you know.
—Yeah, he said. —What's the smell, Davy?
—Is there a smell?
—I think so, yeah.
—A bedsore.
—A bedsore?
—A fuckin' bedsore, yeah.
—Christ.
—It's the stuff they use to mask the smell, I said. —It's in the dressing.
—Grand.
—Zinc, I think they said.
—Really?
—I've lost track, a bit, I said. —The HSE women tried somethin', different things, to mask it – the smell. And that got changed in here – the dressing they're usin'. I don't notice it now, really. The real smell's horrific.
—Must be.
—Fuckin' horrific, I said. —Embarrassin'.
—How come?
—Just is, I said. —I didn't look after him properly.
—Ah, Davy.
—I had to change the dressing, myself, I said. —The weekend before he came in here. I couldn't do it properly. I tried –
—'Course you did.
—So fuckin' inadequate.

303

—He's very old, Davy.

—I know.

—You're not a nurse – a fuckin' health professional.

—I know.

—Are you alright? he said. —Do you want something to drink?

—There isn't a bar.

—There's a vendin' machine – lay off. We fuckin' passed it.

We laughed quietly.

—Can he hear us?

—They say he can, I said. —Or could. He might be too far gone – I don't know. It's hard to imagine he can hear us. Lookin' at him.

—If they say he can –.

—Maybe – yeah.

—D'you want somethin' to drink? A Coke or whatever.

—Lucozade might be nice.

—Fuckin' hell, he said. —Can I have that in writin'?

—I like the occasional bottle, I said. —I've low blood pressure – sometimes.

—An' it helps, does it?

—Seems to.

—Okay.

—The sugar, I said. —D'you want to hold his hand?

—No – can I?

I stood up and leaned across my father, and lifted the blanket and sheet enough for Joe to see his hand, and take it.

—Is this okay?

—Of course.

—It's warm.

—He's alive.

—Yeah –. Yeah.

—That thing beside you there, I said.

He looked at the lamp – the blue, then green, then blue lamp – on the locker beside the bed.

—That helps with the smell as well, I said.

—Clever.

—They put somethin' in it. Some kind of oil.

—Wha'?

—They told me, I said. —I can't remember.

—You're shite.

—I know, I said.

I looked at Joe looking at my father. I looked at my father.

—They prefer to call them pressure sores, I said.

—Sorry?

—The bedsores, I said. —They call them pressure sores. It's marketin', I think.

—Wha'?

—Men our age – which sounds worse? Bedsore or pressure sore?

—No competition. Bedsore.

—So, just change the fuckin' name, I said. —That's what I mean. They should be ashamed of themselves – the HSE, the fuckin' system. For lettin' the man develop a bedsore like tha' – for lettin' me look after him on my own for that long –.

My mouth was full of water – I didn't know where it had come from. I waited, then swallowed it back.

—So, I said. —Call it a pressure sore an' it's not too bad.

—You're being hard on yourself, Davy.

—When I was doin' it, I said. —Changin' the dressing. I had to get him to stand, hold on to his walker,

305

you know. I was tryin' to clean it without lookin' at it, at his bum and – you know. And he was half conscious, half himself, an' I just wanted it to be finished. I was tryin' not to breathe till I was done. I had all the windows open in the house. It was hot back then, two weeks ago, too. I was tryin' to get the bandage thing to hold an' to get the nappy onto him. And he said –.

I was choking again, my head full. There were tissues behind me on the windowsill. I grabbed a couple and blew my nose.

—Sorry.

—What did he say? said Joe.

—This is no kind of a life.

—He said that?

—Yeah.

—Well –. He was right. Wasn't he?

—Yeah.

—He wasn't blamin' you, Davy.

—Yeah – no. I know that. Just –.

—The end's so fuckin' messy, isn't it?

—Your father, I said. —That's the way to go, isn't it? Gone before you hit the ground.

—You'd still be leavin' a terrible fuckin' mess, though, Davy. Believe me.

—Yeah.

—The shock, the grief, he said. —Dealin' with the siblings. There's another word I hate, by the way. Siblings. Jesus, the tension. You're kind o' lucky you've none.

—Okay.

—You don't sound convinced.

—I wouldn't mind a few now, I said.

—Right, he said. —I think I know how you feel.

—Yeah.

—I'll ask again, he said. —I don't mean to be snotty.

—No – go on.

—Where's Faye?

—At home – I told you.

—Why isn't she here, Davy?

—Ah, well.

I looked at my father. I hadn't stopped looking at my father.

—I didn't want her to be here, I said.

—Why?

—It's somethin' I had to do on my own, I said. — Somethin' like that, anyway. He's my father.

I shrugged.

—Okay, said Joe.

—I don't know, I said. —I might have treated him badly. I might have been unfair. I *was* – unfair.

—Okay.

—Years ago.

—Right – okay.

—I felt, I said. —I thought I should do it – this – on my own.

I was wrong: I knew that now. This time, I'd been unfair to Faye.

—He said thank you, I said. —That time. When I was pullin' up his pyjamas.

—Now – that's fuckin' amazin'.

—It is, a bit.

—It's fuckin' brilliant, said Joe.

He let go of my father's hand. He was wiping his eyes. I leaned across the bed, held out the tissues for him.

—Thanks, he said.

He took one, and another. He took off his glasses and put them on the bed, close to my father's shoulder. He put his hands to his face and kept them there. He moaned, softly. He took down his hands. He looked at the tissues. He turned in his chair and put them on the locker. He looked at my father. He got his glasses from the bed and put them back on.

—Strange night, he said.

—Yeah.

—A good night.

—Tell me about Jess, I said.

—Jesus –.

—Go on.

—I've been tellin' you.

—Go on, I said. —Please.

—Your da might be listenin'.

—Go on, I said. —He liked women. I think. That's what's so fuckin' sad, I think. One of the things.

—He lived alone?

—For so long, yeah.

I'd kept Faye away from him, and Róisín – she'd never really known him. I loved all three and I'd been cruel to all three.

—We all dream o' that a bit, now an' again, said Joe.
—Do we? Livin' on our own.

—Probably – yeah. Now an' again.

—So, he said. —Trish –. This is a while back.

—A year.

—Yeah – a bit more. But yeah. She was drivin' me fuckin' mad. That's not fair, but fuck it. She was drivin' me mad. She wanted to move house – an' we're only just finished with the fuckin' mortgage, by the way. Then she wants to knock the whole back o' the house an' put in glass. This is in the same breath as sayin' she wants to move. It seems like that, anyway. An' it's all money. That's not fair either but it is – money. An' I'm fuckin' sixty, Davy.

—You're not.

—I nearly am. An' so are you. An' I don't know –. I was thinkin' I'd love just to live in one room, on me own, like. Just deal with myself. An' I met Jess. An' it was like all that fuckin' pressure – everythin'. Gone.

The rhythm changed, shifted. My father's breathing – it quickened. There was a new click in it now, like something had loosened, broken away.

—Will I get the nurse?

—Hang on.

I watched my father. His face – the mask – didn't change. The breaths, the gaps between them, were definitely quicker. Then, as if he'd stopped snoring or had turned in the bed, the click sound stopped. He was grabbing air in little gasps but the rhythm was steady again.

—Will I get her?

—No, I said. —She'll be in in a bit anyway. He sounds alright again.

—Does he?

—I think so.

I sat back. I couldn't help yawning.

—What about your Lucozade? said Joe.

—He'll die if one of us stands up an' leaves the room.

—You don't believe that.

—I kind o' do, I said. —I went out for a pint with you an' look where we ended up.

—Fair enough.

—But no, I said. —Not really. I don't believe it. But then – I've hardly been out of this place since he came in. It's horrible, walkin' out. Walkin' away from him.

—Includin' tonight.

—Yeah, I said. —Go on, though.

—Jess?

—Yes, please.

—Right, he said. —Jesus. I feel like I'm doin' a job interview now.

—Chief executive adulterer.

—Fuck off.

—The job's yours. Go on – you met her.

—Yeah, he said. —And everything. Lifted. After I realised tha' we wouldn't be shaggin' in the back of the car or anythin' like tha'. And tha' now – it was a relief, really. But. Anyway. We'd be chattin' away and I realised – it occurred to me, gradually. But there *was* a moment, a for fuck sake moment. One o' those – when it occurred to me. I loved listenin' to her, Davy. Her voice. Just that.

I nodded. I knew exactly what he meant.

—Just that, he said again. —But then as well, I realised when I was listenin'. She'd be talkin' abou' somethin' that had happened years before but she wasn't just tellin' me. She was remindin' me.

—Of what?

—There you go, he said. —She was assuming –. What it was. She was includin' me. The things she was talkin' about – the houses, the places, family. The children. I was there too, as far as she was concerned.

—Did you say anythin'?

—No, he said. —No, I didn't. Because.

—What?

—I'm thinkin' – sorry. I'm tryin' to express it. How's your da gettin' on, d'you think?

—It's even again – is it? The breathin'.

—Not even, no. He's breathin' like he has a tiny chest. A bird's chest – lungs.

—But it's regular.

—It is, he said. —Fairly regular, yeah.

—Go on.

—Fine, he said. —Okay. I don't feel like I've been drinkin' all night. Do you?

—No, I said. —I don't. Not now.

—What's that, d'you think? The shock?

—Maybe.

—It sobers you up or somethin', he said.

—Adrenaline.

—D'you think?

—I don't know, I said. —It wouldn't surprise me.

—Nothin' would surprise me any more, Davy, he said. —Fuckin' nothin'. So – right. You asked me if I said anythin' to Jess. About me not actually bein' around in the things she was talkin' about. And I didn't. I didn't say anythin'. Because – this sounds mad. But I don't care. She seemed – she *was* happier when I was there with her.

—In the stories.

—Yeah, he said. —An' so was I.

—Happy?

—Yeah, he said. —I think so, yeah. I went along with it, you know.

—With the flow.

—That's it. I went with the flow. Her flow – so to speak. I let it happen.

—You indulged her.

—No, he said. —No.

—Sorry.

—No – you're grand.

—Give us an example, I said. —A story.

—Well –.

—Nothin' private, if you don't want.

—No, no, you're grand. I know what you mean. A holiday.

—Where?

—France.

—And you were there?

—Accordin' to her. Yeah, I seemed to be.

—But you weren't.

—No, he said. —But – like. It didn't matter. When I saw the impact it was havin' on her.

—Joe?

—Wha'?

—Is she ill?

—No, he said. —No. She's not. She's – lonely would be part of it. Alone. Unappreciated, under-appreciated, somethin' like that. Unfocused.

—Okay.

—An' sad, he said. —Definitely that. Not sick, though. I don't think. Or if she is – fuck it.

—Okay.

—It doesn't matter. We're all fuckin' mad.

—True.

—Somehow or other. Am I right?

—Probably, I said. —Where in France?

—The Dordogne.

—Was it nice?

—Lovely, he said. —Fuckin' fabulous.

—I didn't mean to belittle her there, I said. —Or you.

—No, no – I know, he said. —The funny thing is, though. I *was* there.

—With Trish?

—No, he said. —Like – actually – I've never been in tha' part of France. But it doesn't matter. I was there with Jess.

—And her kids?

He sat up. He shrugged. He looked at my father.

—It doesn't matter, he said.

—Does it not?

—And there are the things I definitely do remember.

—There's a balance?

—No, he said. —But kind of. Remember tha' party? In her house. D'you remember it?

—Yes, I said. —I do. The beer in the bath.

—That's right, he said. —I'd forgotten tha' detail. You remember it better than I do.

—Her little brother guardin' it, I said. —It must have been her brother.

—That's right, he said. —Yeah. A prick, by the way.

—Is he?

—God, yeah. Grew up into a right little cunt. But anyway, she was playin' the cello. In the kitchen.

—Yeah.

—Amazin', he said. —Jesus. Mesmerisin'.

I thought he was waiting for me to agree with him.

—Yeah, I said.

I stared at my father.

—And later, he said. —After she'd finished playin'. I plucked up the courage. I got talkin' to her. Couldn't believe myself. Tha' was the night I got off with her. D'you remember, Davy?

I was looking at my father. I looked at Joe – I made myself look at Joe. He was looking at my father.

—Yeah, I said. —I remember that night.

It was Jess's engagement party, the little brother had told us. She was going to marry a chap called Gavin.

—I remember it well, I said.

I smiled.

—So, like, said Joe. —There are some things I can definitely account for. And others –.

I looked at him again. He was still looking at my father.

—It's one o' the big advantages o' gettin' older, he said. —Probably the only fuckin' advantage. If you live long enough, you can add to it, make it up. You can even believe you lived it. Things you make up bleed into things tha' definitely happened. Like describin' an event, an actual occasion. You add to it, you take things out. You forget exact details. I don't think it's dishonest.

—No.

—It's human. I'd say.

—Yeah, I said. —I think you're probably right.

—I think so too.

—So, I said. —You were in that part of France. The Dordogne.

—Yeah.

—With Jess.

—Yeah, he said. —Exactly.

—Exactly?

—Yeah.

—Literally?

He shrugged. He made himself smile.

—I don't know what to say.

—Okay, I said. —Is it not hurtful?

—To Trish?

—Is it not?

—The details aren't, I don't think, he said. —To be honest, I don't know. But.

—What?

—With Jess, he said. —I don't care if it's true or not. I mean, factual.

—Okay.

—I remember some things, not others. Like everyone.

—Okay.

—Now I'm kind o' rememberin' things that I shouldn't be able to remember, he said. —It's subtle.

—Is it?

—I think so.

—Okay.

—It's the best thing, though, Davy, he said. —Makin' her happy. It makes me feel – I don't know. Powerful.

—Really?

—I think so, yeah, he said. —And good.

—Okay.

We stopped talking for a while. We looked at my father. Joe stood up. He stretched. His hands went to the ceiling, his shirt came out of his jeans.

—I'll go get those Lucozades, he said. —Did we pass a toilet on our way in?

—Yeah, I said. —Go back past the teddy bears.

—Gotcha.

He took change from his pocket and looked at it on his palm.

—I think I've enough, he said.

—You sure?

—I've loads here. Back in a bit.

—Grand.

I looked at him as he opened the door. He looked back as he left and smiled. He shut the door, slowly.

I looked at my father. I got up and leaned in, close to his face. The skin was blue, and tight against his skull. It was like his hair had vanished. It was there but faded, diminished; strands of it danced in the breeze coming in from the open window behind me. I put my hand on his head. I listened. To his breathing. I'd been falling asleep every night on the bench below the window; falling asleep, fitfully and unwillingly, to a different rhythm. This was feebler, but more urgent.

—Alright, Dad?

This is no kind of a life. It was the one occasion, the only time he'd conceded that he wasn't well and that he was never going to be well. I'd spent the months pretending I was just visiting. I'd put him to bed. I'd helped him sit on the side of the bed. I'd given him his last pill of the day, a sleeping tablet. Then I'd helped him lie back and lifted his feet and legs and straightened him, centred him, in the bed. Every movement had hurt him, no matter how slow. I'd covered him with the duvet. I'd lifted the rail so he wouldn't roll out. I'd leaned over the rail and kissed his forehead. I'd slowly closed the door. It was a hospital bed and it was downstairs, in the front room. The kitchen light was on, down the hall. I'd close the door until he'd tell me to stop. He had the three inches of light he wanted. He'd become afraid of the dark, afraid he wouldn't be coming back out of it.

We didn't speak about it. We didn't speak about him, me, the two of us, Faye. I fed him his pills, anxious – afraid – that I was giving him the wrong ones, too many of the right ones, unwilling, unable, to trust my own competence. I was poisoning the man. I was killing the man.

We chatted but we didn't talk. He told me about the time he met my mother. It was a story I'd heard before.

—I was drunk, I'm afraid.

—You?

—Yes.

—You were never drunk.

—I used to be young, David.

It was at a dance, a tennis club hop, and she told him to go away and come back the following Saturday.

—Do you believe in an afterlife, Dad?

He didn't answer. He told me he'd love a boiled egg. He ate the first spoonful and none of the soldiers.

I heard the door. I looked, and saw Joe slip back in. He shut the door.

—Here you go.

He held out a bottle, over the bed. It looked like a torch, or a stunted sword.

—Thanks, Joe, I said.

I stood, stretched, and sat back down.

—I never asked you, said Joe. —What is it?

—What d'you mean?

—Your father, he said.

—Oh, I said. —The cancer, d'you mean?

—Yeah. Which one is it?

—A selection of them, Joe, I said. —He's fuckin' riddled.

—Ah, no.

—Yep.

—Ah, God love him. What started it – which was the first? Do you know?

—I was told, I said. —I have it all written down. But.

My head was filling again.

—I'm fuckin' hopeless.

—Stop.

I opened the bottle, twisted the lid and listened to the short hiss. I drank carefully. I was afraid the stuff would rush out at me, or I wouldn't be able to swallow it. But it was good, it was cold.

—It was his GP phoned me, I said. —He was surprised I hadn't been in touch. That Dad hadn't told me.

—He didn't tell you?

—No. He didn't. But I should've known – I did fuckin' know. The last time I came over to see him. He could hardly walk. I found him leanin' against the radiator. I rang the bell, you know – the front door. I always did it. Before I put my key in the door and went in. So he wouldn't be surprised to find someone else in the house. And – Jesus. There he was. In the hall. Holdin' onto the radiator. Fuck knows how long he'd been there. He said he'd been comin' to answer the door but I don't think he was. I had to help him back to the kitchen. Fuck –.

—What?

—And I went home.

—What d'you mean?

—I stayed a night and went home. He told me he was fine, just a bit stiff. And I decided to believe him. He didn't get up to see me out to the door. I decided it wasn't important. Significant. My father's manners, Joe – d'you remember?

—Always very polite.

—Yes.

—Gentle.

—Yeah.

—He always spoke to me like I was an adult.

—Yes, I said. —And he'd have brought you to the door when you were leavin' – I don't know if you remember that. If he'd known you were goin', I mean.

—I know.

—Not that he was tryin' to get rid of you.

—No, I know.

—But anyway, he didn't stand up when I was leavin' for the airport and I decided that it didn't really matter.

—You're bein' hard on yourself, Davy.

—I shouldn't have left.

—You have a family.

318

—I should have kept at him – to tell me what was wrong.

Joe opened his Lucozade. He lifted it to his mouth. I heard him gulp.

—It's fuckin' sweet, this stuff.

—It works.

—Whatever that means.

—I'm exhausted, Joe.

—You must be.

—Fuckin' exhausted.

—It's nearly over, he said.

We were both looking at my father, both listening to him.

—Yeah, I said. —I'm not sure.

—You don't think he's goin' to go tonight?

—No, I said. —I mean, I do. But –. It doesn't mean I'll sleep or feel better or – I don't know – clearer. When I wake up. I'm so fuckin' tired.

—You have to be.

—I don't phone Faye. I hardly ever phone her. I can't think of the words – things to say. I dread it – the decisions. How to say things. It's not just the sleep. Fuckin' hell, Joe, he'd wake me up half an hour after takin' the fuckin' sleepin' pill. I was wonderin' if he was hiding them under his tongue – like Jack Nicholson.

—In *One Flew Over the Cuckoo's Nest*.

—Yeah, I said. —He could hardly talk but he was able to shout – like, screech. He still wakes me, even though he's been like this for four days now – asleep. Unconscious. I still hear him.

—That'll stop.

—Then I won't hear him at all.

I sat up straight. I wiped my eyes.

—Sorry, I said.

—You're grand.

—Self-pity.

—For fuck sake, Davy. Your father's dyin' in front of you. Take it easy.

We both heard the door. We turned, to see who it was.

Maeve seemed to fill the door and frame. There was a younger nurse behind her; she was pushing a trolley. Maeve smiled as she moved to the top of the bed. Joe had to stand, make room. He shifted his chair – the legs squealed on the floor.

—Sorry.

I laughed – two short barks; they burst out through the water. Joe laughed back. It was a school moment and I was sixteen, for a second. For a great, floating second.

—He's very comfortable, said Maeve.

—Thanks.

—He's exactly the way you'd want him, she said.

—I'm not sure about that, Maeve, I said.

Joe laughed again. So did Maeve. So did the other nurse.

—You know what I mean, said Maeve.

—I do.

—We'll turn him now, she said. —You can wait in the room beyond. We'll only be a few minutes.

I felt like I hadn't walked in months.

—How long? I asked her at the door.

—It'll be soon, she said.

—Okay. Thanks.

We stood outside.

—Let's get some air, said Joe.

—No, I said. —We'd better not. They'll need to know where we are.

—Right, yeah – okay. How long are we here, by the way?

I took out my phone and looked at the clock.

—Less than an hour, I said.

—Jesus, said Joe. —I feel like I live here.

—I do live here, I said.

—That'll stop.

—Yeah.

—What's the food like?

—Not bad, I said. —It's alright. An' there's a café across the way, at the Hilltop. They do a good soup an' sandwich.

—Tha' right?

—And the coffee's very good.

—That's good, he said. —To have it near.

—Yeah.

We needed my father. We needed him there before we'd start talking properly again. It already seemed like a long time since we'd been in the room. We stood outside while they turned him in the bed, gently, professionally; we waited while they cleaned him. There were voices, further up the corridor and around a corner – up where my father had been until he'd stopped waking up. People talked quietly, someone laughed.

The door opened. The younger nurse wheeled out the trolley; she smiled at us. Maeve had stayed in the room. Joe got to the door before me but he stopped, and stepped back.

—After you, he said.

He was eager too.

I walked in.

It was different – my father was different. He was facing the window now, the same shape, reversed, like the negative of a photograph. But his face was different. His mouth was open wider, in a silent howl. I couldn't hear his breath.

—Is he alive?

—Yes, she said. —But he's nearly there.

—Okay. Thanks.

—It'll be soon.

—Thank you.

She left. She shut the door. I sat in the same chair. He was facing me now. The mouth, the howl: he wouldn't accept it was happening. I leaned in, put my hand on his head. I took it away and searched for his hand, just under the sheet. It was dry, and tiny. Not cold.

—Alright, Dad? I said, again.

The mouth – the pain. The end.

—I can't hear him, said Joe; he whispered. —Can you?

—No, I said. —I'm not sure.

I stood and put my head, my ear, closer to my father.

—I can, I said. —I think.

I sat again. I had to – I felt dizzy. I stayed still, shut my eyes. Took in breath, let it go. He'd die while my eyes were closed. I opened them. The mouth was there, staring at me.

—I wish –.

—What? said Joe.

—I wish I'd spent more time with him.

—You're with him now.

—When he was well.

—You're with him now, Davy. He knows you're here.

—He does in his hole, Joe.

—You've been with him for the last four months, he said. —He knew that.

322

—Okay.

—Stop beatin' yourself up.

—Okay.

I looked at the mouth.

—He liked you, I said. —Did I tell you that already?

—I liked him too, said Joe.

My head was full again, a rush of water and Lucozade. I gasped, I coughed. I pushed it back. I sat up, pushed my back against the back of the chair.

—Where did you sleep? Joe asked.

I pointed at the bench.

—There.

—Every night – since he came in here?

—Yes.

—No wonder you're fuckin' exhausted.

—It's not too bad.

—If you insist.

—I do.

—You're a better man than I am, so.

I was looking at my father.

—I'm glad you're here, Joe, I said.

—So am I, he said. —I'm glad too.

—I'm glad.

—Grand, said Joe. —We're all fuckin' glad.

There was a gasp, a hiss. An explosion we hardly heard.

—Was that it?

—Think so.

—I'll get Maeve.

I didn't notice her arriving. My father hadn't changed. His hand wasn't cold. She put fingers to his neck, his pulse. I watched her.

—Yes, she said.

—He's gone.

—Yes.

—He's dead.

—Yes, she said. —He's gone. I'll leave you with him for a little while.

—Thank you.

Joe was standing beside me. He put a hand on my shoulder. I let go of my father's hand. I knew: it would be cold the next time I touched it. I let it go, and stood.

Joe hugged me.

—I'm sorry for your trouble, bud.

—Thanks.

—It's shite.

—It is.

—You did well, Davy.

—Okay.

—You did.

—I'm goin' to phone Faye.

—Good man.

I went to the door.

—No, he said. —Come here. You stay here, I'll wait outside.

—No, I said. —It'll be easier –.

—Okay, he said. —I'll stay.

—You don't mind?

—It's an honour – go on.

Faye must have been awake.

—Hi, Dave.

—Hi.

I couldn't speak. I couldn't say the words. She must have realised, or heard me; I might have moaned.

—Oh, David.

I could speak now.

—He died, Faye.

—I know.

—A minute ago.

—I'm so sorry, she said. —I'm so sorry. I wish I was there.

—Yes.

—Do you want me to come over now? David?

—Yes.

—I'll be there tomorrow.

—Good.

—I love you, David.

—I love you too.

—I do.

—I know. I'm sorry, Faye.

—Stop it.

—Okay, I said.

—The kids, David.

—I'll phone them.

—You sure?

—Yeah, I said. —Thanks.

—I'll be there soon.

—Yes.

—In a couple of hours.

—Yeah.

—He had a good innings, she said. —So he did. Isn't that what they say?

I smiled; I knew I was smiling.

We stood outside the hospice. It was five o'clock, already day. Joe's app told him the taxi was two minutes away, on its way up from Raheny village.

—We could find an early house, he said.

—God, no – fuck.

—Ah, go on, he said. —Molloy's or the Windjammer.

—No way, I said. —I'm bollixed.

—I'm only messin', he said. —You'll have things to do, anyway.

—Yeah.

—The undertaker an' tha'.

—Happy days.

—You're an orphan now, Davy.

—Yeah – yeah. For fuck sake.

—A big orphan.

—Yep.

—What's keepin' this fucker?

—Ask your phone.

He looked down at it. He brought it up to his face.

—One minute, he said. —It says, anyway.

—Grand, I said. —There's no mad hurry.

—What about –? he said. —Do you want to come an' meet Jess?

—No, I said. —No. Thanks.

—The early breakfast, no?

—No, I said. —Thanks.

—You'd like her.

—I know.

I didn't want to see her. She'd be too real and too human. I'd leave them be, her and Joe, with the things that had happened and the things that hadn't happened.

—Another time, he said.

—Definitely.

—Here he is now, look.

We watched the taxi come up over the hill, down, and towards us.

—Pity it's not our man, said Joe. —The lad who brought us here.

—He was sound, I said.

—He was, said Joe. —Sound.

We watched the taxi slow, and stop.

—You'll soon be home, Davy, said Joe.

—Yeah, I said. —I will.